DETECTIVES, SLEUTHS, & NOSY NEIGHBORS

A. BALSAMO

Copyright © 2024 by Inkd Publishing LLC

Death of a Mage Professor Copyright © 2024 by A.R.R. Ash

Murder on a Dark Stair Copyright © 2024 by Mark Beard

What Can I Getcha Copyright © 2024 by Cassondra Windwalker

The Case of the Saintsville Cattle Killers Copyright © 2024 by L.N. Hunter

Urban Swamp Copyright © 2024 by Joe Giordano

Shagra the Untangler Copyright © 2024 by Kay Hanifen

The Good Thief Copyright © 2024 by Mary Sophie Filicetti

Angelita Copyright © 2024 by Robert Richter

On the Rocks Copyright © 2024 by Tiffany Seitz

Secret Family Recipe Copyright © 2024 by Tracy Falenwolfe

God's Truth Copyright © 2024 by Veronica Leigh

A Corpse in the Martian Sand Copyright © 2024 by J.F. Benedetto

The Ghostly Lady's Curse Copyright © 2024 by N.M. Cedeño

When the Evidence Leads Upstate Copyright © 2024 by Michelle Kaseler

Route 90 Copyright © 2024 by Kevin A Davis

All rights reserved.

No part of this book may be reproduced in any form or by any electronic or mechanical means, including information storage and retrieval systems, without written permission from the author, except for the use of brief quotations in a book review.

DETECTIVES, SLEUTHS, & NOSY NEIGHBORS

Contents

Introduction	vii
THE GHOSTLY LADY'S CURSE N M Cedeño	1
DEATH OF A MAGE PROFESSOR A.R.R. Ash	21
ON THE ROCKS Tiffany Seitz	41
MURDER ON A DARK STAIR Mark Beard	62
GOD'S TRUTH Veronica Leigh	92
ROUTE 90 Kevin A Davis	113
THE CASE OF THE SAINTSVILLE CATTLE KILLERS L.N. Hunter	135
SECRET FAMILY RECIPE Tracy Falenwolfe	147
URBAN SWAMP Joe Giordano	165
SHAGRA THE UNTANGLER Kay Hanifen	185
WHAT CAN I GETCHA Cassondra Windwalker	211
WHEN THE EVIDENCE LEADS UPSTATE Michelle Kaseler	226
ANGELITA'S NIGHT OUT Robert Richter	239

A CORPSE IN THE MARTIAN SAND J.F. Benedetto	265
THE GOOD THIEF Mary Sophie Filicetti	285
Tuckerizations	303
Acknowledgments	305
Also by Inkd Publishing	307

Introduction

Welcome to Detectives, Sleuths, and Nosy Neighbors, a collection of mystery stories to keep you guessing *whodunnit*. We have put together an eclectic selection of stories that span all genres. Within these pages you will find suspicious neighbors, amateur detectives, a mysterious highway, and everything in between. The authors chosen for this anthology come from a wide range of backgrounds and writing experience. Some are published authors that you may recognize and others are previously unpublished. You may just find a new favorite author within these pages. If you find a story that you love, please give the author a like on their social media!

A Balsamo, Editor

The Ghostly Lady's Curse
N M Cedeño

Tina's father had said, "Don't go in the attic, or you'll die a sudden, terrible death. Going up there summons a lady ghost's curse. Several family members died because of the curse." What the heck was that supposed to mean? Since when did her usually level-headed father believe in curses? Tina Jones was utterly confused as she exited the dilapidated family home with those words ringing in her ears. Tucking her short black curls into her helmet and zipping her leather jacket, she climbed on her motorcycle and cruised into Sloop, the map-dot Texas town her grandfather had abandoned well before her birth.

Tina's father, Aloysius, a semi-retired petroleum engineer, first mentioned purchasing the century-old house in his ancestral hometown only yesterday, Thursday. Tina agreed to come to the Hill Country west of Austin to see it since she wasn't scheduled to work Friday or Saturday. As an Austin PD homicide detective, she'd just wrapped up investigating a particularly gruesome murder case, so escaping the city for the countryside sounded like a relaxing break. She was flabbergasted when her father warned her about a curse. "How do you know it's a lady if you've never been up there?" she asked, hoping it was a joke as she sipped coffee with him at the scarred oak kitchen table.

"I saw her once. Her face glows," Al said with a nod that shook the few grey hairs remaining in his bald spot. He hadn't touched his own coffee.

"If you saw her, why are you alive?" Tina asked, waiting for a punchline.

"I didn't go into the attic. I peeked from the ladder."

"Huh?" Tina noted that her father's face was serious, as if his words were reasonable. She was perplexed. She thought her parents exhibited their sole eccentricity when they named her Faustina Eudocia at birth thirty years ago, giving her a unique name to counter the plainness of the surname Jones. Even though he wore the relaxed weekend attire of pocket tee and faded blue jeans that she'd seen him wear all her life, Tina felt like she was seeing her father for the first time.

"I'll explain," Al said with the same paternal patience he exhibited when teaching her calculus. "My grandparents owned this house and raised my dad Cornelius, and his siblings, Jedediah and Antonina, here during the Great Depression. In 1942, Dad and Jed enlisted in the military as teenagers. Dad fought in the Pacific and Jed invaded Normandy Beach and marched into Germany. After World War II, Jed moved home to recover from shell shock and leg injuries. He's lived here ever since. Dad said Jed was a different person after the war." Al whispered his last sentence, with a concerned glance at the old man across the room.

Tina's green eyes drifted across the faded country kitchen and studied the frail centenarian, Great Uncle Jed, sitting in a corner watching television. A crocheted afghan was draped over his legs leaving his tattered slippers exposed. His rheumy eyes were alive and intelligent. She tried to picture him young, wounded, and plagued by the ghosts of war. Tina asked her father, "Who died here?"

"First, Dad's Aunt Margie."

"What happened to her?"

"In 1946, Margie came to live here after her sons died in the war. She climbed into the attic to store some clothes and barreled out of there shrieking about a lady ghost. She fell from the fold-down stairs to the landing at the top of the stairwell. Momentum carried her down the steps to the ground floor. She died of a broken neck."

"Did anyone check the attic?" Tina asked.

"No. My grandparents had bad knees. My dad wasn't living here. His younger sister Antonina– they called her Nina – was away at college. And, Uncle Jed hadn't recovered from his wounds yet.

"Who else died?"

"In 1952, Aunt Nina invited a boyfriend over to dinner. Her boyfriend heard the ghost story and wanted to prove his bravery, so he climbed up to the attic. When he came down, he said he would tell what he saw after dinner. Everyone sat down to eat. The boyfriend took two bites and his face started swelling. They rushed him to the hospital, but he died. The doctors said he had an undiagnosed food allergy."

"How is that a ghost's fault?" Tina asked.

"I don't know. But, once a decade, someone entered the attic and died shortly thereafter. Margie died in 1946, Nina's boyfriend in 1952, and my cousin Philo in 1965. I almost died peeking up there in 1971. My grandparents died in a car accident that same week!" Al slapped his hand on the table sloshing his coffee.

"Uncle Jed has lived here alone since 1971?"

Al lowered his voice to a whisper again, "After my grandparents died, Jed discouraged Dad and Nina from visiting and then stopped answering Dad's phone calls. Jed didn't even acknowledge Dad's death fifteen years ago. Before social services called me, I'd lost track of Jed."

Tina turned to face the old man, "Uncle Jed, have you ever been in the attic?"

"Not since before Margie died," Jed said in a raspy voice. "My leg ain't been right since the war."

Tina turned to Al with a skeptical look. "Tell me about the ghost. What did you see?"

"It was Easter 1971, and I was 12. Your Uncle Perseus, who was 14, dared me to peek in the attic and I dared him right back. So we lowered the steps and climbed up. I stuck my head in and saw the top half of a woman floating in the darkness. I yelled and fell as Persy jumped down. I would have fallen down the stairwell like Aunt Margie and Philo, but Persy caught me. My grandparents died in a car accident that week when their brakes failed. The curse got them instead of me and Persy."

"What happened to the other guy–Philo?"

"Philo fell down the folding steps and stairwell and died right where Margie died."

"Did someone investigate all these deaths?" Tina completed a mental tally. Five people had died unexpectedly over four decades.

Al waved a hand dismissively. "The sheriff's department investigated everything. Your detective skills aren't needed."

Tina's eyes strayed to the warped linoleum and cracked walls. The house reflected Jed's deterioration. Some rooms had been abandoned for years, left to molder and disintegrate. The few rooms still in use were as threadbare and sun faded as Uncle Jed himself.

The neglected yard around the two-story house had been the old man's undoing. The yard was well-tended until Jed fell and broke his leg two years earlier. Neighbors complained about the overgrown yard. The town's code enforcement officer, discovering a centenarian alone in the house, took the problem to social services. Soon, Jed's nearest relative in the state, Aloysius Jones, Tina's dad, was contacted. Al Jones and his wife evaluated the situation and offered to purchase the house to help the old man relocate.

Tina couldn't imagine her parents leaving their Port Aransas beachfront condominium for this depressing money pit. "What do you intend to do with the house?"

Al looked at her with amusement. "Relax. I haven't lost my mind. We're going to demolish the house and sell the land. Nobody wants a cursed house."

Tina exhaled with relief. "So, we only have to clear the house out before it's wrecked?"

"Yes. The furniture is antique and salable."

"What about the attic? If your grandparents used it for storage, you might find valuable items up there."

Al hesitated and glanced at Jed. "I agreed with Uncle Jed that nothing up there is worth dying for. We'll clear the lower floors, but not the attic. Then, we'll bulldoze this place."

Tina disagreed but didn't argue. "And Jed?"

"Jed is going to an assisted living facility. He'd like the house torn down soon. Kids might vandalize it once it's empty."

Jed said in his husky voice, "I can't let anyone else die. This house is cursed, and the curse needs to die before I do. I've kept visitors away for decades, knowing that telling folks to stay out of the attic was like challenging them to enter it. Fools never listen! Like Philo, your father, and that idiot boyfriend of Nina's! This place is too dangerous to leave standing once I'm gone."

∼

Passing hills covered with scraggly cedar and prickly pear at sunset, Tina arrived in downtown Sloop, and felt a sense of déjà vu. The main street held antique shops, a café, and multiple spaces for lease. The sheriff's department was inside the pink granite, neoclassical former courthouse. Tina recognized the granite as locally sourced, noting it matched the pink granite batholith at nearby Enchanted Rock State Park, one of her favorite places to hike and camp in the fall.

How had she not known that her father's family had lived nearby? Had he driven her through Sloop when she was a child, perhaps on one of their many trips to visit Enchanted Rock? Dad had passed his love of the park to her. Had her father learned to love the park on trips to visit his own grandparents? She realized how unaware of her father's history she was. Her grandfather had moved away and left his roots behind, not knowing her father would someday be pulled back to the town.

Parking her motorcycle, Tina walked inside the courthouse. She was pleased to see that, despite the hour, a middle-aged woman with tightly permed gray hair occupied the reception desk inside the sheriff's department. The name placard on her desk said Ellie Reginald.

"Hi, my name is Tina Jones. I'd like to review some old case files from the 1940s to the 1970s. Are they kept here or are they stored elsewhere?"

Ellie stared at Tina. Recognition came into her grey eyes. "Wait just a moment, please." She picked up her phone, jabbed in an extension number, and spoke, "Sheriff, Ms. Tina Jones is here asking to see old case files. I imagine she wants the records on the Jones House deaths." She surveyed Tina from her dark curls to her steel-toed, leather boots.

"I want to see the file on my great grandparents' car accident, too," Tina said.

"She wants the car accident file too," Ellie said into the phone. She listened, said, "Yes, I'll tell her," and returned the phone to its cradle. "The sheriff will be right out. We scanned some of the old files into the computer, but the oldest ones are on paper in the basement. We'll have to dig them out."

The sheriff appeared in a doorway behind the receptionist. "Ms. Jones? Hi, I'm Quinton Harell," he said, extending a hand toward Tina. "Word in town was Old Jed sold out to relatives. We wondered who would show up." He shook Tina's hand enthusiastically with a warm smile on his sunburned face. The sheriff was sixtyish and wore his starched uniform shirt over a wide belt buckle.

Tina returned his smile, surprised at his genuine warmth. "I'm not the new owner. My dad, Aloysius Jones, bought the property."

"Al Jones bought it? My dad knew his dad, Cornelius. He was your grandfather, right?"

"Yes." Tina realized from the receptionist's interest and the sheriff's warm greeting that her family may have left town, but they were clearly not forgotten.

"That house has seen plenty of grief," the sheriff said.

"I never heard about any of it until today, when my father told me to avoid the attic if I don't want to die."

The sheriff smiled broadly. "You had trouble with that, did you? I don't blame you."

"When I hear about that many deaths in one place, I

get suspicious. I'm a homicide detective with the Austin Police Department." Tina presented her badge.

The sheriff glanced at the badge. "City detective! Welcome. I've seen the files. Had a look at them years ago. Your family's bad luck is legendary around here. From what I remember, the deaths in the house were accidents. Responding deputies observed that the fold-down ladder to the attic aligned with the stairwell to the ground floor. People fell down the ladder and then continued to fall down the flight of stairs, resulting in broken necks."

"That explains Aunt Margie and Philo, but not the boyfriend who died at dinner."

"What boyfriend? I must have missed that case."

"In the 1950's, Jed's sister had a boyfriend who dared to investigate the attic. He came out of the attic, sat down to dinner, ate two bites, went into anaphylactic shock, and died at the hospital. At least, that's the version I got from my dad."

The sheriff tilted his head. "Hmm. He didn't die at the house, and he was under medical care. It sounds like another unfortunate accident. Of course, people see unrelated accidents and have to make connections. They decide the attic is haunted or the house is cursed."

"Generally, I agree with you, but I want to know what caused the brakes to fail on my great grandfather's car. Do the records indicate that he failed to maintain his vehicle?"

Sheriff Harell put his hands together and rubbed them lightly. "Your great grandparent's case – that was the one that troubled me. Reports are missing. My dad was sheriff here in the 1970s. I asked him about it before he passed, but he said to let it alone, that they did what needed to be done to prevent mob violence, to stop a riot."

Tina stared at the sheriff. "A riot? Why?"

"I was only a kid then, so I don't know for sure. All I

know is that the investigator's findings on the brakes aren't in the file. I don't know where they are, and I haven't had the leisure to look into it. Deputy Keelan, who led the investigation, probably knows more. He's retired now, but still sharp."

"When can I see the files? I'm staying in Sloop this weekend, but I can come back to town if needed."

"Can you come tomorrow afternoon around 1:30?"

"Perfect." They shook hands, and Tina returned to her motel for the evening.

Tina and Al spent Saturday morning hefting furniture into a portable storage container while Jed packed china and tarnished silver in the kitchen. According to their agreement, Jed would live off the money from the sale of the house. The sale of the contents would pay for the demolition.

After lunch, everyone needed a break. While Al and Jed retired for an afternoon siesta, Tina returned to the sheriff's office.

A deputy escorted her to an empty desk and gave her a new manila folder containing several older files that were foxed with age. Tina reviewed the records for Margie and Philo. The case files were legible, mainly typed but with some handwritten notes. The responding officers arrived to find what appeared to be accidents and didn't question that presupposition. Since the county didn't have a medical examiner, a justice of the peace ordered the bodies be sent to a local doctor who took X-rays and photos. In both cases, the doctor observed bruising on the victim's neck, attributed the bruises to tumbling down the stairs, and declared the victim had died of a broken neck subsequent to an accidental fall. No formal autopsies were conducted.

Comparing the cases, Tina found the level of the cervical fractures and the bruises were identical for both victims. That couldn't be a coincidence. Reading the reports, Tina discovered that only her Great Grandfather Hezekiah and Great Uncle Jed were present in the house for both deaths.

The car accident file, as the sheriff mentioned, was incomplete and raised more questions than it answered. A note from the sheriff indicated that no file had been found for the food allergy death.

Tina considered the cases. The deaths stopped with Hezekiah and his wife Mary. Could Hezekiah have hidden something in the attic and then killed people who found it? Could Jed have found whatever was in the attic and decided to protect his father's secret? Maybe Jed isolated himself because he didn't want the secret exposed, but was unwilling to kill to protect it. Then again, maybe Jed believed that he had to prevent death by ghost. Or maybe the secret was Jed's.

The car accident was the key. Tina would have to track down the lead investigator, Diego Keelan. Once she had more details about the collision, she'd question Jed. Surely a decades-old secret would be inconsequential by now. If she couldn't convince Jed to divulge the truth, Tina would inspect the attic herself.

She returned the files and asked Ellie, the receptionist, where to find retired Deputy Diego Keelan. The receptionist directed Tina to a local café called Annie's Haven, where Keelan spent Saturday afternoons reading and doing crossword puzzles until chess games started at three o'clock.

Tina found Diego Keelan sitting in the 1950s-themed café with a Vietnam veteran's ballcap at his elbow and a newspaper in front of him.

"Excuse me, Mr. Keelan. My name is Tina Jones. Could I ask you a few questions about a case you worked while you were a deputy?"

The man's dark eyes evaluated her. "Tina Jones? Please, join me." He folded his newspaper. "You must be Al's daughter since rumor says he's buying Old Jed's place. Your whole family has a thing for unusual first names, though you seem to have escaped it. Would you like a drink while we talk? Coffee? Iced tea?"

"Iced tea," Tina replied, sitting down across from him. "I didn't escape the naming tradition: Faustina Eudocia."

"Faustina Eudocia? Yep. That's sounds like your family." Keelan turned his head toward the back of the café. "Gracie," he called out to an employee, who looked up from rolling silverware in paper napkins. "Could you bring two iced teas, please?"

The woman rose from her stool at the counter. "Sure, Diego."

Tina showed Keelan her badge and explained about her dad's purchase of the house and her trip to the Sheriff's office to review files.

The drinks arrived, and the former deputy took a sip before speaking. "You're here because the file on Hezekiah and Mary Jones is incomplete." Keelan's voice held no defensiveness.

"Yes. What can you tell me about the case?"

"Your great grandfather's brakes failed when he tried to stop at a stop sign. He entered an intersection at the same moment as a pickup truck driven by young man who was late for a movie date. The truck rammed your great grandfather's car broadside, killing your great grandmother instantly. Hezekiah died in the hospital an hour later."

"That's in the report. I want to know why the brakes failed."

"Someone damaged the brake line, cut it through."

"Then, it *was* murder?" Tina wasn't surprised.

Keelan drummed his fingers. "We think murder-suicide. We couldn't determine where your great grandparents were going that day. Hezekiah's last words were 'Tell the sheriff. It can't go on.' The family doctor reported that Mary had a brain tumor. She would have been incapacitated in a few months, and dead not long after that. The old sheriff believed that Hezekiah cut the brake line to prevent her suffering. For the sake of the town, the sheriff didn't want to label the case a murder-suicide, though."

While Keelan paused to drink his tea, Tina said, "Sheriff Harell said y'all needed to prevent a riot. Why would anyone riot over a car accident?"

"Fear of the unknown does terrible things to the populace. After your great grandparents' deaths, rumors were circulating that dozens of people had died from a curse on Hezekiah's house. People blamed a ghost in the attic. Talk of burning the place was spreading, and the sheriff wanted to deescalate the situation. He was concerned calling the deaths a murder-suicide would provoke the folks who already thought that something evil was involved. So, he pronounced the collision an accident to the newspapers. He had me withhold the report on the brakes, Hezekiah's final statement, and our findings. I can return the paperwork if you want. The original documents were misfiled, but I know where they are." Keelan folded his hands on the table.

"I'd appreciate that," Tina said. "Was Jed told about the findings?"

"Yes. He agreed to the cover up."

Tina drank her glass of iced tea and considered the evidence. Perhaps Hezekiah felt he could no longer protect his secret in the attic and grew remorseful over the deaths that had already occurred. When he learned Mary was dying, he decided to end it all.

"Thanks for telling me this." Tina leaned back in her chair. "While reviewing the case files, I found some unlikely similarities in two of the earlier deaths, which made me suspect murder. If those two previous deaths weren't accidents, and someone cut the brake line on my great grandfather's car, then we may have three or four murders. Hezekiah's last words might mean he realized he couldn't keep killing people who found something secret hidden in the attic. Whatever is in the attic seems to be at the heart of it, and I don't believe it's a murderous ghost. I'm going to check the attic."

Tina left the café and returned to the dilapidated house. Upon entering, she found siesta-time had ended and the cataloguing of antiques had resumed in the faded kitchen.

Jed's head swiveled around as the screen door banged closed behind Tina. "Where you been? We thought you abandoned your post."

"I had an appointment," Tina said.

Her father turned to peer at her.

Tina could see the questions in Al's eyes, wondering what appointment she could have in a town she'd never visited before yesterday. "The sheriff allowed me to review the files on the deaths related to this house. One of the files was incomplete. I had to hunt down the original investigator to get the missing information."

Jed sighed in annoyance. "You know, then?"

Al looked from his daughter to his uncle. "Know what?"

Tina kept her green eyes on Jed. "Jed's parents' deaths weren't an accident."

"What are you talking about?" Al asked.

"Why couldn't you let them rest in peace? No one needed to know," Jed said with anger choking him, making his words sound harsh and gravelly.

Tina faced her father. "The sheriff officially categorized your grandparents' deaths as murder-suicide because someone cut the brake line on the car, and your grandmother was dying of a tumor. They think Hezekiah killed the two of them so that Mary wouldn't have to suffer. His last words were, 'Tell the sheriff. It can't go on.' The sheriff hid the findings because people were panicked by rumors that the house was cursed. He was afraid a mob would try to burn the place. He told everyone the collision was an accident to calm public fears."

Al blinked several times. "I can't believe it. My father never said a word."

"Cornelius never knew," Jed said. "I didn't tell him."

Tina crossed the kitchen and stood in front of Jed by the oak table. "What's in the attic, Uncle Jed?"

Jed's eyes narrowed. "The Ghostly Lady. We told you that. She curses this place and kills people. That's why we need to destroy the house."

"I don't think so. Is it something shameful your father couldn't face? Whatever the secret is, it must be irrelevant by now."

"Rubbish! There's no secret," Jed said.

Tina put her hands on her hips. "The only people present for *all* of the deaths were you and Hezekiah. And the deaths stopped with Hezekiah. Your parents died

The Ghostly Lady's Curse

shortly after my father and his brother tried to peek into the attic. Did Hezekiah kill himself and Mary because he was afraid his grandkids would find his secret? Did he balk at killing children?"

Jed banged one boney hand down on the kitchen table. "The ghostly lady's curse killed everyone."

"Then, if I go into the attic, I won't find anything except the ghost of a lady?" Tina crossed the warped linoleum toward the stairs.

Al blocked his daughter's path. "No! You'll die if you go up there. I saw the lady and almost died because of it."

Tina sidestepped her father. "You saw something, Dad, but I don't think it was a ghost. You grew up with this story, and you believed what you were told as a child. Look at the facts, not the story."

Movement caught Tina's eye, and she turned to see Jed hobbling toward a closet, leaning on his cane. Jed opened the closet and reached inside. Tina lunged forward as Jed lifted a rusty shotgun. She knocked the gun away. The heavy weapon clattered to the floor. Tina picked up the gun. "Stop, Jed!"

Jed grabbed Tina's leather jacket. "It's not your business. Your father agreed that no one goes up there!"

Tina shook free of Jed's grip. "Dad agreed. I didn't." Facts shifted and a new theory assembled in her brain. "You returned from World War II, and people started dying. You hid something in the attic. Your Aunt Margie went up there and found it. She confronted you, so you broke her neck and threw her down the stairs."

"She fell!" Jed gasped, leaning against the kitchen table.

"And Philo fell and landed with the exact same bruises on his neck? With his neck fractured in precisely the same location? It wouldn't have been hard for a young man to snap someone's neck. You probably learned how during the war."

Jed glared at Tina.

Tina stood toe to toe with Jed. "Did you even pause before you damaged the brake line on your parents' car?"

Al intervened, moving between his daughter and his uncle. "What proof do you have?"

"None," said Tina. "But, if Margie and Philo were murdered, only two people could have killed them both. One of those people, Hezekiah, died under questionable circumstances. If your grandfather didn't cut the brake line himself, the only other suspect for all the deaths is Uncle Jed." She pointed to Jed. "And he's hiding something in the attic."

Jed rapped his cane on the floor. "I'm not hiding anything! I'm trying to save lives. Anyone who goes in the attic dies. My father went up there before the accident! The ghost cursed him, too!" Jed's face reddened. "You can't go up there!"

Tina said, "Think about this, Dad. Jed severed contact with family and kept everyone away for decades. Why? Not because of a ghost. A ghost didn't cut the brake line." Tina gave Al the shotgun and mounted the stairs. "Dad, keep an eye on Uncle Jed."

"Okay," her father said at last, watching Jed, who stood seething in the kitchen. "Be careful!" he called after her.

Tina climbed the creaking stairs to the second floor and pulled down the ladder to the attic. Unlike other parts of the house where doors long unused were jammed shut on rusted hinges, the attic ladder fell into place without protest. Tina climbed up.

"What do you see?" Al called anxiously from downstairs.

Tina entered the dim, dusty attic. "Trunks and furni-

The Ghostly Lady's Curse

ture." She turned around and saw the ghostly lady. A shaft of light illuminated the woman's face and white sleeves. In the darkness, she appeared to be floating. But it wasn't a ghost. Standing on an antique dresser was a portrait of a woman in old-fashioned clothing.

Tina lifted the painting and studied it. She called down to her father. "I found the lady! It's an exquisite portrait of a woman, probably a museum piece. I bet Uncle Jed found it during World War II. Maybe he stole it or looted it from a damaged building, then brought it home."

"Bring it down," Al called.

Tina carefully descended the attic ladder with the painting.

Jed's voice rang out, "Don't touch her! She's mine!"

Tina returned to the kitchen. "You killed them, didn't you?" She held the portrait in one hand and wrinkled her nose in disdain. "You murdered *family* for this useless piece of canvas and paint." She pretended to flick at the paint with one finger.

Jed's arthritic hands reached for the painting. "You will die for this! No one else can see her. She's mine!"

Tina withdrew the painting from Jed's reach as her father restrained him.

Jed struggled to break free from Al's grasp. "I saved her. I won't give her back to them. Do you know how many they killed on the beach?" Spittle flew from the old man's mouth. "Do you know how many friends I lost? They were all gone! Then she came to me."

Tina rocked backward on her boots, out of spitting distance. "Dad, we need to call the police."

Al shook his head while forcing Jed into a chair. "He's one-hundred-two years old."

"He's threatening to kill to protect this painting. We can have him held for a psychiatric evaluation. And we need to contact the authorities to find out where this painting belongs. Artwork that vanished during World War II is catalogued. Our lady ghost needs to go home." Tina laid the painting on the kitchen table, pulled out her phone, and began to dial.

Ten minutes later the sheriff arrived. Jed screamed obscenities as an ambulance took him away for evaluation.

~

Two weekends later, Tina rode her motorcycle back to Sloop to help her father finish emptying the house. She and Al met the sheriff and Diego Keelan for lunch at Annie's Haven.

While they waited for their food, the sheriff relayed what he'd learned. "Jed claims the portrait began speaking to him when he found it in Germany in 1945. He said she silenced other voices he heard before that. He's apparently been hearing voices since he was eighteen and went to war. He hid his illness by isolating himself and killing anyone who saw the painting."

Tina asked, "He confessed to murdering them all?"

"Yes," Sheriff Harell said. "He admitted to killing Margie, Philo, and his own parents. He said Hezekiah went up to the attic one night when he thought Jed was asleep. Jed overheard Hezekiah and Mary talking about the painting and questioning Jed's sanity. They planned to see the sheriff. Jed damaged the car's brake line that night to stop them. We filed charges, but at his age, he may not live to see his case concluded."

Al shook his head sadly. "Jed's not mentally competent to stand trial anyway. But, what about Nina's boyfriend? Did Jed kill him, too?"

The sheriff said, "Jed says he didn't kill Nina's

boyfriend because he never had the chance. Jed believes the lady killed him."

Diego Keelan cleared his throat. "Jed never appeared crazy back then. I'm sorry our conclusions were so wrong on Hezekiah's and Mary's deaths."

"At least Uncle Jed didn't kill anyone else after the car accident," Tina said. "He must have realized that people wouldn't stand for any more sudden deaths." She nudged her father. "Are you still planning to demolish the house?"

Al said, "Yes. The house needs too much repair to be worth fixing. Most of the studs are rotten from unrepaired leaks."

"Thank you for demolishing it," Sheriff Harell said. "If the place sat empty for months waiting for a purchaser, I'd have to assign a car to guard it every night to stop kids from daring each other to go inside."

Tina asked the sheriff, "Did anyone identify the painting?"

"We've been informed it's by Caravaggio, one of 417 artworks belonging to the Kaiser Friedrich Museum that were presumed destroyed in May 1945. Officials had stored the art in a tower that burned during a bombing raid. Our government will be contacting the German government about returning it," the sheriff said.

Al put his arm around Tina's shoulder and squeezed his daughter. "Thank you. Jed's illness was consuming him. Part of him must have wanted to be free of the voice in his head. Otherwise, why would he want me to demolish the house with the painting inside? With the portrait gone and with proper treatment, maybe he'll find peace before he dies."

Leaving Jed's vacant house for the last time later that day, Tina paused on the weed-choked lawn, pondering the family history she'd never known. The ghostly lady's "curse" was gone. Tina wondered what other family secrets may have formed her parents and, by extension, her. Despite the fact that she had never lived there, Sloop felt more like home than anywhere else she had lived. Everywhere she went, people welcomed her as if she belonged. Tina had always loved the Hill Country. Was it time for her to make a change and leave the city for the country? Could she reconnect with the roots Jed's illness had severed? Whatever she decided, first she would sit down with both her parents and have a long talk about family history.

~

N.M. *Cedeño is a Plan II graduate of the University of Texas at Austin. A native Texan, she lives in Round Rock and writes crime and mystery short stories and novels that vary from traditional to romantic suspense and from historical to science fiction.* Her paranormal mystery series, Bad Vibes Removal Services, *currently includes two novels and fourteen short stories. Her short fiction has appeared in anthologies and magazines including* Analog: Science Fiction and Fact, After Dinner Conversation: Philosophy and Ethics, Black Cat Weekly, and Black Cat Mystery Magazine. *Her short story entitled "A Reasonable Expectation of Privacy" tied for third place for Best Short Story in the 2013 Analog Readers Poll.*

Ms. Cedeño is a member of Sisters in Crime and its Heart of Texas Chapter, where she has served as chapter vice president and president. She is a member of the Short Mystery Fiction Society. Ms. Cedeño blogs with several other Heart of Texas mystery writers at InkStainedWretches.home.blog. *For more information please visit* nmcedeno.com.

Death of a Mage Professor
A.R.R. Ash

Taela shrank back in her chair from the ravings of Mage Professor Didamedes as he paced around his cluttered office, hands waving about as if fending off a swarm of offending insects. She was not afraid for herself from Didamedes's gesticulations, though she had never seen him in such an excited state for anything less than an argument over some esoteric experiment to calculate the magical conversion coefficient to an extra significant digit or a debate over whether Wylar Darkcowl or Nylyr Longfeather was the first to formulate Magical Field Theory.

"They've decided to stop funding my research. *My* research! We have only until the end of the semester."

"Yes, mage pr — "

"But they continue to fund the work of that upstart and mediocrity Sohla. What could they possibly be thinking?"

"I th — "

"I mean, really!" Didamedes swung his arms about at the swarm that only he could see. "My research into magical flux is going to change the way we understand magical energy, and they complain that it's *not marketable*."

Didamedes had started to repeat himself, and Taela's attention began to wander about the office. As an adjunct mage professor and assistant to Didamedes, Taela was as familiar with the room as she was with her own sleep chamber. Yet she took the need for a distraction as an opportunity to reacquaint herself with the room's contents.

Located in the basement beneath the university's Magimetry wing, the office had no windows, its brick walls concealed by sturdy bookshelves or slate boards. Books on every branch of Magical Dynamics, from Epistemagiology to Physiomagiology, filled the shelves and sat in piles atop buried desks. The majority of the tomes, however, covered various fields and topics of Magimetry, the theoretical framework describing the measurement and quantification of magical energy. Reams of parchment, containing calculations that would wrap around the entire wing of the Mageion, lay sprawled about. Glass globes of flameless light sat, here and there, upon tripods or hung from the ceiling upon iron chains.

In its place of importance, upon a slate board at the front of the office, was the formula underpinning all their work:

$$d\bcancel{M} = \int_{t1}^{t2} \iint \bcancel{F} \cdot d\mathbf{A} dt$$

Didamedes's reaction notwithstanding, Taela understood the mage professor's outburst. To her, the work they did was a more essential calling than a holy vocation, and the collection of books more valuable than any holy relic. The slate board displaying the formula describing magical flux was their altar, and the smell of paper and leather, incense.

Because Didamedes expressed her own outrage through his tirade, she was able to maintain her demeanor of calm thoughtfulness. Yet she was no less concerned about the consequence that the retraction of funding would have upon their work and —

"Taela! Are you listening to me?"

Taela flinched in her return to awareness. "Ah, yes, of course, Mage Professor. The university is demonstrating its lack of discernment in choosing to continue to fund Sohla's research over yours."

Didamedes blinked twice and frowned, as if surprised at Taela's answer and unsure whether to be pleased that she had been listening or vexed that he'd been denied the opportunity to reiterate his complaint. "Well. . .ah. . .yes. Yes, they are." He nodded once, curtly, to punctuate the statement, as if to claim credit for Taela's summation as his own.

Didamedes's rage temporarily spent, he ceased his pacing and stood quietly in the middle of the office, his breath coming loudly and quickly.

Taela maintained the silence, her hands clasped upon the lap of her red robe, two gold stripes along the cuffs indicating her position as an adjunct.

Finally, Didamedes's breathing eased, though his eyes were narrowed and focused. "Taela. . .if something. . .were to happen to me, you must carry on my research. It is important."

Taela sat straighter, her face bunched. "Happen? What's going to happen? What do you mean?"

Didamedes shook his head and gave a dismissive wave. "Nothing. I just happened to notice some unsavory characters following me as I left the Merry Toucan

Alehouse. I'm sure it's nothing at all. Just in case, you know?"

Taela most certainly did not know, and, she thought, neither did she *want* to know.

∼

One afternoon, the better part of a fortnight later, Taela sighed as the neophyte students filed out of the auditorium classroom. Mage Professor Didamedes had failed to show, and Taela had been forced to expound on the Postulate of Mathematical Describability. She gathered her papers and strode purposefully to the stairwell that would take her to Didamedes's subterranean office. This was not the first time he had become so engrossed in a calculation that he'd forgotten he had a class to teach, but Taela was intent to make it the last.

Exiting the stairwell, Taela came to a sudden halt. At the far end of the corridor, where sat the entrance to Didamedes's office, stood two guards in the black scale armor of the warriors of the city watch.

For a moment, the fleeting urge to turn and abscond nearly spurred Taela back up the stairs. However, the knot in her throat and the void where her stomach had been propelled her forward.

Light from the open door spilled from the office into the passage, and the guards turned toward her as she approached. Taela smelled the lingering odor of smoke, and she feared someone had brought an open flame within Didamedes's office — the potential loss of books and scholarship caused water to well in the corner of her eye.

"Wha-what happened?" Taela asked, craning her neck to see past the guards and into the office.

One guard raised a black-mailed hand. "Who are you?" Even through his black dragon helm, his voice was clear and firm.

"I — I'm Taela. I work with Mage Professor Didamedes. Is — "

"Come with me," the same guard said and turned his body to indicate that she should follow.

"Ah, yes," Taela said, nodding twice. She stepped past the guard, who followed her into the office.

At their entrance, those in the room turned to face them. Present were a number of official-looking types, some in the silver robes of the university's leadership, some in the black cloaks — hence their name — of the mages of the watch.

One of the silver robes, Hegimenus of Tyracuse, Mage Chair of the Magimetry Department, greeted her, his expression relaxing. "Ah! Taela, I was just about to send the guards in search of you. When we found . . . Didamedes, I feared the worst."

Taela shook her head, trying to clear the confusion that muddled her thoughts. "When — what? What happened to Didamedes?"

Taela tried to swallow, but she found the lump in her throat had grown. Where *was* Didamedes?

Hegimenus moved aside and indicated a pile of ash that lay upon the stone floor in the middle of the office, the largest open expanse in the chamber where Didamedes was wont to pace when considering a problem.

Taela was a moment understanding just what it was she looked at, as if her mind had frozen. From the void that was her stomach, a burning acid rose to the back of Taela's throat. "I — I don't understand." She swallowed the rancid bile. "I saw him this morning."

"I am sorry," Hegimenus said, his tone somber and

eyes kind. "The protective magics alerted the water mages to a significant flame. Yet, when they came to inspect, they found only that pile of ash. They immediately brought it to my attention, and I requested the assistance of the Black Cloaks and the city guard."

Taela shook her head in confusion and denial. "That could be anything."

"No, Taela." Hegimenus's voice had fallen even lower, and he spoke slowly. "The Black Cloaks have their methods and, I'm afraid, they assure me that. . .those are the remains of Didamedes."

Taela had difficulty breathing, and her chest ached. Was this what drowning felt like? Her legs shook and threatened to give out under her own weight.

"Where were you during the attack?" The voice was rough and held none of the sympathy of Hegimenus's.

Attack? Nothing was making any sense. Who would attack Didamedes? Taela had been so focused on Hegimenus and the pile of ash that she had paid no attention to the others in the office. "Huh?"

The Black Cloak stepped toward her. The cowl of his cloak was lowered, and she could see the harsh intensity of his deep blue eyes. Even as discombobulated as she was, Taela thought that, under other circumstances, those eyes would have been striking. "I — I was teaching a — his class."

"And how *do* you know when the attack occurred?" the same Black Cloak asked, his voice smug. "I never specified."

"I — I don't." *Calm yourself.* Taela took several deep breaths. "I saw him, briefly, this morning. His class was to start at midday, but he never showed. I just came from there, so I assumed that that was when. . .it happened.

Though, I suppose it could have occurred earlier. I was working on some calculations before that."

"Alone?"

"Come, now," Hegimenus said, slightly chiding. "You cannot believe Taela had any involvement here."

The Black Cloak turned his gaze on Hegimenus. "Thank you, Mage Chair Hegimenus. This investigation is now under the purview of the Black Cloaks, and we will conduct it as necessary."

Hegimenus held the other's gaze for a moment before nodding and looking away, his body relaxing in resignation. "Very well. We stand ready to assist in any way to gain justice for Mage Professor Didamedes."

"The Black Cloaks thank you, Mage Chair." Though his tone did not convey any sense of thankfulness. The investigator turned back to her. "Adjunct Mage Professor Taela, please have a seat, that we might speak more fully." He indicated the very chair in which Taela had sat those days before when Didamedes paced about, raving at the loss of his funding. How quaint and how long ago that day now seemed.

Taela nodded in acknowledgment and, her legs giving out, veritably collapsed into the chair.

The Black Cloak came to stand before her, looking downward. "I am Vael, day commander of the Black Cloaks."

Taela nodded in greeting, as if only now meeting him.

He raised a pale hand that held a bejeweled ring upon each of his five fingers. "I have several more questions for you. And know: I *will* know if you lie. If you lie, we have numerous ways of learning the truth." He paused to allow Taela time to dwell on the implications of that statement.

Taela nodded in understanding, a shiver running through her. The day commander's tone was casual, if not pleasant, yet the undertone of a threat unmistakable. "I have nothing about which to lie."

Vael nodded. "That is good. Now then, were you alone when you were conducting your calculations?"

Taela again nodded. "Yes. I prefer the quiet." Her palms were sweaty, and she felt sweltered in her robe. Why was she so nervous? She had nothing to hide.

"I see." The day commander's tone somehow made the simple statement sound like an accusation. "You are, of course, aware that the wards on the Mageion's buildings and campus prevent any teleportation or blinking in or out, and bar the entrance of undead or other malicious creatures?"

"Yes, of course." Taela's mouth was dry and her voice hoarse.

"They also suppress any spells cast in offense."

"Mm-hmm."

"Then how do you explain the fact that the door was locked from the inside when Didamedes's remains were found? No casting upon the door itself was detected."

"I — it was. . .I guess someone had a key."

"Ah, so you see my dilemma?" His tone had changed to almost sympathetic. "And you have a key, do you not?"

"Yes, I do, but — "

"And who else?"

"I don't. . .I'm not sure. Other assistants over the years."

"I'll need their names."

Taela began to breathe easier, and the sensation of overheating lessened as the questioning moved away from her. "I can't imagine any of them would do anything like this, though."

That was the wrong thing to say. Vael's eyes narrowed, and his voice lowered. "Oh, is that right? Do you know at whom I should be looking more closely?" He leaned in toward Taela.

"No. I don't know. I was just saying." Taela did all she could to not break into tears at that moment.

Vael stood in silence, staring at Taela, who looked away and fidgeted under that glare.

Finally, the Black Cloak asked, "Can you see if anything was taken?"

"All right." Taela glanced about the room. Her eyes came to rest on the slate board, and she froze. For several moments, the office was utterly silent. The equation to calculate magical flux had been altered. Not only that, but it was incorrect. She'd been so frightened and in shock before that she hadn't noticed.

With narrowed eyes, Vael asked, "Do you see something? Is something missing?"

Vael's voice startled Taela back to awareness. "Ah, no. Nothing missing. May I. . .May I get up and look around?"

Vael frowned, as if expecting a lie and was disappointed to have not found one. He nodded in answer.

"Thank you." Taela stood and walked about the office, the day commander following closely.

She examined each table, scrutinized every shelf. Finally, she came to Didamedes's desk, yet she found nothing amiss there either. "Nothing."

"What about the drawer?" Vael asked, indicating a drawer in the desk.

"It's locked," Taela said.

"Do you have they key?"

"Yes, but — "

"Open it."

Taela swallowed. Didamedes didn't like anyone going through his desk. She pulled the key from a pocket in her robe and inserted it into the hole. Despite the apparent mundanity of the mechanism, most locks in the Mageion were magical in nature, and the keys had not only to fit the mechanism but had to be attuned magically to a particular lock. Something very difficult to do if one was not the person who originally cast the protective magic.

Taela opened the drawer, glanced inside, and gasped. "His research — all his master copies are gone."

Vael stood straighter. "And you didn't know? That's not why you didn't want to look in there?"

Taela shook her head. "No. No, of course not. I just didn't think anyone could have gotten in without disabling the magic."

Vael narrowed his eyes, though, again, he did not contest her answer. "Do you know who would have, and could have, taken them?"

Taela again shook her head. "No." Her back straightened as a memory returned to her suddenly. "Mage Professor Didamedes had said something about, 'if something were to happen' to him."

Vael made a sound that, in an animal, Taela would have called a growl. "And you're just telling me this now?"

"I did — I just remembered it now. I'm sorry." Taela looked downward to the floor of dark wood paneling.

"Did he say what he meant?" By his slow and low tone, Vael was certainly losing his patience.

"Um. . .he didn't go into detail. But over the next few days, he asked me if I'd noticed anyone following me. I said I hadn't. He told me to be careful. It was likely nothing, he said, but he'd thought someone might have been following him. Someone interested in his research."

Vael scoffed. "Is there anything else you're forgetting to tell me?"

Shaking her head emphatically, Taela said, "No. I don't think so. No."

Vael gave a frustrated sigh. "Adjunct Mage Professor, you may go — for now. Do not leave the city. We will call upon you if we need anything else."

Taela nodded, loosing a sigh of relief. "Thank you." As she passed, she gave a curt nod to Hegimenus and whispered, "Mage Chair." Putting her head down to avoid eye contact with the other Black Cloaks and two Black Scales at the door, Taela hurried to her room.

Taela sat in her favorite chair, whose plush cushion had long since conformed to the shape her body. Eyes closed, she considering all that had happened. There, in the quiet and solitude of her room, she could understand why the watch would have suspected her. Except that she was a researcher; she did not know any spell that would have immolated someone, let alone having the skill to overcome the wards to attack Didamedes. To say nothing of the fact that it was something she would never do even if she could!

Her eyes shot open, as if attached to springs released from compression. The equation. She had stared at it every day for years, so she'd easily recognized the changes, whereas Mage Chair Hegimenus likely paid no attention to it or was too distracted to notice, as she had been at first. Taela doubted that the investigators would know a magical flux density from a magical density. She wasn't quite sure why she hadn't mentioned it to Vael, but she had an inkling that it was meant for her.

Taela retrieved parchment, ink, and quill and set to recreating the changed formula she'd seen:

$$dM = \int_{t1}^{t2} \iint T \cdot dAdt$$

Below it, she jotted the erroneous terms. The differential of the magical energy referenced the notation for a single mag, M — an unmeasurable, quantized unit of magical energy — rather than the measurable and more practical molar mag, $\mathcal{M}$, equivalent to $6.02214179 \times 10^{23}$ mags. The differential area showed the scalar quantity, A, rather than the vector quantity, **A**. Lastly, the magical flux, $\mathcal{T}$, was incorrectly written as mundane flux, T.

For some time, Taela simply stared at the three terms: M, A, and T. Mage Professor Didamedes would never have made such mistakes. But then, if purposeful, toward what purpose? Could he have left a clue as to the identity of his killer?

Taela shook her head. How would he have had time to adjust the formula while engaged in a battle for his life? And if he did have time, why not just be more direct as to his murderer's identity? She sighed in growing frustration and rubbed her eyes with the heels of her palms. She had more questions without even an inkling as to where to look for an answer.

Taela rearranged the correct formula into alternative forms, hoping they would offer some new insight:

$$\iint \mathcal{T} \cdot dA = dM/dt$$

Then:

$$\mathcal{T} = d^2M/(dAdt[\cos \theta])$$

Nothing. After staring at the equations long enough that

she had to light a new candle, Taela gleaned no epiphany from the manipulated formulae as to the intent of Mage Professor Didamedes. In some corner of her mind, she heard and felt her stomach rumble and recognized that she was hungry. However, Taela was accustomed to engaging in long nights of lucubration and put the distraction out of mind.

She considered what she knew of the relationship between the erroneous terms. Magical energy, unlike mundane energy, was not a derived unit but was a fundamental quantity — the substance of magic — both a thing unto itself and a property of all things in Existence. A molar mag was defined as the amount of magical energy that passed through an area of one square pico-meter per second. Area had the dimension of length squared. Magical flux, like the mundane equivalent, had the dimension of quantity per length squared per time.

Taela shook her head again and gave a deeper sigh, born of profound frustration. The three terms had no greater meaning or other relation to one another, as far as she knew. Without further information, she had no context to focus her analysis.

"What aren't I seeing?" she said aloud. Feeling as if she were failing Didamedes, tears welled in her eyes, and she choked back a sob. He must have left those clues thinking she was smart enough to discern their meaning, yet she had no notion what it might be.

A, M, and T. *Maybe I'm overthinking it.* Taela sat up straighter. What if the letters were just that, letters? She arranged the letters into their six possible combinations — AMT, ATM, MAT, MTA, TAM, and TMA. She grunted and ran a hand through her hair. Those acronyms could mean anything. *Magical theory analysis. Too much alcohol.* She gave a sardonic laugh.

No, the order of the letters must have meaning — she hoped. So, Tacla concentrated on the acronym MTA.

Perhaps Didamedes had learned the identity of the one who'd followed him and left the individual's initials on the chance that something nefarious occurred. Taela closed her eyes and put her head into her hands. Realizing that her breath was rapid and shallow, she efforted to ease her respiration. Her mouth was dry, and she took a long draft of water, then continued to stare at the letters.

Whom did she know with the initials MTA? Try as she might, she couldn't think of a single person. Taela recalled the last conversations she'd had with Didamedes. Perhaps he'd given some hint that she hadn't realized at the time.

Taela sat bolt upright as if struck by lightning. Didamedes had mentioned being followed near the Merry Toucan Alehouse. It had to be a coincidence. Or, maybe, Didamedes saw his killer there; perhaps the killer even rented a room there.

Taela stood, stretched, and yawned. She had been sitting for the better part of the day, and her legs were stiff. It was likely nothing but, at least, a visit to the Merry Toucan Alehouse gave her something to do. For a short time, she could feel like she was making progress. She donned her walking boots and a mantle against the slight chill of the evening and walked from the campus of the Mageion and into the city proper of Magipolis.

What was she doing? What would she do if, indeed, she found the culprit? She was a researcher, not a spellcaster.

Taela stopped abruptly in the middle of the avenue, forcing other pedestrians to circumvent her like an obstacle dropped in their path. She should go back and tell the Black Cloaks or Mage Chair Hegimenus. She took a deep breath and shook her head in response to her inner argument. No! Didamedes had left those clues for her, of that she was certain.

With renewed determination, she continued onward. Soon, she stood outside a three-story, stone brick structure with a sign depicting a toucan with its beak plunged into a tankard. Orange-yellow light glowed from the windows to either side of the door.

With a deep breath to steel herself, Taela entered and inhaled the pervasive smell of beer and spiced meat and potatoes. The conversation was a continuous buzz but not raucous. Several heads turned in her direction, though none lingered on her.

Taela walked to the bar and caught the barkeep's attention. "Good day, good sir, do you recall Mage Professor Didamedes visiting your establishment?"

The aging man, dressed in a tunic and leathers, nodded. "He paid for a month in advance." He reached under the bar and retrieved a key. "He said to give this to a woman asking after him."

Taela felt dizzy, like her head floated on waves separate from her body.

Already turning toward another customer, he handed her the iron key. "Room four, third floor."

Without her mind willing it, her hand took the key — forgetting to thank the man — and her legs, of their own volition, carried her to and up the stairs.

The key slid into the hole and rewarded Taela with a click when she turned it. She almost *hoped* the key wouldn't work, for then she could postpone learning what was in the room — what her murdered mentor had left for her alone. Postpone the further reality of his death.

With another deep inhalation and a quick wipe of the tear that escaped down her cheek, she opened the door, crossed the threshold, and closed the door behind her. The click of the bolt seemed ominously loud.

Whatever Taela had expected to find in the room — her mentor actually alive and well or an enemy lying in wait — that wasn't it. The room could have been any other in any inn or hostel in Magipolis. Kempt bed, simple but comfortable chairs, a desk, a bureau, and a wardrobe. The only item that spoke to the uniqueness of the chamber was a single, folded sheet upon the desk.

The leaf was sealed with unstamped red wax and had her name in Didamedes's script scrawled upon it. With a shaking hand, Taela broke the seal and unfolded the sheet, then wiped the water that blurred her sight and read:

> Taela, I never doubted you would solve my riddle. I am the one dead, but I must apologize for what you have, no doubt, endured. We were so close to a breakthrough, and I simply could not allow the university to end my research. With my death — I do hope I did not suffer (one can only self-immolate once, after all) — and the apparent theft of the documents, even that politicking bureaucrat Hegimenus must conclude that I had been killed for our work and will see the benefit in its continuation.
>
> As I write this, I imagine the play of emotion you must be feeling, particularly anger and betrayal, as you realize the import of what

I have done. I can picture your scowling face and fuming denunciations. I can only assure you that, despite the great sacrifice, it is one I believe worth making. The research is all that matters, and I am nothing without my work. A parent would risk everything for their child, and I can do no less for something that means as much to me.

You will find the missing research documents in the drawer of this desk. You do not need me to complete the work. Take all the credit if you will. All that matters is the work — the magic.

Yours ~ Mage Professor Didamedes

The letter fell from Taela's numbed hand, and she stood immobile; even her thoughts seemed frozen and her tears stagnant. When she was, finally, again capable of movement, Teala reread the letter, thinking it must be another cryptogram of some sort. It couldn't mean what it seemed to mean. Didamedes had *not* been murdered; he had taken his own life for the sake of the continuation of their work.

Taela opened the drawer of the desk and found all their missing research. She shook her head in stubborn denial.

A creak of the floorboards outside the room and the click of the bolt on the door shook Taela from her stupor. She had just the time to put the documents and letter into the drawer and close it before the knob turned and the door opened.

Black Cloak Vael stood in the doorway, cowl down, with two Black Scales standing indomitably behind him in shining ebon armor. They may have been the same guards as before; in their armor, they all looked the same to her.

Taela clasped her hands behind her back so Vael would not see them shake.

"Do not look so surprised," Vael said. "Surely, you did not believe we would not have you under observation." He looked at the nondescript room and frowned. "Why are you here?"

Taela nearly answered before remembering that the Black Cloak would detect a lie. She quickly rephrased her response. "The loss of Mage Professor Didamedes was overwhelming. Everything at the university reminded me of him."

Vael's eyes narrowed, and his frown deepened, again frustrated at her apparent lack of falsity. "And, so, you came here?"

Taela shrugged — neither affirmation nor denial. She hoped his magic would not register it as a lie.

"I needed to think," Taela said. "And I'd like privacy to grieve, if you please." Her voice grew harsh and indignant. "I don't know why you waste effort pursuing me when I am obviously not the killer."

"Perhaps not," Vael said, "but I believe you know more than you say."

Taela felt as if her heart leaped into her throat and choked her. Did he know? No, it was only a general statement, a provocation. "If you please, I'd like to be alone."

Vael continued to scrutinize he for several moments before nodding, turning on his heel, and departing. The Black Scales closed the door behind them.

As soon as he was gone, Taela fell onto the bed and sobbed until her tears went dry.

Taela stood on the stage before the assembled luminaries of the various fields of Magiology. Her body tingled with excitement and nervousness . . . and a touch of fear. Through her water-clouded vision, she saw, in the crowd, a pair of intense, deep blue eyes beneath the hood of a black cloak. She could not see his expression, yet she did not believe that he was one to let a crime go unsolved, a perpetrator unpunished, even after so many years. A cold shiver shook her body, and she forced herself to look away.

Taela's conscience bent nearly to breaking under the weight of the guilt represented by the medallion she held. Through tear-shrouded eyes, she looked at the starburst pattern on the platinum medal — the most coveted recognition for any magical researcher. Despite her protestations, they had even named the scientific law after her — Taela's Law of Magical Diffusion.

Even now, she would have given up the recognition and the award and the significant monetary prize if the sacrifice would have returned her mentor to her. Yet no one could know the truth without destroying everything Didamedes had died to make possible. And that was a worse betrayal than taking credit for his life's work.

Holding aloft the medallion in a tremulous hand, Taela said, in a voice equally quivering, "I accept this Lauder Award in the name of Mage Professor Didamedes, without whom I would not be standing here."

A.R.R. ASH

A.R.R. Ash is a lifelong fan of both science fiction and fantasy, though he typically focuses his talents on writing grimdark. His first independently published novel is The Moroi Hunters. He has had short stories appear in several anthologies — including Hidden Villains, Hidden Villains: Arise, and Behind the Shadows by Inkd Publishing, as well as Socially Distant: The Quarantales *by Impulsive Walrus Books* — and he has received a Silver Honorable Mention and five Honorable Mentions from the L. Ron Hubbard's Writers of the Future Contest. Xy: Descent, *the first book of his* The First Godling *trilogy, as well as* The Tribe of Fangs, *the prequel to* The Moroi Hunters, *are undergoing editing. He is currently working on* Xy: Ascent, *the sequel to* Xy: Descent, *as well as other short stories that pique his interest.*

In other trivia, his favorite dishes are burgers and sushi (but not together), and his favorite series is Dune, *though* The Expanse *by James S. A. Corey is making a run for the title. His sense of humor is decidedly an acquired taste. You can contact A.R.R. Ash and watch his interview with Cursed Dragon Ship Publishing through LMPBooks.com.*

On the Rocks
Tiffany Seitz

"No! Come back!"

It was a hot and dreary morning, and Georgie was no match for the scruffy mongrel's determination to sneak into the building. She imagined what the gruff landlord would say about an animal in his domain as the stray disappeared down the hall. A glance at her surroundings proved the dog wasn't the only creature housed inside the walls. She hadn't visited in several years, but she didn't remember the building being so decrepit. Carefully avoiding rat droppings and scurrying roaches, she walked down the same dingy hallway the dog had gone.

The dog forgotten; she stopped outside of a wooden door; its clean surface hid the horrors within. Bold, black lettering on the frosted glass proudly announced the business name: G. Powers, Private Investigator, Est. 1946. Georgie traced the letters with a gloved fingertip. Her lips lifted in a trembling smile at the memory of Gordon's pride in his new venture. Having left as a boy, he'd come home from the war as a man with fancy decorations on his uniform and a dream of owning his own business. She had watched as he painted his name on the glass almost ten years ago, saying, "I can help people, Georgie." Her eyes had rolled as only a sixteen-year-old sister's could.

"Oh, Gordie," she sighed. Her eyes weren't rolling now. They were damp with fresh tears that she refused to let fall. "You helped many people. Including me."

Shaking her head to relieve the stinging in her eyes, Georgie fumbled in her handbag for a handkerchief. The only one she found was wrapped around the key to the office. Ned Novis had provided everything from a shoulder to cry on to a handkerchief to dry her eyes. He had dealt with many of Gordon's business associates but was occupied when the landlord approached her with the key, a reminder that the office needed to be cleaned, and that rent was due by the fifth.

Delicately blotting her nose, she sniffed as she unlocked the door and turned the brass doorknob. The door clicked open, letting a wave of stale air hit her. Although she wasn't sure she could trust him, she now wished she'd accepted Ned's offer of help. It was too late to change her mind.

With a glance down the hall to ensure no one lurked, she placed a hand on the doorframe to steady her nerves and leaned through the doorway far enough to see that a tornado had swept through the dimly lit office. Gordon hadn't been the neatest man in the world, but he wouldn't have left the filing cabinet lying on its side with files and papers strewn about.

Georgie's teeth worried her bottom lip. The police had released the scene, but it seemed that they had taken no care for her brother's belongings. She couldn't say with any certainty if the chaos was Gordon's, the murderer's, or the investigators' — or all three.

"Hello?" Her voice sounded timid. Gathering her wits, she tried again. "Is anyone here?"

Silence.

Determined to get on with her mission, Georgie turned to shut the door but stopped as a hint of color on the door's window caught her attention. She leaned in for a closer look: blood-red ruby flecks marred the glass. She shuddered, swallowing the bile that threatened to come up. Thankfully, the coroner had spared her the sight of her brother's bullet-ridden chest — having cleaned him up for identification. The memory of Gordon's lifeless form lying in a cold steel slab would remain with her forever.

A sob escaped. The funeral had been the day before. Maybe she shouldn't do this so soon. Ned had offered to sort through Gordon's things for her. Maybe. . . No. She could go through Gordon's things. She could continue his dream. She could. . . No. She *would* find his killer.

Stepping into the office, the only sounds came from the swish of her fashionably full skirt, the crinkle of paper, and a drip from the washroom. Georgie removed her gloves and hat as she looked around. Taking a deep breath was a mistake. The stagnant air, tainted with the metallic stench of aged blood, forced her toward the window. The lock was stuck, but she managed to wrench it open, breaking a fingernail. She gulped several breaths of humid summer air into her lungs before turning back to her task. A mental list formed: gather and sort the papers, clean up the bloodstains, and determine the status of the current investigations.

The jangle of the phone interrupted her thoughts. It took her a moment to locate the device under the debris. Touching the receiver was a mistake: sticky, garnet-colored blood coated the handle and transferred onto her hand.

Sickened, she ignored the insistent ringing and stumbled to the washroom. She shut the door, and the phone fell silent.

After scrubbing her skin raw, Georgie finally looked into the small mirror that Gordon had hung especially for her. Her bobbed chestnut hair and amber eyes might be considered ordinary by any fashion standard, but at twenty-six, she received her fair share of masculine attention. None had captured *her* attention nor gained Gordon's approval. Being twelve years older, he had taken his role as big brother and protector to annoying levels, insisting on a code so she would know who he considered trustworthy. Upon their parents' deaths seven years ago, he pushed her to pursue her interests and to become a successful woman in her own right.

She had made him proud.

"What happened?" A grumpy voice called from the office. "Powers?"

She hesitated. She wasn't expecting anyone. "One moment, please."

Georgie quickly finished drying her hands, smoothed her hair into place, and checked her Hot Coral lipstick before returning to the office. A tall man waited, illuminated by the light coming from the hallway. His charcoal suit was exquisitely tailored, and his wingtips had never seen a scuff. An onyx fedora pulled low hid his face from view.

"Ma'am." He yanked off his hat to reveal dark, wavy hair, an olive complexion, and eyes the color of sapphire. A scar cut across the right corner of his otherwise firm lips, giving him a permanent scowl. She realized he was the handsomest man she'd ever seen, but also one of the most dangerous. "I didn't realize Powers had a dame — excuse me — a woman working for him."

She caught the hint of an accent — French, maybe?

"What can I do for you, Mr. . . .?" Georgie wasn't about to offer this man any information, not without him using the code name. Gordie had taught her that much.

The man hung his hat on a hook by the door, then took his time to answer. "Name's Nicoló DiAngelo. Mr. Powers was gathering some *information* for me."

Italian. Definitely, Italian. "Mr. DiAngelo, Mr. Powers is — unavailable. Do you wish to leave a message?" She moved to the desk, hoping to locate pen and paper amongst the debris. If nothing else, she could appear confident and efficient.

The man glanced around before reaching to flip the light switch. Georgie shielded her eyes from the sudden brightness. As her eyes adjusted, she saw more than the scattered papers and the toppled file cabinet. She saw the blood. There was more than she'd initially thought. A small puddle sat near the side of the desk where Gordie might have spoken to his killer. The phone cord lay in a second pool. Streaks on the floor between the twin puddles told the horrible tale of a dying man dragging himself toward the phone to summon help. Help that arrived much too late.

Fighting to maintain her composure, Georgie focused on her guest. "Please excuse the mess, Mr. DiAngelo."

The man waved her apology away. "By unavailable, you mean Powers is dead."

Fresh tears sprang to her eyes at the sharp sting of his words. "I don't — "

"You must be Gordon's sister." DiAngelo moved closer, stepping over the debris. "He spoke of you often." One rough fingertip gently brushed away her tear. "You have my condolences."

"Thank you." A hard lump in her throat refused to go away. She glanced away, realizing for the first time that she was alone with a strange man, in the same room in which her brother had been murdered. She moved, placing the desk between them. Her fingers drifted below the desk surface, searching for the Luger P08 that Gordon always kept there.

It was gone.

His eyes followed her movements. He stepped back, holding up his hands. "I mean you no harm, Georgiana. Gordon was not simply an associate — he was my friend."

A friend Gordie had never mentioned, but his knowledge of her full name told her Gordie had trusted him. But someone Gordie trusted had shot him. She couldn't take that risk.

Georgie placed her hands on the desk and squared her shoulders. "What can I do for you, Mr. DiAngelo?"

The side of his lips twitched in a hint of a smile. "Powers said you had spunk. Glad to see it." He wandered around the room, seeming to observe every detail. "I've been out of town for several weeks and didn't receive the news. Gordon had some information about an — issue that has come to my attention. Did he leave a message for me?"

"I — " Georgie stopped herself from revealing her ignorance. "I have yet to go through his things. If you'd leave me your contact information, I can let you know what I find."

The man's face blossomed into a grin. "And if you don't find my information? What then?"

She knew he was teasing her. "Then I will get it for you."

The smirk slid off his face. "No! That won't be necessary. I can't allow — "

"I will uphold my brother's obligations, Mr. DiAngelo." Georgie stated firmly, feeling her nerves stretch to a breaking point. "Now, please excuse me, I have much to do."

He studied her before jerking his head in reluctant agreement. From an inside jacket pocket, DiAngelo retrieved a pen and a small white card with black lettering. He quickly jotted something on the back before handing it to her. When she reached to accept the calling card, he held on to it. He waited until her eyes met his to speak: "Information only, Miss Powers," he said. "That is all that I require."

After holding her gaze for another moment, he released the card, turned, and left the office, grabbing his hat along the way. He didn't look back.

Georgie didn't breathe until she heard his steps fade to silence, then her air whooshed out. She glanced at the card. Bold, black letters said:

Nicoló DiAngelo
HI5-2574

She flipped the card over and read the words aloud. "Leonid Novikov." *Now why does Mr. Nicoló DiAngelo need information on Leonid Novikov?*

There was only one way to find out.

It took three days to put the office mostly to rights. The bloodstains were still visible, despite her efforts to scrub them away. An untouched mound of paper and debris lurked behind the door, and the file cabinet was heavier than Georgie could lift on her own, but she had sorted many of the files and paperwork into manageable piles. She found no reference to DiAngelo among Gordon's files, nor did she discover anything about Leonid Novikov. The name didn't even appear in the telephone directory.

Today, Georgie was finally able to tackle the desk. She arranged the phone and desk accessories, centering two paperweights as tributes to the parents she'd lost at the age of eighteen. A silver airplane sitting on a heavy onyx base had been her father's retirement gift from the F.A.A. The other was an amethyst crystal the size of her fist that had belonged to her mother. Both parents had served as inspiration for the life that Georgie had chosen. With Gordon's support, she had pursued her dreams. Now, her family was gone, and she was left with trinkets and memories.

Wiping away a stray tear, she began replacing the drawers that had been dumped, intent on organizing them neatly. The right-hand top drawer refused to close. Remembering the missing weapon, she dropped to her knees to search underneath. Interfering with the drawer slide was a broken, hidden compartment where she found a leather notebook. Even though she was accustomed to Gordie's habitual precautions, she would have missed the journal if she hadn't tried to reattach the drawer.

Flipping the book open, she discovered it was a datebook. An emerald ribbon marked the current month. Notations of appointments and important events littered the page. One notation caught her attention two days before his death: L.N. — rocks/balls — Cordova. She found the same entry twice more in the previous month.

"L.N. — Leonid Novikov? Cordova?" she murmured to herself. "What are 'rocks' and 'balls'? Drugs, maybe? Isn't 'goofball' slang for bennies? Rocks could mean several things — drugs, diamonds, or a location."

The phone rang; she jumped. Releasing her breath, Georgie answered, "Powers Investigations."

"Miss Powers," a husky, accented voice answered, "Nico DiAngelo."

"Good afternoon, Mr. DiAngelo."

"Please, call me Nico. About our discussion earlier this week — did you locate anything?"

Georgie glanced at Gordie's datebook. "I may have a lead."

"Please, tell me."

"Ever heard of someone named Cordova?" She nibbled her lower lip.

The line went silent, then, "I've *heard* of it."

She reached for a pen and paper. "Who is it? Where can I find them?"

"You don't."

"Why not?"

"It's — no place for a lady," DiAngelo said. "It's a bar. A rough one."

"I see." She really didn't. Bars weren't her favorite locales, but she could suffer through to finish Gordon's business. She pulled out a telephone directory and opened it to the Cs in the yellow pages.

"Listen to me, Miss Powers." He sounded concerned. "You can't go there. Tell me what you found, and I will go."

Georgie recognized the address as being a few blocks away. "Thank you for your advice, Mr. DiAngelo. I'll get back to you soon." She hung up on his protest.

Her finger tapped on the page as an idea formed. She glanced down at her outfit — pedal pushers and an old button-up. Her broken fingernail had been filed smooth and the others cut in length to match, but the cleaning she'd done had made her hands appear ragged.

"This will work," she murmured. She picked up her

handbag and went to the door. Hesitating, she turned back to the office and said, "For you, Gordie."

It was later in the evening than she'd wanted, but preparations had taken longer than expected. Georgie checked her reflection in the store window. It was closed, so no one bore witness to her new look. Marnie, her best friend and hairdresser, had been aghast when asked to trim Georgie's cute bob. Georgie was pleased with the resulting masculine cut. Using Brylcreem, Marnie styled the shorter hair to a side part and wave, similar to Tony Curtis's style. The resulting effect was a younger version of Gordon. She decided she might keep the new cut when she was done being undercover.

A raid on Gordon's closet yielded nothing that would fit. Fortunately, Marnie had two younger brothers. With her help, Georgie outfitted herself with a pearl button-down and tan trousers, belted at the waist. A brown box coat finished the look and covered her curves. The boys' shoes had been much too large, so she settled for her leather loafers. She prayed no one would notice they were ladies' shoes.

With a final adjustment of Gordon's favorite hat — for luck — Georgie shoved her hands in her pockets and ambled down the street toward Cordova's Bar. As she passed a darkened alley, she heard a whine that sent shivers down her spine. The whimper that followed had her change her direction. She searched the shadows for the source of the noise and found a ball of dirty fluff among the trash. Recognizing the scrawny mutt from Gordie's office, she whistled. His dark, pitiful eyes met hers as she extended a hand for the dog to sniff. A tentative pink tongue licked her fingertip.

"What are you doing — snooping in the garbage like that?" Glancing around, she saw no one close. She leaned close and whispered, "You're not the ugliest thing I've seen, but you're close." More licking. "I'd take you with me, but I have a job to do."

Lick. Lick.

She stood and dusted her pants. As she moved to the mouth of the alley, the little dog followed. "You can't come with me, Mutt. Sit!" The mutt sat. "Okay. So, you have some manners." She thought for a moment. "Here's the deal. If you're still here when I get back, I'll bring you some peanuts. Okay?" A dirty tail thumped the ground. "I'll take that as a 'yes'. Stay!"

Georgie turned and headed for the bar. At the door, she glanced back. The dog hadn't moved from its spot. "I'll be back, Mutt."

She entered a smoke-filled, dimly lit bar. The place wasn't swarming with bodies, but did a fair business. Populated primarily with men, a handful of scantily clad women served drinks or sat in the laps of customers. Conversations lagged as attention turned in her direction.

So, it's that *kind of bar.* Remembering that she was posing as a man, Georgie squared her shoulders and swaggered toward an empty seat at the bar. The bartender glanced at her and grumbled, "What'll it be?"

The others perched at the bar, in varying degrees of cognizance, had glasses ranging from beer mugs to shot glasses. She opted to keep it simple and ordered Gordie's preferred, "Whiskey sour."

The man hesitated, looking her over. "Comin' up."

A prickling sensation told her she was being watched. Unobtrusively, Georgie searched the room for the culprit.

A shadow in the corner caught her attention, but she couldn't make out any features. Uneasy, she reached for a bowl of peanuts and flipped a few into her mouth. A handful went into her pocket as the bartender turned to set her drink down. "Thanks."

She took a sip, fighting a grimace as the smoky sweet and sour taste hit her tastebuds. Before she could force herself to take a second sip, a heavy hand landed on her shoulder, spinning her around on her seat, spilling her drink. "Hey!" She recognized the familiar face. "Ned. It's you."

Gordon's friend gave her a grim look, taking her by surprise. As he did he hissed, "What're you doing here? And why're you wearing that getup?"

The shadow in the corner leaned forward, ready to intervene. She didn't want a scene. Thinking quickly, she replied, "I'm following up on Gordon's business. I need information."

Ned stilled. "What information? For who?"

Ned had always been nice to her — flirty even — but this was different. "That's privileged."

"Get out of here," he warned. "This isn't the place for you."

Glancing around, Georgie caught the stares of the bartender and several customers. The shadow had disappeared. "I need to find someone with the initials L.N., and —"

"You need to leave." Ned growled as he gripped her arm and hauled her off the seat. Tossing a few bills on the counter, he dragged her to the door. Once outside, he spun her around. "You're hunting for his killer, aren't you? Where'd you find those initials?"

Georgie shook off his hands. "Gordon's datebook."

"You should have called me. That's a job for professionals."

A growl caught her attention. Georgie looked around to find the little dog watching them from the alley.

"Looks like you've got a friend there," Ned sneered. "You should take your little doggie home and let me take care of business."

She narrowed her eyes at his rudeness. "I don't need your help."

He scoffed, "Do you *know* where you are?" He didn't wait for an answer. "Men — *dangerous* men — conduct business here. They aren't having tea and biscuits. They get drunk and hire people to. . .do things."

Fighting the urge to slap him, Georgie played innocent. "What kind of things?" She had a pretty good idea of the business conducted in Cordova's. Gordon had been an excellent teacher.

"Things you have no business knowing." He glanced around before staring into her eyes. "I'll get information for you. What do you need?"

She debated what to tell him. "Nicoló DiAngelo came to the — ."

"DiAngelo!" Ned's face turned a vivid red. "I should've known."

"Do you know him?" She hoped Ned could help her. If he didn't, she might have to tap into Gordon's *other* resources — the dangerous ones.

"I know him," he growled. "What'd he want?"

"Information," she blurted. "Gordie had an appointment with this L.N. two days before he died. I need to figure out what this person knows. Do you know him?"

"I know him." He didn't speak for several seconds. "Did it say anything else?"

She watched him closely. "It mentioned 'rocks' and 'balls'."

A thoughtful look spread across his face, accompanied by a lazy grin. "I'll tell you what, you go home and take off that ridiculous outfit. Put on something fun. I'll see what I can find out, then I'll pick you up for a late dinner and some dancing. What do you think?"

She knew what he was doing, and she didn't like it. "I'll take a raincheck on dinner and dancing, Ned. I'm rather tired."

His grin widened. "No problem, Georgia. Whatever I find, I'll bring it to your place in the morning."

She stilled. Goosebumps rose on her skin, but she stayed calm. "No. I'm still sorting through Gordie's office. Meet me there."

"You got it, dollface." With a chuck of her chin, Ned wandered back to the bar, whistling as if nothing were wrong.

Everything was wrong. She didn't know what to think, but Gordon had drilled it into her head to trust her gut.

~

One second the peanuts were in her hand, the next — gone. The dog sniffed her palm, licking to ensure every morsel was devoured.

"That was all I could grab, Mutt," Georgie cooed. "Don't worry. I'll come up with something else for you."

As she spoke, the back door to Cordova's opened, and the bartender stepped out, cigarette in hand. He jerked when Georgie rose and stepped forward. The dog scampered around the corner.

"You!" he exclaimed.

She lowered her voice. "You remember me?"

"Yeah." The man glanced around nervously, shutting the door behind him. "Whatcha doin' out here?"

"I wanted to talk with you. I didn't catch your name."

"Wilson." He eyed her. "What d'ya want with me?"

"Just some information." Georgie stepped closer. "Do you know an L.N. or anything about rocks?"

"You trying to get me killed, kid?" Wilson glanced around again.

"I'm trying to find information about my brother."

Wilson shook his head. "Powers, right?"

She tilted her head to one side. "How did you know?"

"Look, kid," he grumbled, "Powers wasn't a regular, but when he came 'round, he meant business. We all knew him, and you're his spittin' image. Don't go lookin' for the same kinda trouble."

That just made Georgie more determined. "Did you know who he met with the last time he was here?"

"The usual suspects," Wilson opened the door and hauled out trash bags to dump into a nearby bin. "He had his informants. Then there was his buddy."

"What buddy?" she demanded. "What were they discussing?"

Wilson raised his hands and backed away. "Look, I mind my own business. It keeps me from wearing concrete shoes."

"What questions?" Georgie growled. She'd had enough of secrets.

He glanced around, then leaned in and whispered, "Rocks. He asked about some rocks. That's all I heard." He opened the door, then turned back. "I'll tell Dottie you came by."

With that, Wilson was gone, slamming the door behind him.

Gordon had mentioned a Dottie once. Georgie got the

impression that Dottie was her brother's on-again, off-again girlfriend. No girlfriend — current or otherwise — had come to the funeral. She made a mental note to locate the woman — but it would have to wait until she was finished with the investigation.

With a huff of frustration, she turned to speak to the dog when movement caught her eye. "Who's there?"

"Your instructions were for information only, Miss Powers." The shape matched the one that had watched her in the bar.

"Mr. DiAngelo?"

He stepped away from the shadows. "You've done well, but I'll take the investigation from here."

"But — "

"Go home, Georgiana." With that, he walked away. At the corner, he turned back. "Thank you for your time. Forget everything you've seen — including me."

~

"The nerve of that man!" Georgie fumed as she entered the office building the following morning. "As if he was worth my time. If I didn't have. . .Hey!" A blur of matted fur slipped by her feet before the door completely shut. "Mutt! What are you doing?"

Slowed by her agate pencil skirt and rose pumps, she followed the stray down the hall. She found him sniffing at Gordie's office door, which stood ajar. Mutt nosed the opening wide enough to slip inside.

Georgie held her breath and peeked through the door to see a man dumping a desk drawer while a second man tore through the neat stacks of papers ready to be filed.

She couldn't see Mutt, but neither man seemed to have noticed the little dog.

She stepped back from the door. Before she could turn, she was grabbed from behind. A gloved hand silenced her surprised yelp. She was helpless to do anything but grip her purse to her chest.

"Boss said you'd come 'bout," a low-pitched voice muttered in her ear. Stale cigar-and-onion-scented breath accompanied the voice and made Georgie's eyes burn. "Shoulda stayed home like a good'un. Hey, Boss! Look what I got."

Georgie struggled, but she was no match for the stronger man as he dragged her into the office and kicked the door shut. The two men she'd seen straightened and looked menacing.

"Let her go, Walt." A familiar voice came from the corner of the room. She wouldn't have seen him without entering the office. "Leave us."

Walt shoved her toward the desk before following the others from the office. Georgie turned to face the man who had pretended to be a friend. "Ned."

He stepped forward with a Luger P08 aimed at her heart. "Georgia. You aren't surprised."

"Should I be?"

Ned shrugged. "Your brother stole something valuable from me, and I think you have it. Hand it over or — well, let's just say that life will become uncomfortable."

"I don't know what you're talking about," she responded. "What did Gordon have that's so important?"

"Don't play dumb," Ned waved the gun, indicating she should move. When she didn't, he grabbed her and shoved her against the desk. She grabbed the edge to keep from falling to the floor. "You found them. Where are they?"

Georgie kept her composure. "That's Gordon's gun. How did you — you didn't!"

"Didn't what? Kill him?" He barked a laugh. His usual midwestern accent now sounded thicker and heavier. "He stole what was mine and refused to cooperate. I need them back."

Georgie thought quickly. "You're Leonid Novikov. What did he steal? The rocks?"

He no longer hid the Russian accent. "DiAngelo told you, didn't he? I didn't think Gordon had enough to call for backup yet. Then, I realized he knew everything. I liked Gordon. I like you, Georgia. Unfortunately, you know too much."

"No!" she gasped as he raised the gun. Her hand landed on the silver airplane. She threw it at him as she dove behind the desk.

Thunk!

"Ow!" Georgie heard his yelp as the paperweight hit its mark.

GRRR!
CRASH!
BANG!

Georgie's ears filled with growls and shouts that accompanied the sounds of a fight and the blast of a gun.

"Stupid mutt!" She heard Ned yell.

"Got him!"

"Good. Get Novikov out of here. Put him with the others. Down, dog." That command came from Nico DiAngelo.

The fight was over in seconds. A wet tongue licked her hands and face before rough, but gentle hands lifted her from under the desk where she had landed.

"Georgiana!" Those same hands steadied her when the room spun. "Are you hurt?"

"No. I'm fine." Trembling, she glanced around to find her father's airplane bent but in one piece, and a hole in one of the tin ceiling tiles. Both could be easily fixed. With Nico's help, she moved to sit in the chair. "What happened?"

Nico glanced around before calling the dog over. "Your pooch is quite the guardian. He bit Novikov. That gave my men time to get in here and make the arrest."

"Mutt!" She gathered the dog into her arms, ignoring the matted fur and questionable odor. "You're my hero!"

Nico laughed. "He needs a better name."

"You're right." Georgie considered the little stray. "Jasper. For courage." After promising Jasper a juicy steak, she turned to Nico's concerned gaze. "How did you know Ned killed Gordon?"

"We weren't certain." Nico hiked his hip on the desk and faced her. "Gordon called me after he uncovered a Russian smuggling ring."

Georgie studied the man before her. "Who are you?"

Nico removed a thin wallet from his jacket and flipped it open to reveal a U.S. Customs and Border Protection badge. "He said he had proof and would keep it safe until I arrived to set up a sting. With Gordon's death, we had to stay back and wait. With you cleaning the place, Novikov figured you found what he needed. You were smart to not trust him."

She smiled. "That was Gordie's doing."

"How?"

She gazed at the man before her. "Gordie gave me a code. I knew I could trust you from the start. Ned gave himself away last night."

Confusion evident, Nico asked, "What code?"

She shrugged. "You knew to call me Georgiana. Ned called me Georgia. It doesn't matter now."

"You can explain it to me later." Nico shoveled a hand through his wavy hair. "The evidence is still missing. We don't have a case."

"I wouldn't say that." Georgie reached for her handbag and removed a bulky envelope. "This arrived today in my mailbox. I believe your proof is inside."

He flipped it in his hands. "How do you know? You don't know the case, and you haven't opened it."

"This wasn't the first time Gordie sent me sensitive evidence."

He stared at her for several seconds before opening the envelope. Several paper packets of varying sizes and one thick white envelope addressed to her landed on the desktop. Georgie studied the evidence Gordon had sent as Nico opened the packets. When she looked up, she gasped at the sight of glittering green stones. Within moments, open packets of multi-colored gemstones covered the surface. Other packets contained white tablets and inhalers labeled Benzedrine.

"The drugs are easy to verify, but I need someone to authenticate these stones," Nico announced with a grimace. "It'll be difficult to determine where these came from."

"That won't be a problem." Georgie handed him the documents before reaching into her purse a second time. "Did Gordie ever mention my studies?"

"No."

She withdrew a jeweler's loupe and gemstone tweezers from her purse. "I'm a certified gemologist with a degree in minerology. I've investigated jewel thefts all over the world, but I specialize in the Russian trade. This is a collection of imperial gems, including Yakut diamonds, emeralds, alexandrite, topaz, and garnets. Most likely from the Ural Mountains."

"Is that right?" Nico pulled her into his arms. Jasper jumped up on her leg. "Brilliant *and* beautiful. May I suggest we continue our collaboration over dinner, Miss Powers?"

Georgie smiled as she scratched Jasper's ears and leaned into Nico's embrace. "Please, call me Georgie."

T*iffany Seitz began writing in 2013 and has since independently published four romance novels under the name T. A. Seitz. Her first paranormal suspense,* And They Danced, *was published in March 2023. She has won several short story awards including those from* Granbury Writer's Bloc, Writer's Guild of Texas, and Writer's Police Academy. *She currently serves as President of Writer's Guild of Texas and Secretary of Sisters in Crime North Dallas.*

More information can be found on her website and blog, www.taseitz.com. *She can also be found on Facebook, Twitter, and Goodreads.*

Murder on a Dark Stair
Mark Beard

Smokey Sparks watched the late afternoon goings on in the neighborhood from the front seat. While most might have been bored at the ordinary events, Smokey took in the subtle details.

The snow had departed weeks before and an older man shoveled dirt from the edges of his stone slab walkway. A woman rubbed smudges from her car while another buffed the inside bottom edges of her windows furiously, only her face and arms visible from the dim interior.

They, like everyone else, ignored the stranger goings-on in Wildervalley. The smooth domed mountains cupped the out-of-the-way valley to keep it from the world, but little protected the citizens from one another, other than thin walls of their old two-story homes and tall pines and oaks that shaded them from above. Smokey and his junior high friends would sometimes hatch rumors about the residents of the sleepy, secluded town, but no one ever took them seriously.

"It looks like Mrs. Green went up to the park after all," he commented. The woman would only have collected those bugs on her windshield on the mountain highway. "She said she wasn't going."

His mother spoke as if responding. "Blair will be out here any minute. You should move to the back seat."

Smokey sighed at the non-answer and imagined her response instead. *Is that so? How interesting.*

He sighed and unbuckled. "I think Mr. Deen hurt his shoulder again." He flicked his eyes her way for an instant, hoping she might have interest or say something like, *Mr. Deen should be more careful at his age.*

"What's taking her?" His mother asked, instead.

"She always does this," Smokey responded while climbing in the back.

The woman across the street finished her window and disappeared from sight. "I thought the Hornbergs said they weren't going to babysit again." He flicked a glance at the rearview mirror to gauge his mother's reaction. *Maybe her grandchildren visited.* It was the wrong time of the year, but his mother *might* have responded that way.

Mom delivered her next words with timing and tone as though she were responding to his statement. "We won't tell Blair what we know. We'll let her tell us. That's how my husband did it."

"Mom, no." Smokey hoped she would not finish the rote and often-repeated iterations about his father, but he knew she would.

"He showed me how the detective business worked, and I picked it up pretty fast," Mom went on, impossible to stop. "I'm quite a detective myself at this juncture."

Smokey nodded and replied, "Okay." He had to say something, or she might circle back around to the beginning to drive home her point.

"Oh, there's Blair now," Mom said. "Hush, hush."

Blair Briar exited her house and her shoes clapped

against her wooden porch and steps loud enough to hear with the windows rolled up. The stone slabs of the Briar household sidewalk next told of Blair's approach, and Smokey could see her with his peripheral vision; swift small steps and a big head of hair that attempted to compensate for her thin frame.

Blair Briar clutched the purse at her elbow. *She's excited. She thinks Mom hasn't heard the news.* Smokey only hoped the gossip would not ruin their trip to the store. Mom had revealed the addition of picking up Mrs. Briar only after they pulled away from the house, condemning Smokey to fend off the nosy woman's inevitable prying questions.

Mrs. Briar entered and closed the door behind her. "Candice, did you hear?" She didn't wait for a response. "Someone died on the steps at the old graveyard." She gripped her purse with both hands at her chest. "They say it might be murder."

"Well, yes," Smokey's mother replied. "I mean, no." She pushed out a frustrated breath. "We only heard a brief bit. That's why I called. I was hoping you knew more." She tilted her head. "The cemetery has stairs?"

"The stairs used to go up to a mausoleum out front where they stored ashes," Mrs. Briar said. "Of dead people."

"That's called a columbarium," Smokey offered. Holly had told him so recently during study hall hour.

His mother put the car in drive.

Mrs. Briar stiffened, but it only lasted an instant. She then gave a brief glance and smiled over her shoulder. "A columbaria, yes. I'd forgotten that's what used to stand there."

"Columbarium" Smokey said. "It's a — "

Mother spoke over him. "I heard the county coroner mentioned something odd about the body."

Mrs Briar's purse trembled in her grip. "He said it was murder."

A slight frown appeared on Mom's face. "The coroner said that?"

"Well, no," Mrs. Briar's eyes darted to the side for a moment. "He said the fall didn't kill the man."

"Then what did?"

"Murder!" Mrs. Briar clutched her purse against her chest.

Smokey wondered what the coroner might actually have said. Mrs Briar had surely filled in some of her own invented information.

Smokey tried to imagine how the old building atop the stairs might have looked. Only a set of granite steps amid knee high grass reminded the world it had ever been there. They had played capture the flag there once, until the preacher's wife had chased them away.

"Well," Mom stated, tilting her head down while making eye contact with Mrs. Briar. "You know my husband was a detective." *Dad's ghost would live again.* "I know quite a bit about the craft myself."

Mrs. Briar spoke through a stationary smile. "Yes, Candice, you've said." She attempted her politest tone. "We've all heard."

"Yes." Mom replied, ignoring Mrs. Briar's attempt to stop her. "I would study what he did and after a while, I was able to help him find the culprits." She nodded to assert her words. "Perhaps we could do a little snooping around? I wouldn't mind putting my detective skills to work."

Smokey pressed his eyes closed.

A moment later, Mrs. Briar spoke in a tone with a crisp, business-like edge. "We need to visit Sheriff Pike."

Smokey opened his eyes. Frank Pike hated Blair, and he

didn't try to hide it. If Blair wanted to actually go and talk to him, it meant she was going after information without reservations.

"Well, okay," Mom responded with a treble of uncertainty. The car accelerated, taking on a more purposeful vector.

Smokey realized that a stop at Frank Pike's house would delay their arrival at the store for quite a while.

The talk of murder had absorbed Blair Briar, sparing Smokey and his mother from an onslaught of questions. If not, the entire ride would have consisted of Mrs. Briar prodding them for news. Then, of course, that information would find its way, rather swiftly, into any ear willing to listen.

When Mrs. Briar turned in her seat to face him, he realized with discomfort that the reprieve had ended.

"You look so much taller," she said. Her lips pursing.

"I grew — "

"He's four inches taller since just the beginning of April," Mother spoke over him. "His hands are bigger too."

"Oh." Blair responded with a coy smile that made Smokey cringe and wish he could open the door and roll across the pavement to freedom.

"I don't think he knows what to do with it all," Mom rattled on and Smokey felt his insides tighten further. "He tripped on his feet a few days back and hit his head on the lamp just yesterday."

"I was trying to avoid the cat," Smokey rushed in. "It was on the back of the couch with — "

"I think we'll be buying new socks and underpants soon," Mother went on.

"Mom," Smokey protested.

"Haden, please." Mother used his real name. She

refused to call him Smokey. When someone else used his nickname she would make sure to insert the name Haden into her next sentence.

"There he is." Mrs. Briar pointed up the street. Sheriff Frank Pike stood in his front yard with a running hose in hand.

Frank tilted his head forward and back to stretch his neck. That would mean he had worked the night before. His perfect crew cut could hold up a mug of root beer, one of Smokey's friends had joked. He went easy on ticketing but would take no nonsense from anyone. If he was in his front yard, that would leave his deputy running the show. The Sheriff was nice enough to the boys that Smokey and his friends referred to him as Frank rather than Sheriff or Mr. Pike. He would listen to the wilder rumors the boys shared with him. They had once tried to convince him that a chupacabra roamed the mountains surrounding the town. Frank had given a dismissive chuckle but hadn't denied their truth outright. Framed by the trunk of a hundred-year oak, the sheriff appeared oblivious to the approaching danger.

The car slowed and pulled up to the curb in front of the sheriff's house. Across the street, Mrs Sanders rose from her porch chair, her eyes on Blair Briar in the front seat. Mrs. Sanders hurried inside through her wooden screen door and her curtains drew closed a moment later.

"God bless it," Frank uttered when Mrs. Briar popped into view. Her small steps were gone and she strode up to the sheriff with a longer, more elegant stride. Smokey could not help but grin when Frank unconsciously looked to the hose as if the spattering water might be used as a weapon against Blair Briar.

"We heard about that poor Mr. Franklin," Mrs. Briar

said. "We're so distressed to hear what happened to him. Is it true?"

"Roger Franklin didn't live in Wildervalley, Blair." Frank tossed the running hose onto the lawn. "He was a land developer from out of town. Don't pretend to know him."

Mom had already gotten out of the car. "Victim's full name and profession," she said under her breath, as if checking off a list. She exited the car and strode forward, stopping where the granite slabs of the sidewalk met the lawn.

And he's from out of town. Smokey got out and leaned his elbows on the car top. He grinned. He hadn't been tall enough to do that before.

"Well, I've met the man," Mrs. Briar countered, a hand on her chest.

The other hand clenched a fist at her side. Smokey sighed. She had not met the developer.

"Really?" Frank asked.

"I was handing out pamphlets," Mrs. Briar lied.

"I haven't received any pamphlets lately." Frank shook his head. "I suppose if you suspected the man was up to something interesting, you would drive to that old cemetery and hand him a full newspaper in the middle of his inspection."

Smokey tilted his head. *Inspect the graveyard? To buy it and build something there?*

The garage beyond Frank rested in darkness and inside the shadows, something moved. Smokey watched as Holly Pike stepped into the cloudy daylight. The discussion of the adults faded to a muffled drone of voices and he could hear his heartbeat in his ears. Holding a sandwich, Holly wore a simple t-shirt and a pair of shorts that someone might wear around the house. She looked amazing.

She swallowed and smiled at him. He smiled back, feeling his cheeks flush.

Smokey knew her from school. She was one of the prettier girls. The two of them did not share the same circle of friends, and they never really spent time together, or at least they hadn't until they shared a study hour in the same room that year. Once in a while since then, they had talked about something she had learned at the library, or something new he had noticed in town. He was always ready for her to push him away or ignore him, but she never did.

With a quick look at her father to make sure he wasn't watching her, Holly mouthed a pair of words. *Thomas Zoric*. She then made a subtle pushing motion with both hands.

Smokey inhaled. Thomas Zoric? At the graveyard? Pushing a man down the steps? A creepy man at a creepy place. Smokey and his friends had been afraid of Thomas Zoric all their lives.

The conversation among the adults halted. Smokey realized that Frank was looking at his daughter. Frank flicked an evaluative glance Smokey's way before looking back to Holly. "Did you leave your brother in there alone at the table?"

"Mom's in there," Holly said.

"Why are you out here without shoes?" Frank stated. "You'll catch a chill from the slab." He waved a hand about as if uncertain what to say next. "Go check on your brother."

Holly put her head down and retreated.

Frank half glanced in Smokey's direction a second time. The exchange unsettled Smokey. Frank was known at school for being mean to boys who showed interest in Holly. Smokey's heart skipped a beat. Did Frank think he was one of them?

Blair Briar made her move. "Is it true someone shoved the developer down those old stairs? The ones from the old columbaro?"

"What?" Frank blurted. "Colum — "

Smokey sounded out *columbarium* in his mind.

"Columbard." Mrs. Briar waved a dismissive hand. "It's a mausoleum for ashes." She then added. "Ashes of bodies."

Frank's shoulders dropped a notch and rubbed his forehead.

Smokey could not shake the idea that Frank might suspect him of liking his daughter. The unbidden question popped into Smokey's mind. *Did he like Holly?* More importantly, did he like Holly in a way that would anger Frank?

"Well," Blair pushed on, "everyone in town knows it was murder."

Frank's eyes went wide and he bared his teeth when he spoke. "No official statement has been made. God bless it, Blair. No statement, no facts. You're running off of rumors."

"So you always say," Blair turned a shoulder to him, not meeting his gaze. Smokey noticed the rigidity in her poise had melted. She had gotten what she came for. "Well, we'll leave you to your chores, I suppose."

"Please do." Frank shook his head. "For the sake of our town, go home and do your own."

Blair's big head of hair wobbled while she crossed around the front of the car toward Smokey. "It looks like chores are all you're doing."

When Mom nodded to herself, Smokey's gaze flicked to Frank again. *No denial of Mrs. Blair's accusation.*

Mrs. Briar opened the door and plopped inside. Smokey heard her mutter, "A murder in town and he's watering the lawn."

Mom bid the sheriff good day, but then turned back to him. "You know, my husband was — "

"Was a big city detective," Frank finished for her. He held up a hand to stop her and said, "This isn't that big city. This is Wildervalley."

"Well, yes," Mom replied. "All right then. Good afternoon." Mom climbed back into the car and, when the door shut, her smile faded.

The city was almost an hour away. Dad had been gone often, until that day he hadn't returned at all. Smokey had been young and remembered only some of the images.

He leaned in his seat to wave farewell to Frank. Frank gave a nod, although it had an uncustomary hint of a frown that time, which he followed with a glance at the garage where Holly had disappeared.

When Mom started the car, Mrs. Briar spoke one word. "Library."

Smokey groaned as quietly as he could. He had only wanted a candy bar from the store. It dawned on him that his mother might have already forsaken the stated purpose of their trip.

Mom grabbed the gearshift. "That's next door to the church."

The sound of Blair Briar's fingers drumming her purse stopped suddenly. "We need to know."

Mom nodded and pulled the car away. "Time for some detective work." Smokey felt himself wilting and observed Mrs. Briar stiffening. "My husband would say we now have a location and a motive." She raised a finger. "I think the developer wanted to buy land somewhere nearby."

"Maybe the graveyard," Smokey said. "You should find out who he worked for and — "

"Perhaps someone wanted to prevent the sale." Mom spoke to Mrs. Briar, ignoring Smokey's statements. "Or, maybe, a competitor shoved him down those stairs. A rival."

Mrs. Briar waited through Mom's guesses with a stiff smile. Only when the other had run out of options, did she brighten. "Someone waited for the developer to get to the top of the stairs, and then stuck the knife in his back." Blair made a stabbing motion with a snarling expression.

"Knife?" Mom asked.

"He didn't just fall." Blair Briar spread her hands, as if pleading innocent of some accusation.

A tall house with dark asbestos shingles covering the exterior walls appeared on the left. A square widow's watch rose to a third-floor tower at the corner. Thomas Zoric's house. Smokey and his friends believed the man came out of his house only after nightfall; that he might not even be human. A sleek black car with a high polish sat in the driveway.

A pale face peered out of the picture window under the shadows of the front porch.

Smokey gasped and sank down. His knees struck the back of Mrs. Briar's seat.

"Are you all right back there?" she asked.

"Buckle up," Mom scolded.

When the library appeared ahead, Mother and Mrs. Blair went into observation mode. Smokey joined them, but with none of the rigidity the women showed. Somewhere ahead lurked Pricilla Pommel.

The library looked as old as the rest of the buildings in town, despite having paint over its aged stucco.

A section at the back rose to a second story, and that's where the county records were stored. That's why Mrs. Briar had aimed them that way. The danger, however, waited just beyond the library.

The entrance faced Main Street, a parking area filled

the left side, but, on the right, a fair swath of lawn dipped down to a driveway, and then up again to the walls of the church.

The church rose tall and elegant, its walls the same white stucco. The narrow steeple reared at the front. It occupied a similar piece of land to the library, grass-covered, with well-manicured trees. The open grounds allowed for a view of the home a fair space back from the two buildings. The two-story white house had a wrap-around porch and a turret on the corner with a second-floor sunroom. It was the residence of Reverend Wilfred Pommel. It was also the home of his wife, Pricilla Pommel.

It was the fear of running into the preacher's wife that had the three of them scanning the grounds. The school kids called her Pricilla to one another but never dared to do so in her presence.

Smokey spied a set of flowers sitting in store-bought containers next to the garden that lined the side wall of the church. There were already a full set of early spring flowers sprouting, but if any of them had dared to wilt, Pricilla would discard them for more compliant replacements.

Pricilla wouldn't leave a job half done. Her return was imminent.

"We'd better hurry if you want to miss Mrs. Pommel," Smokey warned.

"She's not here," Mrs. Briar assured. The car pulled into the small library parking lot. "We'll find out who that developer worked for,"

"Well, of course," Mom said.

Smokey crossed his arms. *Like I said.*

They exited the car and rounded the front of the library.

Blair Briar pursed her lips not breathing for an instant,

before inhaling and stating. "We'll find out why he wanted that land the old graveyard is on.

"Good thinking," Mom said. "We can find out what value the developer saw in that plot."

Smokey looked askance and spoke barely loud enough for them to hear. "A deed might help."

"Is there a deed?" Mrs. Briar asked.

"Exactly." Mom wagged a finger at Blair Briar. "Those are the questions a detective needs to ask."

"I thought as much." Mrs. Briar put her nose up.

"Oh, hello," the voice of Pricilla Pommel rang, congenial yet crisp, like a whip.

Gray streaks whisked through the hair she had mounted in buns atop her head. A flowered garden apron covered pants and blouse. A narrow face bore a long-bridged nose.

"Oh, Mrs. Pommel," Mom's hands moved as if uncertain what pose to take.

"There you are," Blair Briar smiled, her cheerful expression locked in place as if made of wax.

"Hello, Smokey." Mrs. Pommel tilted her head in a quizzical manner and she glanced up and down his height.

"Haden is joining us on some errands," Mom inserted his given name.

"Something to do with the church?" Pricilla's eyes scanned each woman for cracks in their facades.

"The library," Mom said.

Mrs. Briar's marionette smile had not budged.

"Blair." Pricilla turned to her. "Didn't you sign up for the April 20th potluck? We had you down for potatoes."

Mom stepped back half a pace, putting Mrs. Briar in a space by herself.

Mrs. Briar stood still, but Smokey watched the tips of her fingers moving next to her hips. Did her fingers provide the only outlet for her nerves she had when standing so still? "April 20th?"

Mrs. Pommel spoke her next words with well-honed perfection of impatience and politeness. "It had been on the bulletin board since January 1st."

"I thought it was rained out," Mrs. Briar said with an extra movement of her fingers.

"It was inside." Pricilla's tone stiffened.

The moment stretched, but then, as if by magic, Blair came back to life, her entire body loose and mobile again. "Did you hear about the murder?"

Pricilla cast the potluck discussion aside with ease. "I'm the one who informed the police of it." She cast a half-glance over her shoulder, indicating her house. "You can see the old graveyard from the second-floor sunroom."

"You saw the stabbing?" Mrs. Briar asked.

"He was stabbed?" Pricilla's eyes narrowed. "How fascinating."

"Quite possibly." Mrs. Briar nodded to back up her information.

Pricilla stiffened an increment at the response. "From my vantage, it appeared the other person simply let go of him. The man fell down the stairs to his demise. Drunk probably. The other person made off into the tree line."

"Did you see his face?" Smokey asked.

His mother opened her mouth to fill in where an answer would have gone, but Pricilla spoke first. "Not per se."

"Dark clothes, pale face?" Smokey watched her face for any reaction. *Thomas Zoric*.

The slow rise of Pricilla's chin brought silence. "Did someone show you the police report? I didn't tell anyone else what the perpetrator looked like." She let the garden gloves clutched in one hand swing. "Perhaps I'd better get back to my planting. I wouldn't want the new flowers to atrophy."

Smokey eyed the plants. They might survive in their store-bought containers for another month. Pricilla Pommel's reaction confirmed that the perpetrator's appearance matched that of Thomas Zoric.

He frowned. How had Holly known? Had her dad told her? That was unlikely. The sheriff wouldn't casually reveal the identity of a suspect to his family. Smokey's gaze settled on the library. The building was like Holly's second home. He eyed the second story public records section. If Holly had heard anything about a land sale of the graveyard, she'd have been there when the doors opened.

They were hours behind her.

"Good day, ladies," Pricilla said. "Smokey." She almost looked his mother's way but turned decidedly before the other woman could insert the correction of Smokey's name.

Mrs. Briar smiled. "Nice work, Smokey."

"Please don't encourage, Haden." Mom flicked a glance his way. "He interrupts when he shouldn't."

"I have to go," Smokey said. He had to get to Holly Pike's house.

"Now he wants to skip out on searching the records with us?" Mom said to Mrs. Briar.

"This was supposed to be a trip to the store." Smokey felt desperate. If Mom insisted, he might have to stay at the library. "I need to — "

"The library won't be open too much longer," Mom said to Mrs. Briar. "Let's all get inside."

"Yes," Mrs. Briar said but she looked at Smokey rather than his mother. "You like digging up information. I thought you would have fun with us, looking all that up."

"I don't understand that stuff," he said.

"Let's go," Mom said. "I'll be the detective and you two can help me do the detective research."

Blair Briar avoided looking at Mom, still facing Smokey. "You love reading and working things out." Her tone became kind and beckoning. "And I thought you might understand the city records rather well. You might find some tidbit of information," her hands moved in front of her as if she might not know how to phrase her thoughts, "like you do."

If Mrs Briar didn't stop, there would be no way out.

"Mom," Smokey pleaded. "I just want to walk home."

"From here?" she asked.

"I walk here all the time." He had little left to offer.

His mother sighed, her shoulders cocked in a manner that showed disapproval. "Go ahead. Pick up your room though." A balance for losing the battle "It's not officially free time until you do."

"Okay." He dashed away, hoping to avoid any further response.

"You should have made him stay," he heard Blair Briar say.

He almost turned onto the road that led directly to Holly's house. He corrected his course, veering down the first lane that might appear to lead toward his house.

Tall oaks filled the tree lawn next to the road. Ahead, the setting sun on the horizon shone in his eyes. His short-cuts through neighborhood backyards soon led him onto Holly's street.

Frank Pike leaned over his car engine, hood up. Smokey came to a stop as fast as he could. He shifted course and ducked behind a fence five houses up. Had Frank seen him?

The reality sank in. Holly was not allowed to visit after dark, at least not with boys. The thought of upsetting a man like Frank Pike sent a bolt of fear through Smokey. He huddled beside a fence while the light drained from the sky. He had evidence that Thomas Zoric was guilty. Holly knew something too. They had to talk about it.

Mustering his courage, he dashed into the backyards that would lead to Holly's. Darkness and hedgerows hid his approach. At long last, the lights of the Pike house shone through the bushes.

He slunk forward, keeping low. Holly appeared at the kitchen window. The house sat up a few feet from the ground. He arrived at the back of the house and put his hands on the sill, which ran level with the tip of his nose.

Would Holly welcome him? The new thought caused him to step back. What would she think of him snooping at the window? He didn't really know her well enough for that.

Holly saw him and gasped. Smokey froze. It was too late. Holly rushed forward and crouched at the window and slid it up an inch. "What are you doing?" she hissed. Her tone betrayed interest rather than outrage.

"We have to talk about Thomas Zoric."

She froze, eyes flicking to the side. "I'll meet you outside."

"Where?" Smokey shrugged.

"It can't be here or your house." Her eyes flicked from side to side. "I've got it. We'll meet at the scene of the crime. That's what Dad would do."

"The graveyard?" Smokey sagged. He had just run all the way from there to her house. On the other hand, he might get a ride home from his Mom from the nearby library.

He opened his mouth to warn her that his mother would be nearby, but the sound of approaching footsteps stopped him. They could only be Mr. Pike's. Holly whirled about and stood and Smokey ducked.

Fear of Frank Pike filled him. He had never considered being at odds with the man before. If Frank caught him peeking in his windows, who knew what he might do?

"Are you hanging around that Sparks kid a lot?" Frank asked.

Smokey's heart raced. Frank was asking about him?

"Smokey?" Holly asked. "Just some. I see him at school."

Smokey sank down into a ball, his eyes wide.

"That's fine," Frank said. "If you see him outside of school, though, you can't be alone. You have to have friends with you, or me or your mother. And you need our permission."

"Okay, Dad," Holly agreed.

Some clanking and moving of chairs occurred and then Holly said, "I have a thing tonight. It's at Christina Weaver's house."

Smokey drew a breath. She was leaving?

Frank groaned. "All the way over there?"

Smokey recalled the location of Christina Weaver's house and smiled. Christina lived over by the old cemetery. Holly knew what she was doing.

"It's a five-minute drive," Holly said. "You said you didn't want me walking after dark. It starts in 15 minutes."

"Fifteen minutes?" Frank's voice rose but another groan followed it. His footsteps left the room and Holly reappeared at the window.

She hissed, "Graveyard. Twenty minutes." Smokey nodded and dashed away.

He avoided Main Street. It would have been a shorter route, but Frank would surely use it. Smokey took the side street just beyond that ran parallel to it. It was dark and lined with big trees and old houses. Many of the lots backed all the way up to it from the main road. The streetlamps shined on Main Street but their light only reached him from the spaces in between houses.

Two figures ahead exited their home and walked in the murky shadow toward the darkened lane. Smokey wanted to avoid them, but, somehow, the couple moved too fast. They stepped onto the sidewalk in front of him.

Smokey recognized the black asphalt shingles on the walls of the house too late. It was the Zoric estate and standing before him was none other than Thomas Zoric.

Smokey stopped. Staring at Zoric and his companion, their pale faces ghostly in the darkness.

A woman in a dark gray dress, almost black, accompanied him. Smokey thought he might have seen her once or twice. Was her hair black or gray? Her face appeared too young for gray hair. Some of the long strands floated in the light breeze.

Smokey tried to speak but only made a sound.

"In a hurry?" Zoric asked. An unidentifiable accent tainted the words. He smiled at the woman. "Young people rushing about, as if time were out of their grasp."

"As if their lives will pass by in a blink," she cooed back at him. She also had an accent.

Smokey could only stare. He wanted to run, but he didn't want Thomas Zoric to suspect that he knew something about him. The fear of Frank Pike paled in comparison. Frank might get angry, but this man might kill him, the way he had killed the land developer.

"Have we met?" Thomas Zoric asked.

Smokey could only stutter. "Uh."

"I'm Thomas Zoric," he extended a gloved hand to Smokey.

Smokey took the hand, feeling flesh beneath with bones

all too present. The glove felt cold, as if the hand within offered it no heat. The brass buttons on Zoric's jacket had images crafted in relief.

Zoric tilted his head with a mild bow. "And this is the dame Shelly Nemirov,"

Shelly gripped Smokey's hand in both of hers, her bare skin smooth and cold. She rubbed thumb and fingers across his palms and the back of his hand. "So young and strong. So full of life. A fleeting moment, that type of youth. Be sure to mark this time so that you can recall it later, should you get the chance." Her dress looked like something from Smokey's great grandmother's closet.

Her words were soft and might have been kind, but something hid beneath them that chilled the flesh of Smokey's back.

Though colder to the touch than Zoric, her cheeks flushed healthier, her grip pressed stronger. Thomas, in comparison, appeared a bit gaunt.

"And you?" Thomas Zoric asked. "To whom do we have the pleasure of meeting?"

"I'm Smokey." Smokey found the ability to breathe again. "Smokey Sparks."

"What a lovely name," Thomas Zoric replied and smiled ever so slightly so that only a bit of his teeth might show. "I shan't forget a name like that."

Shelly Nemirov raised a hand to stroke a cold finger across Smokey's cheek. "Smokey Sparks."

"Where are you off to on this fine moonless night?" Thomas Zoric asked.

Smokey wanted to run. "I have to go. I have to get to the graveyard. No. I mean the library."

The pleasantry drained from Shelly's face and she withdrew her hand.

Smokey shuffled his feet to get around them but realized he had put himself on the granite walkway to Zoric's back door.

"We wouldn't want to delay you," Thomas said. He motioned past them with a hand, beckoning Smokey to move on. Above the hint of a smile, the dark eyes stared, fierce.

Smokey attempted to walk away in a casual manner. His nerves failed him, however, and he broke into a full sprint away from the pair.

With his lungs heaving and his head spinning, he ran through the darkness. No wonder people shared strange whispers about Thomas Zoric. He was horrifying. Smokey ran until the walls of the library rose before him, the street and sidewalk ending at the parking lot.

He remembered his mother and Mrs. Blair. They would still be upstairs studying. The car sat in the parking lot alone. The library would close soon.

He could not risk them seeing him. The upstairs portion had windows facing in every direction except toward the rear. Once he left the shadows, he would be in full view. If they saw him go to the graveyard, he would have to try to explain himself. If they caught him with Holly, all manner of chaos might follow.

He considered going inside, eliminating the threat of punishment.

No. Holly was waiting for him. He had to see her.

Smokey had broken a sweat despite the coolness of the night. He allowed his heart rate and breathing to slow. He shot one more glance down the dark lane toward Zoric's house. He could see no one on the sidewalk.

Smokey took a breath for courage and ran into the open, his eyes on the upstairs library windows. He hid behind the building, the only lights there coming from the Pommel household some distance away. He arrived at the far corner and looked beyond the church. The grass grew tall on what appeared to be a vacant lot. Everyone in town knew it to be the old graveyard. The newer one, where recent burials occurred, was on the north end.

He was going to have to expose himself to view when he ran between the library and the church. He stepped beyond the corner and looked up just in time to see the lights on the second floor flicker off.

Had his mother and Mrs. Blair finished? That meant no one could see him. He sprinted to the shadows behind the church. Panting, he looked back at the library. The crunch of wheels on gravel preceded the headlights of his mother's car. She pulled into the street and drove away down Main Street.

He had missed his ride and Mom would arrive home to find him missing.

His gut clenched. How would he explain his absence? He thought of racing home. Imagining Holly alone at the graveyard stopped him.

The church had no lighting on its rear or sides. Smokey passed beyond it into darkness. When the manicured grasses gave way to knee high growth, he aimed toward the front of the graveyard. Main street ran in front of the library, church, and graveyard. On a perpendicular side street, Smokey spied someone walking. Still far off, he recognized Holly.

Smokey swallowed when he realized they were going to get to spend time together.

Just like her father had forbidden. Smokey winced.

He hastened to the front of the graveyard. When he realized some of the light from the church still reached him, he slunk over to a tall pair of cedar bushes that rose well overhead. Between them descended a set of stone stairs. The crumbled foundation of the columbarium spread under his feet.

The stone block stairway descended to a stretch of flat land below, significantly lower than that of Main Street behind him. The grasses waived, but the darkness of the night allowed him to observe no details other than dark shapes of tombstones at irregular intervals amid century old trees. He recalled seeing the graveyard in the daylight. Only a small number of the markers still showed above the ground.

Holly's footfalls drew his attention away as she ran the last stretch over to him.

Their purpose returned to Smokey in full. "I have news about Thomas Zoric."

"You do?" Holly asked, her eyes wide. "So do I." She had changed into long pants and a jacket.

"You can — Smokey tried.

"No, you go," Holly said.

He blurted, "Mrs. Pommel saw Thomas Zoric push the man down the cemetery stairs."

"What?" Holly gasped. "Are you sure?"

"Well," Smokey realized the preacher's wife had not actually said those words. "She said someone with dark clothes and a pale face pushed him down."

"You mean dropped?" she asked. "I overheard dad say dumped."

"Oh," Smokey said. "You eavesdropped?"

Holly shrugged.

A cool night breeze blew and crickets chirped. The streetlights were far off and the graveyard slept in shadows. The first inkling that they might be doing something dangerous occurred to Smokey.

"Even if Zoric did only drop the man, he was there when he died. It could have all been an accident."

Holly stepped in close, and her eyes held fear. "The land guy was missing some of his blood."

The top of Smokey's head tingled, and the sensation spread down his spine. "Blood? Like how much?"

"More than a gallon," she answered.

"How much blood do people have?"

Holly shrugged. "I don't know. I just know he was mostly drained."

"Wait," Smokey said. "Why did you tell me about Thomas Zoric?"

"I went to the library." Her eyes lit with excitement. "Nobody owns this cemetery anymore. No. Wait. Actually, a bunch of people own it and they're all scattered across the whole world. To sell it, they would all have to sign a paper or something, which would be almost impossible. But," she leaned closer, "Thomas Zoric has been paying the property taxes for forty four years."

"That's a long time." Smokey marveled. "For land he doesn't own?" His voice lost its sharpness when he realized he could feel the heat of her body on his face.

"You're taller close up," she said.

"I grew a little," he explained.

An awkward silence followed. The unexpected thought of kissing her bloomed in Smokey's mind. He decided at last. He did like her.

"Anyway." Holly stepped back. "That developer guy had friends in the county government, and it seemed like they were going to bypass the ownership issues and acquire the land."

The encounter with Thomas Zoric and Shelly Nemirov burst to the forefront of Smokey's mind. "I ran into Zoric and his girlfriend tonight."

Holly gasped and clutched her jacket. "Did they bite you?"

"What?" Smokey asked. "Bite?"

Her inference struck him and it dawned on him at last. Pricilla Pommel had seen the pale-skinned person dropping the victim down the stairs that descended at their feet — but not before he'd been drained of blood. "You think Thomas Zoric is a vampire?

She put up her palms. "Weird, but what else? He's a creepy old guy who tossed a guy down the stairs after draining his blood."

"They didn't bite me." Smokey knew his eyes had grown wide. He reimagined the meeting with Zoric. He scanned the images in his head. The antique brass buttons and that old dress, their pale features and cold skin. What if it were true? What if vampires actually lived in Wildervalley?

He tilted his head, recalling one more observation. "Thomas Zoric looked all dried out."

Holly gasped. "Like a creature of the night."

Smokey held up a hand to stop her. "But his lady friend didn't." Smokey nodded at his conclusion. "Yea. She looked pretty healthy, almost rosy." He tilted his head, modifying his statement. "Rosy for a pale lady, anyway. She was kind of strong too, for someone with little hands like that."

"Pale?" Holly asked. "Does she wear dark clothes too?"

A boot scuffed on stone.

Thomas Zoric was on the stairs, ascending toward them. His black jacket flowed in the breeze behind him and his pale face peered up at them, framed by raven locks.

The two froze in terror. Zoric reached the top with deceptive ease and stood before them.

"Rosy cheeks," he said, dragging a thumb across a fingernail as if cleaning it. "I hadn't noticed that. I should have." Zoric offered them a smile that didn't expose his teeth. "She still can dazzle me a bit. Especially when I've missed dinner."

He passed between them and then turned around, so that a fall down the staircase loomed at their backs. "You're a perceptive young man." He then pointed at Holly. "You're the sheriff's daughter. You sound quite bright." He paced several steps. "You've put together a lot of tidbits it seems most others have missed, even me. Someone will undoubtedly act on that information." He looked about. "Wildervalley is such a nice place. I would hate to leave here. Perhaps I should take action to avoid that." He strode back and forth in front of them.

An instinct made Smokey reach out and take Holly's hand. She gripped his in return. He could feel her pulse rushing in her palm.

Zoric's eyes flicked their way. "Two youths with bright minds; not something an old fellow like me ought to mess up."

Zoric looked to the moonless sky and then back at the pair. "You ought to be home at this hour, don't you think?"

The pale-skinned man in his dark coat with brass buttons retreated into the darkness, away from the lights while circumnavigating the church with a wide margin. Smokey followed the figure as it trod dangerously close to the preacher's house. Thomas Zoric, however, merged with the shadows in a way that made him hard to follow, until, at last, Smokey lost sight of him.

"Let's go," Holly said, her voice trembling.

Smokey hurried Holly back toward Christina's house.

He at last understood. "It wasn't Zoric who dropped the developer down the stairs. It was his girlfriend."

"What?" Holly's eyes were wide. "She's a vampire too?"

"We — We don't really know that." Smokey's brow wrinkled. "It's all inference."

"Well, I think they are," Holly said.

They stopped at the bottom of the porch stairs to Christina Weaver's house. Somehow, their hands touched and gripped together.

Her skin felt so warm. *This is it. I should kiss her.*

"We know who did it," Holly said.

He considered her safety. "You should get inside." He inwardly cursed. He had ended the moment too soon.

Holly climbed the porch steps and disappeared inside. Their evening together was over.

The thought of his mother returned, and Smokey sprinted away.

Smokey arrived home to find his mother waiting at the kitchen table. "You will do nothing but stay in this house and go to school for the next two weeks." she said. "If you leave this house, it will be with me in the car."

Smokey plodded up to his room. His mother didn't understand. She never did.

The next morning, Mom was in the shower when the phone rang.

It was Holly. She had never called him before. "You're not going to believe this. Thomas Zoric turned his girlfriend in. He walked her right up to my dad's desk at the station and told her to confess. Then she did!"

"No way," Smokey replied. "She admitted it?"

"Yes," exclaimed Holly. She then whispered into the phone. "You must have convinced Zoric to do it."

Had he really?

"Dad was mad because Zoric got her a big lawyer from the east coast," Holly continued. "He said the lawyer has never had a client receive more than about twenty years."

"Which she might easily survive," Smokey said. "You know, if she's a — " He left the word unsaid.

"I know," Holly replied. "It makes me wonder if the lawyer might be one of *them*."

Smokey paused at the thought. He had preferred the idea that the world of the unknown consisted only of Zoric and Nemirov.

When Smokey arrived downstairs, his mother pointed at the chair across from her. He sat. "Where were you last night?"

"I just went for a walk," he lied. He couldn't tell the truth. If she found out he had been with the man suspected of murder, and the woman who had actually done it, he would be grounded forever.

She leaned forward. "Is everything okay? Is something bothering you?"

Her concern for him caused a lump in his throat and pressure at his temples. Out of his mouth issued words he had intended to never say. "Nothing is ever okay. You don't listen to me. You treat me like nothing I have to say is important." He almost choked on the words, and he feared tears might spring into his eyes.

His mother gasped.

"You talk over me." He stood from his chair and picked up his books. "A lot." He made it several steps toward the door but faced back. "You make me look stupid in front of your friends."

His mother stared with her mouth open. "I — "

The doorbell cut her off.

Smokey stepped forward and opened it. Blair Briar strode in and halted midway into the living room. "Candice, you are not going to believe what happened."

Smokey intervened. "Thomas Zoric's girlfriend did it?

He walked her into the police station, and she confessed? Fancy east coast lawyer blah blah blah."

Blair's jaw dropped down to a before-unseen length.

"Old news, Mrs. Briar." He stepped out. "I'll be in the car, Mom." The door closed behind him and he strode to the car.

Blair Briar soon left with swift steps, even taking an awkward shortcut across the lawn in high heels.

Mom did not speak until the car stopped at school. "The world can call you Smokey, but I named you Haden. I'm not going lose that."

Smokey hung his head. The pressure in his temples returned.

One of his friends bounded up to the car. "Hey Smokey, the bell's about to ring." The boy shared his first class with him.

"Haden is — ," Mom cut her correction short with visible effort. "*He*'s coming."

Smokey let go a long exhale. "Thanks Mom."

After the school day began, it seemed like study hall would never arrive. He and Holly sat in adjacent seats.

"I can't believe we solved a crime," Smokey said.

"With vampires." Holly raised her eyebrows.

He smiled. "Maybe."

"Definitely." She smiled but then blushed and looked down. "Are we going out together or something?"

"Um." His breath stopped in his throat and he felt his head spin. "Okay."

Holly exhaled as if she had been holding her breath too.

"Less talk," the study hall monitor called out from his desk. "More studying."

They smiled at one another in silence. Holly then frowned as if recalling something and whispered. "They found an oversized canine print up on the mountainside a couple days ago."

The chupacabra. A sense of exhilaration ran through Smokey. He leaned toward her. "It's a date."

*M**ark Beard is a novelist, short story writer, and has worked as a marketing content writer. He is a resident of Central Florida and enjoys both the cities and the wilds of the Sunshine State. He has published four heroic fantasy novels which encompass the series entitled* The Jeweler of Tirravon. *His trilogy,* Leviathan Brood, *is scheduled to come out in 2024. Keep up with Mark Beard publications at: Lanthanor.com.*

God's Truth

Veronica Leigh

February 1933
Ouabache, Indiana

Sheriff Claire Williams climbed out of her Model A Ford and made her way up the walk. Mr. Howard Chase was sitting on the front porch steps of his house, elbows on knees, face in hands, wailing louder than the blackbirds in the bare tree close by.

His head snapped up on hearing her heels click on the cement and he scrambled to her. "Mrs. . .Sheriff Williams!" Were it not considered unmanly, he would have fallen into her arms and sobbed. It was bad enough to show such outward emotion, or so society claimed. "My-my Helen is d-dead. Some riff-raff boy ho-hobo killed her." His breathing became labored and he went white.

Claire grasped his shoulder to steady him. She couldn't have him fainting; she wouldn't have been big enough or strong enough to carry his dead weight. "Mr. Chase, calm yourself, if you can. And let's not jump to conclusions." Despite her many successes in solving crimes, folks–men especially–tended to think because she was a woman that they could do her job better than she could.

A tug on her coat sleeve drew her attention to the right. A small, bird-like bespectacled woman nodded to her. She wore an old-fashioned sprigged frock and leaned upon a gnarled cane. Ouabache was a town full of gossips, but Iva Kent was the reigning queen of them all. *Every town has one.* Nothing escaped her notice, she seemed to know everything, and what she didn't know she made up. People went to church to listen to her speak as much as they went to hear a good sermon.

"It's God's truth, sheriff." Iva raised up her hand solemnly. "The little trash shot her and I saw him with my own two eyes run out the front door. I happened to be looking out my front window when it happened."

Claire nodded, and retrieving a small pad of paper, she scribbled Iva's statement down. The woman was in earnest, but she had to take what Iva said with a grain of salt. There was no doubt in her mind that Iva saw *something*, but witnesses were notorious for making false statements and contradicting the truth. The upset of the moment, emotions and assumptions were often skewed. Her weak eyesight would be another reason to question her reliability.

"Take me to her, Mr. Chase," she instructed.

Howard shivered and led her through the shotgun house. Iva was on her heels, the clicking of her cane was like a tsking tongue. Sparsely decorated, the furniture appeared old, but the rooms were tidy–until they entered the kitchen. Flour dusted the Hoosier Cabinet that stood in place of customary cabinets, and the floor; the sink was full of dirty dishes and utensils, and the air was thick with the scent of apple pie and gunpowder.

Helen Chase was slumped in a chair at the kitchen table. A streak of blood spatter, along with a hole where the bullet or shell entered, was on the wall beside her. The left side of her face and head lay on the floor.

In an attempt to quell her nausea, Claire inhaled a breath, held it, and released it. Dead bodies generally no longer repulsed her, but seeing a victim in this horrific state was sickening.

She dreaded what she had to do, but there was no way around it. At this angle, she couldn't make out what she suspected was a bullet hole in the right temple. Helen's bent arm blocked her view. She returned her paper pad to her purse, and seizing the corpse by the shoulders, she attempted to draw it upwards. But it was no use. The woman was icy cold as one of the icicles hanging off the house's guttering, and her body was too stiff to straighten. Claire was able to catch a glimpse of the hole in Helen's head and it was where she expected it to be. A dark ring encircled the wound, which was interesting.

The light from the ceiling cast an unnatural halo around what remained of the woman's head, making her appear angelic. In the past, whenever there was a shooting, a halo never formed around the victim. While a believer in miracles, Claire figured there must be a reason for this phenomenon.

"You haven't touched anything?" Claire released the body and took a step back. One would expect if someone found their loved one murdered they'd alert her immediately, rather than waste precious time tampering with the crime scene. Perhaps adjust the light to cause the unique halo. But in her time as sheriff, she learned there was no predicting human behavior.

"No, ma'am." Howard pointed at his wife; his greenish eyes once more filled with tears. A heavy man, his head and jaw were shrouded in wispy gray hair. Only in the winter did he grow a beard, likely to keep his face warm in the cold weather. In the warmer months, he was clean shaven. "This is how I found her. Why?"

"Sometimes people like to move things around." The halo and the dark ring were going to bother her, but she would have to let it go for now. Whatever the cause, the doctor would explain it later. "Now you say a young man killed her?"

"Yes, ma'am." His mouth twisted into a scowl. "A few days ago, Helen, out of the goodness of her heart, had him do some chores in exchange for food. Wasn't enough. He came back, broke in to steal some jewelry, because her cameo brooch is missing from her dresser. She must have caught him and he shot her."

Claire signaled for him to direct her to the bedroom. The bedroom was like the rest of the house, sparsely decorated and tidy. From her observations, nothing looked out of the ordinary. There was also no cameo brooch sitting on top of her dresser. A description of it wasn't necessary. She vaguely remembered Helen wearing it when she was running errands, so she had an idea of what it looked like. Besides, a man like Howard would know as much about cameos as a politician would know about honesty.

She withdrew to the sitting room to gather her thoughts. Iva Kent took a seat on the sofa while Howard stationed himself at the old lady's side. Both waited for her to speak.

She rubbed her brow and said aloud, "Helen caught the boy in the bedroom stealing, so at gunpoint he forced her into the kitchen and made her sit down. Then he shot her and ran away? Why not shoot her the second she found him?"

Howard and Iva exchanged bewildered expressions and looked back at her.

"How did he break in?" Claire asked. When she entered through the front door, there was no damage and when she was in the bedroom, none of the windows were broken.

"Well, we don't lock our doors. Never had a reason to — until now." His lower lip trembled.

"I swear, sheriff, I saw him. Hobo trash." Iva sniffed.

Claire took the pad of paper out again. "What did he look like?"

The description Iva gave was hardly helpful. *Dirty, raggedy clothes, evil look about him, up to no good.* Nothing was said about the color of his hair, his size, or possible age. This would be like looking for a needle in a haystack.

Claire waited until Dr. Jed Loving arrived, briefly mentioning her concern about the halo and the dark ring around the wound. She also asked if he'd dig the bullet or shell out of the wall. Once the body was in his custody and conveyed to his office, she waited a little longer for the Chases' priest to arrive, before departing for the Hooverville a little east of Ouabache.

As Claire left her car and approached the Hooverville on foot, the lively chatter of the community died down and it fell silent as the grave. Folks down on their luck, in various stages of dress and cleanliness, loitered about the makeshift buildings and tents eyeing her suspiciously. The coat she was wearing hid the sheriff's star pinned to her dress, but everyone seemed to be aware of who she was, and from their wary expressions she sensed they would not make this investigation easy for her.

There was a time, in the early days of the Depression, that the hobos would come by the house and if her husband Reginald had been there, he'd invite them in for a meal. If he weren't home, she'd feed the poor souls on the back stoop. After Reginald was elected sheriff, that stopped. He was no longer a friend to those down on their luck. Law enforcement was often used to chase off hobos or demolish Hoovervilles. When he died, she assumed the position through *Widow's Succession*, but the hobos never returned to her property.

A man in a frayed suit with red curly hair, pale skin, and white teeth that chattered from the cold, moseyed over. "What can I do for you, ma'am?" He inquired.

The others – men, women, and the children – kept their distance but observed the exchange keenly.

"I'm Sheriff Williams," Claire nodded to the gentleman politely. From his polished manners, she deduced that he was educated and maybe at one time had money. How far he had fallen! How far they had all fallen! "I'm looking for a young man who may have information on a recent crime."

"A crime occurs, so naturally you come to our little town, wishing to lay the blame at our feet?"

"No, sir. It isn't my intention to accuse anyone, especially the young man in question." She intentionally looked everyone she could in the eye and spoke a little louder for them to hear. The last thing she wished was for anyone to be threatened by her presence. There may come a time when one of them may need her. This was a chance to extend an olive branch. "That is why I came alone, without handcuffs and unarmed. I only wish to speak to the young man, to ask his side of the story."

"Very well, but I will be acting as his attorney." The man produced a billfold and from that withdrew a yellowed wrinkled card, he briefly showed it to her, bearing the name *Archibald Lindley*.

Quirking a finger, he led her past a menagerie of ramshackle structures, consisting of cast-off tin, wood, rocks, brick, newspaper, and fabric. A harsh wind wound its way through the Hooverville. . .she was surprised when it didn't blow the little structures over. *No one can stay warm here.* Aptly named for President Hoover, who belittled the plight of the American people since the crash, shanty towns were called Hoovervilles, Hoover blankets were newspapers used as blankets, Hoover leather was cardboard used in place of a sole inside a shoe, a Hoover wagon was a car with horses hitched to it to pull it. There was hope that the new president would change things. But for now, this was the reality of the downtrodden.

Fires burned, people wore layers and they were wrapped in coats and blankets, but there was a bluish tinge to their bare skin. Guilt settled low in her belly and she averted her gaze. These were unforgiving times, and she experienced hardships, but she had so much while they had so little. These folks had no place to go, no one was going to help them, they squatted where they could and if they needed to move, they rode the rails illegally.

Archibald Lindley brought her to a structure at the far end of the Hooverville. He nudged the door open, revealing a young man laying facedown upon a pallet of blankets. Beneath it was the cold, hard earth and frozen blades of grass.

The man knelt down and tapped the boy's shoulder. "Noah, this is Sheriff Williams. She has questions for you."

"I didn't do anything wrong." His voice was muffled

but his youthful voice squeaked, informing her he was at the age where it was changing.

Claire squatted down next to him. It was impossible to judge his innocence or guilt since he refused to face her. Rather than begin with the shooting, she decided to begin with an easier question. One that might help her understand what led up to the shooting.

"Mr. Chase said you did some chores for his wife?" she said.

"Yeah." Noah sighed and he rolled over and sat up. His dirt smudged cheeks were round and had never felt the sharp edge of a razor before. Unruly curls were longer than was preferred amongst boys his age, though tucked beneath a battered newsboy cap. "I was in the neighborhood looking for work, and she had me shovel snow and chop wood and move things around the house. She paid me in food and clothes. She was a nice lady, she looked like an angel, though sad." Though he didn't say it, Claire could tell he cared about Helen Chase and that he didn't have it in him to harm her. "The last time I was there, her husband showed up and ran me off. Said never to come back or he'd send the law after me."

"Noah," Claire instinctively touched his shoulder and squeezed it softly. "Mrs. Chase died; she had been shot. A neighbor said she witnessed you run out of the house not long afterwards."

A tear trickled down his face but he quickly swiped it away, leaving a patch of skin clean. "I was there — I snuck in because they never lock their doors. I was in their bedroom and I was going to steal something from him." He shuddered beneath her hand. "A gun went off; I saw a brooch laying on a dresser and. . .the devil made me do it, but I took it. Then I ran off. That's God's Truth, I swear!"

The boy rummaged beneath one of the blankets and

pulled out a pink cameo brooch. He laid it in the palm of her hand.

Claire put the piece of jewelry in her coat pocket. His story was plausible enough. He could have denied he was there or that he knew Helen Chase, he could have disposed of the brooch, he could have hidden in the woods to avoid questioning.

If Noah didn't shoot Helen Chase, then who did?

"Where are your parents, Noah?" Claire tilted her head in consideration.

"I'm sixteen, I can look after myself." Noah puffed out his chest, in an attempt to appear older. Or bigger.

"And when you say sixteen, you mean not a day over?" She smiled knowingly.

"Fourteen" Noah admitted.

More like twelve or thirteen. Claire figured, but it was no use arguing over his age. If she angered or upset him, she'd lose whatever chance she had of getting him to trust her. A boy of his age should not be out on his own. The others in the Hooverville, like Archibald Lindley, may have looked out for him, but Noah should be with his parents. She had to wonder if he was a runaway.

"Sheriff, he's just a boy," Archibald interrupted. She felt a pang of embarrassment that she had forgotten he was there. "He stole and that was wrong, yes. But that doesn't make him a murderer."

"I know and I agree." Claire concurred. "Here is what I propose: Noah, you come with me. Not as a suspect, but as a witness, since you were present when the gun went off. You will stay with me and my family until I solve this crime." She turned to the gentleman beside her, in hopes that he would support her plan. "Mr. Lindley will look in on you every day to ensure you're treated well."

"No, I don't want to." Noah crossed his arms over his stomach.

"You are fourteen and on your own. As a sheriff and a mother, I can't leave you here."

Archibald piped up once more. "Noah, I think you should go with Sheriff Williams. You'll be protected and when this is over, you can return." He lifted his brow, hinting to her that they should take this bit by bit.

"Okay." Noah said.

Claire was about to stand and was pleased when both Noah and Archibald chivalrously assisted her. She was further amused when Noah offered his arm and escorted her out of the Hooverville.

∽

Claire was holding her breath as she ushered Noah into the house. She cast a quick glance around and finding the room empty, she exhaled. She pressed a finger to her lips and they tiptoed gingerly on the wooden floors. If she could get the boy into the bath, or at the very least wash his face and comb his hair, she'd have a better chance convincing Mother that his staying with them was a good idea. Unfortunately, Noah's booted foot hit a creaky board and the noise beckoned the older woman from the kitchen.

"What is this?" Mother approached, arms crossed, wearing the same frown she wore when Claire was seven and she brought home a cockeyed mangy cat to keep. "Claire?"

She placed her hand on the boy's shoulder. "Mother, this is Noah." A sly lift of her brow encouraged the boy to hold out his hand in front of him respectfully. "He is a witness and he'll be staying with us for a few days."

Mother ignored the boy's extended hand. She opened her mouth to protest, but Claire moved quickly, sweeping Noah into the kitchen. Her mother trailed; the woman would give her an earful as soon as possible.

Claire grabbed the cookie jar from the counter and passed it to Noah. Since she worked, Mother claimed the kitchen as her own domain and took over the cooking and the baking. The other day she made a fresh batch of oatmeal cookies. "Noah, make yourself at home and help yourself."

The boy plunked down at the table and dug through the cookies, cramming them into his mouth. God only knew when he last had a home cooked meal, let alone cookies.

She ducked into the bedroom, which was off to the side. Her little daughter, Mirabelle, was in her cradle, sound asleep. There was a part of her that hated to disturb the baby's rest, but after a day of investigating crimes and murders, nothing soothed her more than holding the little girl.

Claire lifted Mirabelle out and sitting in the rocker, she cuddled the child close. "How's my girl?" She brushed her lips against Mirabelle's brow.

Mother came in and after closing the door behind her, she hissed. "I heard word from Iva Kent that this boy is a hobo and he killed a woman. Folks are talking of running those tramps out of the valley."

She rolled her eyes, annoyed that Iva made such quick work. "Noah did no such thing. He was in the wrong place at the wrong time. I wish folks would let me do my job before jumping to ridiculous conclusions." The prejudice against the hobos was so severe that she shouldn't be surprised at the lengths people were willing to go to make themselves feel *safe*.

Mother's expression softened a fraction. Her mother had always been strict, proper, and every inch the Victorian lady. But since Father abandoned her, running off with another woman and leaving her alone and without a home, Mother struggled to trust and think the best of others. She moved into Claire's home, kept house, and looked after Mirabelle. There were times when her mother neglected to hide her displeasure in regard to her work as sheriff, but she did try to be understanding.

"So, what are your plans for this boy?" Mother asked.

Mirabelle rubbed her face with her balled fists and cooed.

"I hope to earn his trust and reunite him with his parents. His mother must be worried sick." Claire murmured and shifted the baby, to hopefully prevent her from getting fussy.

Mother harrumphed. "If he robs us blind or murders us in our sleep, it'll be on your head." She cautioned.

"If he murders us, I'm sure I'll be in glory and I'll no longer care. Mother, will you keep an eye on him while I'm at work?"

"Well, you've left me with little choice," she sniffed.

Claire smiled to herself. Mother would come around; the older woman had a good heart.

She called for the boy and he entered promptly, his dirt-smudged cheeks puffed out while he chewed his last bite. *Mother will have to bake another batch.* His eyes darted from her to Mother and back again.

Claire carefully rose from the chair, cradling Mirabelle with one arm, and patted the seat. "Noah, have you ever held a baby before?"

The boy shook his head and swallowing, he sat down. She placed the baby in his arms and as she suspected, he was gentle with Mirabelle, petting the little girl's golden head.

Claire kissed the baby one more time and ruffled Noah's curls. To Mother she said, "I need to see Dr. Loving about Mrs. Chase. I'll be back later this evening." Turning back to Noah, she declared in her most maternal tone, "Mother is in charge, obey her. And no offense to you, take a bath."

"Yes, ma'am," Noah chuckled.

She stood back and marveled at the sight of Noah holding Mirabelle. They looked perfect together, like an older brother and baby sister. The young man had been closed-mouthed about his parents and family. *Is he an orphan?* Orphan or runaway, he belonged in a family. He deserved to be loved and she couldn't deny how much she wanted to take him in and be a mother to him. How anyone could believe him capable of shooting Helen Chase was beyond her imagination!

The grandfather clock in the sitting room chimed, reminding her of the hour and how she had to get to Dr. Jed Loving's office. Solving this case was imperative, especially with the anti-hobo sentiment simmering in Ouabache. Hatred of the unknown drowned out all logic and reason. She had no intention of running those in the Hooverville out, but a handful of irate locals could take the law in their own hands.

"Heard you took in the hobo boy." Dr. Jed Loving greeted when Claire entered the room. He stood behind the autopsy table where Helen Chase resided.

Claire wrinkled her nose. The whole building reeked of death, old blood, and a stale corpse, but she was more disturbed by the fact that her private business was public knowledge. "How-" She threw up her hands, fully exasperated. Iva Kent, that's how! The old biddy never knew when to quit. "I only just brought him home. How on earth did you hear of it?"

"This is Ouabache." He let out an ungentlemanly snort. "Nothing stays a secret here for long."

She thought having Noah at her home would offer him protection during this investigation. If any of the locals were to start chasing the hobos out of the area, he'd be out of harm's way.

"So, tell me about Mrs. Chase," Claire said.

The woman was before them, half her head and face detached and next to her, her bare body laid flat out, the distinctive hole on her temple. The halo was gone now. A yellowed sheet was draped over her for modesty's sake; it was the same sheet used for all of the autopsies Jed performed. By now Claire had memorized every stain, snag, and fray in it. He'd wash it up and store it away for the next body he had to examine.

"Well, I took your thoughts into consideration and had some interesting findings." Jed declared, "Mrs. Chase was already dead when she was shot."

"Really?" Claire couldn't disguise her surprise. There were oddities about the corpse, but she hadn't expected this. "Was it obvious she was dead when she was shot?" She inquired.

"Yes, though I figure rigor mortis had yet to set in. Right now, from the state of her body, she's been dead five or six hours." Jed wiped his hands off on his apron and removed it. He went to the counter and plucked up a shell and held it up for her to see. "Can't be sure, but I think the weapon of choice was a Colt M1902. I have one and the shells somewhat resemble this. Anyway, I believe she was found dead and slumped against the table. The shooter had to hold her up in the chair and pressed the barrel to her temple and shot her. That's why there's this dark ring around the hole – the close proximity and gunpowder residue. The shooter let her droop against the table again. But they would have known she wasn't asleep. There was no mistaking that."

"How did she die? Natural causes?" She suggested.

"Nope." Jed looked a little smug. "Arsenic poisoning. The halo you noticed was a symptom of arsenic poisoning. After arsenic has time to get into the lungs, it can make a person's breath fluorescent. She wasn't breathing when you found her, but I kinda wonder if when you checked the wound and moved the body, the movement caused a pocket of air to release and the halo to return. I don't know, just a theory." He grabbed Helen's hand and raised it for Claire to see. "But look at her fingernails, the pigmentation is different. She'd been ingesting arsenic for a while, I looked through the contents of her stomach, she had eaten a pie and I think it was laced with arsenic," he proposed, and put the hand back down. "Maybe someone poisoned her and someone else shot her? You may have two suspects on your hands."

"Hmm. . ." Claire considered it. There could be two people involved, anything was possible. However, the whole crime was odd. A woman who was poisoned to death and then shot. The one who shot her knew Helen was dead, what reason would they have to shoot her? If she had not been shot, her death might have been shrugged off as natural causes. Nothing was taken, save the cameo brooch that Noah stole and he explained that. Howard Chase and Iva Kent both blamed the boy for it, but Claire couldn't believe Noah had it in him to do it. What would have been his motive? Where would he have found the Colt M1902. Helen Chase had shown him kindness; there was no reason to kill her.

Apple pie. The kitchen smelled of apple pie and Helen had clearly eaten a pie, but when she looked at the crime scene, no pie was found. Not on the table or the Hoosier Cabinet. Where did it go? It had been there at some point. The sink was full of dirty dishes and utensils. The killer must have disposed of it, but why?

"Let me see her clothing." Claire requested.

Jed grabbed a sack from the chair in the corner and handed it off.

She rummaged through it, studying Helen's apron and sleeves. They were dusty with flour. Putting the sack down, she peeled back the sheet and leaning down, she examined the woman's fingernails herself. The nail pigmentation was different, but flour and pastry were corroded beneath the beds.

Claire released the woman's hand, stunned by the realization of what she believed to be the truth. "Helen made the pie, she put the poison in it, and she intentionally ate it. Helen Chase killed herself!" she blurted out.

Jed Loving had been around and seen things, but even his face blanched at learning this piece of information. "Are you sure?" He gulped loudly.

"Yes." Unpleasant as it was, Claire knew she was right. Helen Chase killed herself — The why of it was a mystery, but she supposed the one who shot Helen could explain it. *Howard.* She rubbed the back of her neck, in hopes of loosening the strained muscle. "I think I know the how, I'm not certain about the why, but I intend to find out. Thank you, Jed."

She turned to leave, for she had to confront Howard,

but first she needed to speak to Archibald Lindley on legal matters.

"Hey, are you going to share it with me?" Jed yelled, amusement coloring his tone.

"Come for supper and you'll hear everything," Claire replied, trying not to appear too smug. This wasn't a game or a mystery novel, this was real life. Yet satisfaction swelled within her that she solved yet another case.

The doctor muttered under his breath, but she knew the old curmudgeon wasn't peeved with her and that he'd be prompt for mealtime this evening.

Clare knocked on the Chases' front door, and while she waited for Howard to answer, she gave Archibald Lindley a sideways glance. The man cleaned up nicely and looked every inch a gentleman and an attorney in his new-but-used three-piece suit. He was only too happy to be of use to Noah and help with the case.

The door swung open and Howard's whole face brightened at the sight of her. "Did you catch him?" He jutted his chin towards the red-haired man. "Who's this?"

Claire pushed her way into the house and the lawyer followed.

"Archibald Lindley, Noah's attorney," Archibald supplied, and flashed him a newly printed card.

Howard was puzzled at the mention of Noah. To him, Noah was just a hobo. *Trash.* It never occurred to him that the boy had a name or that he mattered.

"The boy you tried to frame for your wife's death." Claire clarified.

"What? I didn't. . ." Howard looked back in the direction of the kitchen and his cheeks reddened. "I'd never kill my wife. That boy —"

Claire raised a finger, silencing him. "No, you didn't harm Mrs. Chase. Neither did Noah, for that matter. Mrs. Chase killed herself via arsenic poison, didn't she? And you found her?" She took a few steps towards the bedroom. "I imagine if I look around, I'll find a Colt M1902 in the house or on the property."

Howard covered his mouth as tears fell freely. "Helen always had troubles with melancholy, more so after we lost our savings in the crash. I watched her the best I could, took care of her." He said in a small voice. "This time I failed."

"So, you shot her in the head to cover up the truth." Claire concluded.

"We're Catholic." Howard motioned to a crucifix mounted to the wall and crossed himself. "Suicide's a mortal sin; the priest wouldn't have given her Last Rites, a funeral, or allow her to be buried in the cemetery."

"Noah just happened to be in the house at the time, stealing, when you shot her."

"Right, that's how it was." Howard's head bobbled eagerly. "I heard him leave and Iva Kent watched from her window and corroborated what I said happened."

"And that, I suppose, is God's Truth?" Claire said, her words dripping with sarcasm. She took a pair of handcuffs out of her purse. "Howard Chase, you are under arrest."

"What?" Howard backed away.

Archibald Lindley began, "You attempted to frame an innocent person — a boy of fourteen — for Mrs. Chase's death." He crossed his arms over his chest. Though he possessed a mild-mannered disposition, she believed he would be a fighter in the courtroom. When she had a chance, she'd do what she could to see if Archibald Lindley could be hired as a district attorney. He would be the ideal man for the job. "That's a crime, sir."

"Please, have mercy!" Howard begged; hands clasped together.

"You must appeal to the Lord for mercy now," Claire said, and put the handcuffs on him.

Howard whimpered as they led him to the Model A, but despite the tears he shed, she couldn't muster any sympathy for him. He was too eager to place the blame on a boy and let him suffer for a crime he didn't commit. The man deserved jail.

∽

Claire was able to persuade Noah to stay at her home for no more than three days. At the end of the third, Noah put the clothes and books she had gifted him in an old pillowcase. He put his coat on and slung the pillowcase over his shoulder and met Archibald Lindley on the front porch, eager to return to the Hooverville.

Claire trailed him outside. "I can't say anything to keep you here?" She wrung her hands anxiously. The thought of him returning to that dirty, cold place weighed heavily upon her conscience. He ought to be with his family, or at the very least live with her and her family. "Your mother?"

"My mother's dead, and my father — he's not a good man." Noah said simply.

So, there is a father. Claire racked her brain but couldn't recall Noah saying what his last name was or where he was from. He certainly wouldn't tell her now. Was his father *not a good man*? Had Noah fled his home because his father was abusive? Or was it just a yarn Noah was spinning to prevent her from investigating further? This was one mystery that would remain unsolved for now. She would figure out the truth one way or another.

"There's a cat drawn on your fence; that's hobo code for a kind lady, and you are. You do care. This isn't home to me, though." As if he were a mystic and could read her thoughts, he threatened, "And I don't want to go back to my father; I'll just run away again."

"Sheriff Williams," Archibald interrupted, tipping his cap to her. "I'll look after Noah as I would my own son. I promise, you have my word." And she believed him, she had no reason not to. Throughout the whole ordeal he had been Noah's protector and ally.

Sometimes families were created where they didn't exist before. She knew that from experience.

"This feels wrong, but all right." Claire exhaled, her breath turning into white curling whisps. She began to shiver and hugged herself, regretting she hadn't thrown on a coat or a shawl before going outside. "If either of you need anything, come to my office or this house. Anytime."

"I will." Noah abruptly threw his arms around her and whispered in her ear, "Thank you for believing in me."

Claire pressed a kiss to his cheek as they parted.

Archibald put out his hand, which she gladly shook. "Thank you for making me respectable again." He put his hand on Noah's shoulder and they left her property. She watched the two disappear down the road, praying for their safety and well-being.

Claire returned inside and went straight to Mirabelle. She drew the rocker close to the cradle and found solace in watching her daughter sleep.

Mother stood in the doorway and leaned against the door frame. "Don't look so glum. You can't rescue everyone in the world," she stated.

"I know," Claire mumbled.

There was comfort in the fact that Archibald would take care of the boy. The hobos in the Hooverville seemed to look after one another. And knowing Noah, this wouldn't be the last time she saw him. He'd be back.

∿

Veronica Leigh has been published in numerous blogs, anthologies, journals, and magazines. She aspires to be the Jane Austen of her generation and she makes her home in Indiana.

Route 90
Kevin A Davis

As Liz Dixon slowed on Route 90 to turn into a driveway, she smiled at the blooming azaleas outside of her client's house. "Right on time and as pink as a sunrise."

She'd left last night in the dark with the crew who'd replaced the two front windows. Yesterday, she'd hoped the buds might pop. Liz had a showing with the Andersons today at noon, and her job as a realtor went better when the yard gave a good first impression. From inside her Prius, the windows appeared proper as she parked and stepped out. The sole reason she'd come over so early was to check the installer's work in daylight.

"Details matter," she said quietly as she strode toward the steps of the wraparound porch. A faint chemical scent remained from the installation the afternoon before. Four years prior, the single-story house had been remodeled and should sell in no time once buyers saw the kitchen.

At the house next door, Mr. Stuttard had left a light on upstairs in his bedroom, which wasn't like him. He counted every penny. His property would fetch a good price as the frontage along Route 90 stretched over a hundred feet. It would end up a commercial lot someday, likely sold to David Turner who'd tear down the beautiful old house to put up a dollar store.

Liz eyed the outside framing of the newly installed windows carefully; they appeared as perfect as the inside. The beige siding hadn't been scratched and the workers had wiped it neat. The porch was clean of any construction debris. The lawn had been trimmed a fresh, spring green, and now there were azaleas blooming.

She scowled and stomped off the porch. A wet oil stain marred the driveway she'd had pressure cleaned three days ago.

"You've got to be kidding me."

It hadn't been there last night. The installers had left before she did and she'd checked to make sure they didn't leave a splinter. The blasphemous blotch leered back at her as she glared at it. Someone had parked in her client's drive last night.

For a moment, she considered a quick restoration spell, but it was too public along the highway with light traffic. She'd call around, but it was unlikely it could be taken care of by midday, if today at all. Jaw tight, she glanced over at Mr. Stuttard's again. If he'd been out walking his dog, she'd have asked.

Liz lifted her chin and strode for the sidewalk linking the two houses and rapped on his front door. He hated to be bothered, but she did wonder why he'd left his upstairs light on. As he didn't answer, she swallowed and stood back and to the side. Mr. Stuttard was pushing eighty and though she hated to consider it, she couldn't leave if he'd fallen, or worse. With all the noise she was making, his dog should be barking, even if he'd left and taken his golfcart downtown.

Walking up the side of his house, she called the sheriff's non-emergency number. Doris Becker answered.

"Doris, this is Liz Dixon. I'm next door, well, *at* Mr. Stuttard's and he's not answering. Could you send the sheriff over for a wellness check?" Liz didn't mention the light upstairs. "I've knocked a few times."

"Sheriff Calure's out at the moment." Doris's tone was hesitant. "I'll send someone."

"Thank you, Doris."

The reek of gas hung in the air, but the lawn had been mowed a few days ago based on the fresh tips of the green shoots. The old house needed painting in a few spots and a hole in the brick foundation needed to be filled.

Through the opening, a shadow under his house moved.

Liz froze, then leaned in when she heard a whine. "Hey." A gray muzzle highlighted dark eyes before it disappeared again. She had no idea of what Mr. Stuttard called the dog. "Hey boy." What was it doing outside by itself? Her concern over Mr. Stuttard rose, tightening her chest.

The hole was halfway between the front corner of the house and the side door. Liz squatted at the edge, not wanting to kneel in her slacks.

The muzzle appeared again and the whine grew louder.

"C'mon. It's just Liz." She stretched out her fingers and the older Yorkshire Terrier sniffed carefully before edging out. It trembled and her apprehension for Mr. Stuttard furrowed her brow.

Cradling the dog in her arms, she sacrificed her clean blouse and ignored the dirt. She had a change of clothes in her trunk and at her office. "Better to be prepared." The dog studied her with liquid eyes.

Liz juggled the dog into the crook of her left arm and

called her friend, Faith. "Hey. I'm not going to make it for coffee. Old man Stuttard hasn't answered his door, his dog was under his house, and I've got the sheriff's department on the way."

"Damn, Liz. What do you suppose happened? I hope he's okay."

"Me too."

"I mean he's a grumpy old man, but I don't want to see anything happen to him. Think his son would move in? What am I saying — I shouldn't be getting morbid so quick. How'd the dog get out?"

"No clue. Doors on this side are closed." Liz didn't blame Faith for jumping to conclusions, her own mind kept racing there.

"You've got a client next door, don't you?"

Deputy Dale Parsons pulled into the drive, and Liz marched to meet him. "The sheriff's here. I'll call you back."

"You better."

Dale cut his brown hair into a near military shave, but his smile was always warm. "Mrs. Dixon. Councilwoman Dixon."

"Stop it, Dale. It's Liz and you know it." The dog growled and nestled deeper in her arms.

He studied the dog, then the house. "Let me check the doors, Miss Liz. Stay put."

She stood by his car as he checked the front door. They exchanged awkward smiles as he returned and headed for the side door. She adjusted Mr. Stuttard's dog as he grumbled a light growl. "It's okay, honey. Just looking for your daddy."

A minute after Dale knocked he opened the door, glanced at her, then entered, calling out for the elderly man. She wasn't surprised that Mr. Stuttard had left the door unlocked, people did in this town. She approached to get a better view of the back yard, which was fenced in with old, weathered sections. The obnoxious scent of gas grew stronger.

Dale was pale faced and speaking into the mic at his shoulder when he burst out. His face grew tight at the sight of her and she couldn't make out his words as he strode for his car.

The tightness in her chest hollowed out. She didn't doubt Dale was rattled. Something *had* happened to Mr. Stuttard, but what was his dog doing outside? Liz tried to approach as Dale spoke inside his closed car, but he gestured for her to wait and kept talking.

Sheriff Benson Calure arrived a couple minutes later with sirens. She cleared the driveway area before he pulled in. A seventies porn mustache attached impossibly to his thin face, and she caught a glimpse of his bald head before he tucked on a cap and jumped out. "Mrs. Dixon." Pulling on a pair of plastic gloves, he barely offered a nod as he strode toward the side door.

She followed. "Benson, what's going on?" The dog growled lightly in her arms.

The sheriff paused, door half opened, considering the ground before he turned. "I'll assume you're asking as a council member and will keep any information confidential."

"Of course."

He studied her. "This is a murder investigation. Someone bludgeoned Mr. Stuttard with one of his statues. Liz, I'm going to ask you to step back off the property for now."

She blinked as he strode inside without waiting for her response. A chill rose up her neck. Had there ever been a murder in Layetteville? The door the sheriff closed didn't appear to be pried open or broken into. Had it been someone Mr. Stuttard knew? His son, Vic, had approached her to find a buyer for his dad's house. She'd refused because she knew Mr. Stuttard had every intention of spending his last days there. Liz didn't want to believe his own son might have expedited the timeline with the horrific act.

Dale, wearing an apologetic smile, approached her, nodding for her to step back over to her client's yard.

"I'll watch the dog — for now." She could do that small favor for Mr. Stuttard. Her office had plenty of room for a little dog who'd lost their person. Liz could follow up with the sheriff after he announced the investigation.

~

Liz's office was located on the main street of Layetteville Florida, called Jefferson Avenue on maps and signposts. She rented the downstairs of a hundred-year-old brick building on the corner of Route 90. Thoughts drifting as she drove, she dialed her friend as she neared town.

As Liz pulled into a parking space out front, Faith answered. "Hey, any word from Mr. Stuttard?"

"The sheriff will announce it to the rest of the council soon enough, but the poor man's been murdered."

"Damn. How'd he die?"

"Benson says bludgeoned with a statue and I'm guessing he means the angels Mr. Stuttard kept on the mantle." Liz coaxed the dog out of her back seat where it hid. "The door didn't look like it had been broken into."

"You don't suppose it was that sleazy son of his?"

Liz strode for her door, keys and purse in her right hand. "I hate to say I thought the same thing. Horrible to imagine. He did want to sell the house, and there's been plenty of buyers." The sharp scents of cinnamon and nutmeg oils wafted from the potpourri by her front door. "Speaking of buyers; I've got a couple coming out to look at the property by Mr. Stuttard's, but I've got his dog. Feel like coming to the office at eleven and puppy watching?"

"Yes. If you sell, then you're buying lunch."

Liz set up some water for the dog and it drank heavily while she finished her call. The police at the house next door might hamper her sale. Shame rose from the thought, but she was just being practical.

Slipping into the back, she changed her blouse, then called her husband, Mike, to have him set up for a canine guest for a couple days.

"Who's is it? What's its name?" he asked.

She'd have to see if someone knew. "I don't know its name and don't ask me. Council business until I can say more."

Mike chuckled. "You are joking, right?"

"Don't. I'll explain when I can."

"I cannot wait to hear how this ties into the county. I'll call him Scooby-Doo for now."

Liz ended the call, found some crackers for the dog, and fought heading early to her client's house to spy on the investigation. She should have mentioned the gas smell, but surely they'd notice.

Her tall friend, Faith, arrived with her brown hair in a ponytail. She wore a blouse instead of her usual T-shirt, likely because she would be sitting in Liz's office.

When Faith stepped inside, Liz grabbed her bag. "Thank you. I'm going to go see what they've found."

"Share the juicy bits with your BFF." Faith peered around the office. "Where is the dog?"

Liz pointed at her desk. "I made a bed for him at my feet. He seems comfortable there."

Faith peeked under and smiled. "I'll give the poor thing some love. Good luck. Sell the house."

Liz drove down Route 90 with her hands flexing around the steering wheel. The town would be in an uproar over Mr. Stuttard's murder. Hopefully Sheriff Benson Calure would be up to finding the killer quickly.

Three squad cars and an emergency vehicle were parked outside when she pulled up. Liz sighed, shaking her head. "I'm going to have to explain this." The Andersons would expect her to know.

Which mattered more, Mr. Stuttard's murder or her sale? Until it was announced, she would have to keep the sheriff's confidence.

She flushed as she pulled into the driveway, stopping over the oil stain and parking over it. Dale was outside with an EMT driver, but everyone else appeared to be inside. Liz unlocked her client's door, went inside, and circled to the window.

By her fifth lap around the house adjusting what she could, the Andersons had pulled up out front and stood on the driveway watching the activities at Mr. Stuttard's. They likely hadn't noticed the azaleas.

Liz opened the door with a smile. "Right on time. Come on in."

As expected, their expressions were tight as they entered. "What's going on next door?" Mr. Anderson asked.

"I hope nothing serious," Liz lied. "The Sheriff's department is very thorough. Let me show you this living room floor."

Every time they passed a window on the east side of the house, the prospective buyers peeked out at the activity at Mr. Stuttard's. Even the modernized kitchen and stainless steel appliances didn't excite them. Liz wasn't surprised when the Andersons thanked her less than warmly for the tour and fled to their cars.

She waved goodbye and stood on the porch with a forced smile until they had merged onto Route 90. Determined, she marched off the porch and crossed the yards to Mr. Stuttard's house. The scent of gas still hung in the air. From his position talking with the EMT driver, Dale jumped and jogged toward her as she breeched the invisible boundary between properties.

"Do you smell that?" she asked Dale.

"Miss Liz, you can't be over here, ma'am."

She veered toward the back of the house, forcing him to put on some extra speed to catch up. "It smells like gasoline. Mr. Stuttard didn't have a car and he parks his golf cart in the shed on the other side. Lawn hasn't been mowed in a few days." Liz almost made it to the house before he darted in front of her.

"You can't . . ."

Liz waved him silent. "Do you smell it?"

"Yes, ma'am. Gasoline."

"Where's it from?"

"Miss Liz, I don't know, but you can't be over here." Dale glanced furtively back at the house, perhaps worried about the sheriff.

Her cheeks flushed. She wanted to help, but they weren't going to accept even a simple comment. Straightening, she drew a deep breath and nodded to Dale. "I'll leave. But you'll check out where it's coming from. Agreed?"

"Yes, ma'am."

She couldn't be sure he'd follow up, but she'd make

sure Sheriff Calure did. Lips tightening and twisting, Liz retreated off Mr. Stuttard's property.

Mr. Stuttard had been murdered, and there wasn't anything she could really do about that. She would take his dog back to her house and get him settled in. She had the time, since she didn't have a deal to discuss with the Andersons.

∽

In their den, Mike had set out a water bowl and bought kibbles. A yoga mat had been his idea of a dog bed.

"Where are the cats?" Liz asked. Mr. Stuttard's dog grumbled a low growl at her husband.

"Tucked in the bedroom." Mike smiled and let the dog sniff his fingers. "I'll let them out once Scoob is settled." He peered at her face. "Council business still?"

She nodded and headed for the water bowl. "I'm sure it'll be out soon. Sad." Her phone rang in her purse.

Mike nodded, scratched his beard, and headed upstairs.

Sheriff Calure called. "Miss Liz." His voice was firm, not stern or angry. "I understand you want to help, but you're going to have to stay out of this investigation and keep off Mr. Stuttard's property. Mind your business."

Her jaw tightened. As part of the county council, she did have some right to ask questions. "What have you learned?"

"Nothing yet. We are dealing with someone dangerous." Again, his warning for her to keep out of it.

"Have you contacted Mr. Stuttard's son?"

"We have."

She kept her voice even. "And?"

"Vic Stuttard is on his way to town." The sheriff did not make it sound like he considered the son a suspect.

"He lives less than an hour away, in Tallahassee." Surely they would see him as a suspect.

"I'm well aware, Miss Liz. Let me get back to work. I'll keep the council updated with anything new." Benson's tone was firm, but she bristled at the patronizing edge to it.

She hung up, twitching slightly. He'd make sure she kept out of it and warn his deputies as well. It certainly didn't sound like he had any leads, but he wouldn't let on if he did. Did he intend to question, or maybe arrest, the son?

She watched Scoob snack on the fresh food. Sheriff Benson Calure intended to keep her at arms' length either because she was female, or some other insecurity of his.

Three hours later after busying herself with work, a venting call to Faith, and the occasional internet search on Vic Stuttard, Liz couldn't help but call the sheriff. He didn't answer so she called the station. Doris proved cautious and tight-lipped, but she did answer when Liz asked her if anyone had been arrested for the murder yet.

"Lord, no. I mean — You're going to have to wait till Sheriff Calure calls you back."

After she hung up, Liz stared at her cell phone. If the son were in town this afternoon, he might be planning on staying the night. Probably not at the house. He'd stayed at the Brewster House when he'd tried to get her to help him maneuver his dad into selling.

She sat stiff, found the number on the internet, and dialed. "Hello, Vic Stuttard please, he asked me to call."

The voice on the other end was a young woman, probably a high school kid. "He went out for dinner." There was no offer to take a message.

"Damn, I was supposed to meet him. Do you know if he went to Deal's or the Porch?"

"Didn't say." The bored response came slowly and I imagined her scrolling her cell phone.

Liz grabbed her purse. Scoob had settled at her feet, rather than on the yoga mat. "Mike, I'm headed out. Watch the puppy, please."

The cats had come by for a sniff, but had gone upstairs to hang out with the less traitorous member of the household who responded with a muffled. "Got it."

Liz drove into town playing out several conversations she might have with Vic Stuttard. Did she really believe he'd driven into town last night and killed his dad? Someone had.

She found Vic Stuttard sitting alone at a booth at the first restaurant. Thin and dark-haired, he wore a light beige polo shirt and talked with an earpod dangling.

Liz saw a short woman in an apron heading for her and she wormed through the tables to grab a table just to Vic's left. She slid in, her back to him, and smiled at the waitress who'd chased her down. "Can I get some sweet tea and a menu?"

The woman appeared flustered, but nodded and retreated.

" — a few days. Bumpkin lawyers. It'll be worth it though. You'll see." Vic's tone was disgustingly gleeful. "I'm thinking Acapulco to celebrate."

He paused to listen, and Liz had to smooth her frown. No one watched from the other tables, but she did recognize most of them.

"Alright. Let me go. I've got a meeting in about an

hour." Vic rattled his glass, ice clinking. "Redneck waitstaff."

Liz turned, as if just noticing him. "Oh, Vic Stuttard, is that you?"

He glanced at her dully. "Yeah."

She shifted her chair. "I'm so sorry to hear about your father. You have my condolences."

Vic scoffed. "He couldn't live forever." He toyed with his phone, as if he might call someone.

Liz swallowed, her tongue feeling slimy talking to him, yet worse as she spoke. "What are you going to do with the place? I'm sure I've got buyers who would love to look at it."

He picked up his phone, scrolling. "Already got a buyer."

She tilted her head, running through the options. "The Keatons or David Turner?

His head snapped as he focused on her, then his eyes tightened in recognition. "Wait. I remember you. Told me to take a hike when I wanted your help with the old man." Vic relaxed and shook his head. "He would have been safe in a nice nursing home if you'd played along, but no, you got all high and mighty. Well, there you go. Take a hike, sister. You'll get nothing from this deal." He motioned for her to turn around. "Don't even talk to me."

She turned slowly, and as she did, he slid out of his booth. Passing her without a glance, he made for the register. Liz watched from her peripheral vision as he paid, glancing at her repeatedly. Getting up and following him would be too obvious. The waitress left a glass of sweet tea as Vic Stuttard exited the restaurant.

Liz wiped her face, still flushed from his comments. She'd done nothing but make him suspicious of her. She hoped the sheriff wouldn't get wind of her chance meeting.

Mike texted as she brooded. "Scoob is stressed. Took him for a walk. We all miss you. Dinner?"

There was little she could do at this point about Mr. Stuttard's murder. She'd botched any chance to get clues from his son.

∼

On the way home, she tried again to reach the sheriff. He might care that the son had already found a buyer for the property. If Vic had made the deal prior to his dad's murder, it might be evidence.

As she drove down Route 90, approaching the intersection leading to her house, her teeth clenched and she drove straight. It wouldn't surprise her if Sheriff Benson Calure was in his office, avoiding her calls.

She strode into the Sheriff's office and found Dale at the desk. "Tell Benson I'm here," she said.

Dale glanced over his shoulder. "I think he's out."

"Tell him you're horrible at lying." Liz headed for the door from the lobby, happy to find it unlocked.

"Wait, I . . ." Dale stood, face reddening, all the while snatching glimpses over his shoulder.

She passed him, patting his shoulder and strode for Benson's office.

His door was unlocked as well. Leaning toward his computer, he peered up at her over the rims of round glasses. "Councilwoman."

"Did you know that Vic Stuttard has a buyer for the property, already?"

Benson peeled off his glasses, leaned back, and

motioned toward his chair. His eyes tightened when he caught a glimpse of Dale and gestured him away. "I did not."

"Don't you find that suspicious?" Liz remained standing.

He smoothed his oversized mustache. "Not suspicious, no."

Her phone buzzed with a text, but she ignored it. "If not suspicious, what?"

"Sad. Disrespectful."

"Did you even question him?"

"Of course."

"And?"

Benson tapped at his chin. "He has an alibi. I was working on a report now. You would have gotten all this in a couple of hours."

"What alibi?"

His jaw tightened, then relaxed. "Three friends, one a judge's son, were at his house until 4 a.m. A fourth friend crashed on his couch as they were too drunk to drive. We've got corroboration from all of them."

Friends were as tight an alibi as a spouse. They might lie. "Track his cell phone? Traffic cameras? Do you have even one lead?" Her tone edged on accusing, and she stopped.

Benson stood, facing her over his desk. "Nothing substantial. We're processing forensics. You'll get all this in the report. I've sent out a statement as well."

Liz opened her mouth to continue pushing, but allowed him to raise a finger and stop her. She had already made her point.

"Let me do my job, Miss Liz. I'll keep you, and the rest of the council, in the loop. But I don't want to hear you sticking your nose in anything, or I'll bring it to an open meeting and we can discuss your activities there."

County politics as they were, some might enjoy his complaints. She carefully didn't fidget. "I appreciate that you're on top of this, Sheriff."

Blood pounding in her ears, she spun on her heel and headed back toward Dale. Her investigating had done nothing but close down any access to information.

Stepping out into the late afternoon air, she drew a deep breath. The best she could do for Mr. Stuttard was take care of his dog.

After a quiet and unsatisfying meal with Mike, she coaxed Scoob into the living room where they intended to watch a quick show. The cats were annoyed, but feigned indifference. Mr. Stuttard's dog just stayed at her feet.

She glazed at the television with her head swirling around the real-life murder rather than the crime show. When Mike clicked it off, she started. "What?"

"Maybe the dog needs a walk," Mike said.

She peered down. "What makes you say that?"

"Maybe you need a walk."

Liz hadn't been paying attention, and he'd known. "I just can't get my mind off of what happened to him."

"There's a leash hanging from the hook behind the door of your den. Take a drive. Take a walk. Sitting here will just frustrate you." He smiled. "Better if you're frustrated and walking."

Ten minutes later, Liz pulled into the drive of her client's house with the sun low in the sky. The sheriff's department had left tape on the doors of Mr. Stuttard's house, but otherwise it appeared normal. The bedroom light had been turned off upstairs.

She pulled up far enough to expose the oil stain and chastised herself for not calling someone to clean it up.

Again, she peered along Route 90 to see if she might work a quick restoration spell. Not only was there too much traffic, but a sheriff's department car drove by. They couldn't complain if she checked on her client's house.

Quickly, she leashed Scoob and let him out. He sniffed the air as if he might know how close he was to home. Liz kept them along the edge of the property. The gas smell had faded to a mere hint.

She'd worked her way back to Mr. Stuttard's fence when a dark blue sedan pulled up in front of his house. Liz stood beside the trunk of a live oak trying to make out if it were the son returning, or arriving, to the scene of the crime.

The driver just sat there, and she became self-conscious. Scoob whined at her and she slid deeper into the property.

A black SUV pulled beside the first vehicle, and Liz couldn't restrain herself, drifting toward them. The first arrival stepped out of the sedan with a lanky profile and sky-blue shirt. The son, Vic, stood between the cars, waiting.

The second driver, a short man in a dark jacket, climbed out of the SUV and circled around the front of his car to shake Vic's hand.

She walked earnestly down the property line, uncaring if they noticed her. Scoob growled slightly as they got closer. The second man was David Turner, the buyer.

Her pulse rose. They could have murdered Mr. Stuttard together. They hadn't seemed to see her, and she wanted to hear what they were saying. She had a pretext, the dog did not belong to her.

Liz reached the sidewalk without them spotting her. Their voices were a murmur, but a little closer and she should understand them.

As she walked toward Mr. Stuttard's drive, Scoob snarled and barked. Both men turned toward her. David Turner had thinning hair, and his face twisted into a questioning scowl.

Vic Stuttard just rolled his eyes and headed toward her. "Lady, I don't know what your game is, but it ain't happening."

Scoob skittered behind her, looping the leash around her right hip.

David gave her and the dog a dark frown and moved up with Vic to confront her. "What are you doing here?" he asked.

Her pulse rose, and Liz questioned her intelligence confronting both men. One or both could be a killer. She was alone and night was coming. Wetting her lips, she drew in the magic around, and readied a stumbling curse. It wasn't much, but if she had to run, it might help.

"This is your dad's dog. I thought you might want him."

David appeared to relax.

Vic laughed outright. "I don't want it. Keep it or tie it to the bumper for all I care."

Liz forced a smile which cut into tight cheeks. "I wouldn't do that."

"I don't care. Get out of here." Vic cocked his head, daring her to continue.

"Do you know his name?"

"Don't know, don't care. Move it, lady." As he spoke, Vic's face hardened.

She turned to find a vehicle turning into the drive. Sheriff Calure pulled onto the lawn beside the SUV. Liz blew out a breath of relief. Then again, he would likely send her packing.

The two men focused on the sheriff and stepped

toward the front of their cars. Scoob remained hidden behind her. Liz breathed in and out. How would the sheriff react? She'd been advised to let it go. Interference in his investigation would not be tolerated well, especially by a woman. Blocked by the SUV, she didn't see his face when his door closed.

"Mrs. Dixon, you were warned." Benson had a sharp expression as he rounded the front of the SUV. His eyes were steel. "Get off the property now. This will be in my report."

Liz sagged. She had nothing to offer which might lead to even one of the men being involved in Mr. Stuttard's murder. The day had slowly gone down the toilet soon after she'd arrived at her client's house.

She smiled.

"I'm sorry, Sheriff Calure. I mistakenly thought Vic would want his dad's dog. It really is his responsibility." She knelt to retrieve Scoob, knees grinding in the grit of the driveway. Liz glanced in one direction, then the other, before standing.

Benson frowned, scratching at his mustache. "Well, I can get animal control . . ."

Liz stepped forward and opened the back door to David's SUV. "Vic's just going to have to deal with it." She leaned forward, as if to deposit poor Scoob into the car.

Vic laughed. "Not my car, crazy lady."

David snarled, stepping forward. "Do not put that nasty rat in my car."

Benson stepped forward, moving between them. "Miss Liz, you've gone too far." His hand reached the top of the door.

"Can you smell it?" she asked him.

He frowned, forehead wrinkling. "What?"

"The gas?" Liz nudged her chin toward the interior. The sharp scent was strong.

David's eyes widened.

Liz cuddled Scoob. "He's your killer."

Benson sniffed the air, then turned to study David. A tense silence rose as all eyes focused on the man.

David blustered and growled angrily. "I have no idea what she's talking about."

She stepped back from them all, her curse still ready. "I'm guessing he did not come here last night to murder Mr. Stuttard, but burn him out. The first mistake he made was parking at my client's house and leaving an oil stain. The same one he's leaving now. They'll match, I'm sure."

David blinked, then huffed. "Ridiculous."

"The second mistake was not knowing Scoob would wake up Mr. Stuttard. That's when the murder had to happen." Liz's pulse raced as David glared at her. "I'm assuming David Turner doesn't have an alibi which would have him parking in that driveway between 8 p.m. last night and 8 a.m. this morning."

"Bitch." David Turner pushed the gangly Vic into the sheriff, then raced for the driver's side of the SUV. Even roundish and out of shape, he moved quickly.

Benson swore and untangled himself from Vic. Liz backed up a step away from the open door, then let her curse fly at David Turner. Magic doesn't always work cleanly, nor at all with more powerful targets. However, David, the dollar store king, had no natural defenses or abilities of his own. When he opened his car door, he tripped, and fell backward onto his ass.

Liz waited patiently as Benson scooped up David Turner and began reading him his rights.

Vic began pacing and swearing. He stopped, glaring at

her, then pulled his head back and studied her. "Wait, you said you could find me buyers."

Her eyes nearly popped out of her head. "That man killed your dad, and all you care about is money? Don't speak to me."

The door to Benson's car closed, and he came to the back of the SUV, peered at her, then down to the damning oil stain. "Hell."

He gestured toward her client's driveway. "I've got forensics coming." Benson wrestled his mustache and took a deep breath. "I owe you an apology, Miss Liz."

She smiled. "Don't fret, Benson. You've got this all handled. I'm going home now." Liz gave Vic a sour glance and shook her head. "Oh, Benson. I don't know if your boys are any good at getting out oil stains on driveways, but when they're done . . ."

Benson chuckled. "We'll clean it up, Miss Liz."

The thin clouds to the west had started to light up orange and pink from the sunset.

She cuddled Scoob on the way to her car. "Think you want to hang with me and Mike for a bit? The girls will accept you after a while."

In her car, she watched a second sheriff's car arrive at Mr. Stuttard's. The property would sell quickly and Vic would make his money. A dollar store was doomed to decorate this part of Route 90. Liz would have to sell her client's house quickly, before it seemed an add-on to a strip mall.

Mr. Stuttard could rest with the memory of his house as it had been. His dog, curled peacefully on the passenger seat, would be cared for.

As Liz Dixon backed onto Route 90, she smiled at the blooming azaleas. "Pink as sunset."

Kevin A Davis is a contemporary fantasy author with three published series. The six-book Khimmer Chronicles features the spunky assassin, Ahnjü, who does a quick job at making friends and enemies among Earth's cryptid and human communities. The indominable Haddie reluctantly battles descendants of the fallen angels in the six-book AngelSong series. In the paranormal procedural DRC Files, the adept Kristen is quick to use her magic to help protect Earth from dangerous cryptids and artifacts which the other realms provide.

A multitude of his short stories have been published in anthologies in a slew of different genres.

Residing in north Florida, he attends conventions throughout the southeastern US either as a vendor, speaker, or a nerdy fan.

Follow him, join his newsletter, read his books.

Website: https://kevinarthurdavis.com/

FB: https://www.facebook.com/KevinArthurDavis

Instagram: https://www.instagram.com/kevinarthurdavisauthor/

The Case of the Saintsville Cattle Killers

L.N. Hunter

There are plenty of frightening things within the city of Saintsville — I should know, I'm one of them. But beyond the burg's limits, it's worse — much worse.

Regardless, here I am on a hot, dry summer afternoon, accompanying Gordo "The Butcher" Moroni across a field full of cows, trying not to step in deposits from ruminants who have nothing to do all day but eat grass. I take a final drag on my cigarette and flick it to the ground. Gordo scolds me for endangering his farmland, so I step back and press my foot on the butt to extinguish it properly.

The cattle silently watch me from across the field, every now and then blinking their long-lashed eyes. I think they're waiting to see what I do to the one on the ground in front of me. She looks quite peaceful, as if she's merely asleep, but even I know that cattle don't normally sleep on their backs.

Gordo points at the cow's neck. "See there, Solly."

I lean forward for a closer look. Sure enough, there are two tiny holes in the animal's skin, about an inch apart. My gorge rises, which is saying something since I've been post-mortem for five years now. It ain't because of the odor of deceased bovine: dying has rendered my senses of smell and taste so inert that I need to doctor my bourbon with Tabasco. No, it's because I know exactly who did this, and I'm not looking forward to confronting them. I take a dozen photographs of the wounds with my new Kodak Brownie.

As we walk back to the gate, Gordo tells me he called Saintsville PD as soon as he discovered the first of the animals, but they just weren't interested. A better sense of self-preservation than mine undoubtedly cautioned the cops against getting involved.

"I didn't know who else to ask," Gordo says, a hint of despair in his voice.

"Leave it with me." I pat him on the shoulder. "I'll make sure this doesn't happen again."

"I don't know how I'll pay you," he blurts. "Business is slow, and that's the third heifer I've lost in as many days."

"This one's on me." I open the door of my battered Model A. "Forget about it."

I'd worked for, against, and — finally — with Gordo's family over the decades. My first case as a rookie cop was a raid on one of the Moroni speakeasies, but the family's gone legitimate now, more or less. Gordo owns a deli in town and runs a slaughterhouse at his farm, which earned him his nickname. He's one of the best guys around, and helped patch me up after the shootout that put me six feet under. Without Gordo, I wouldn't be here. I owed him big, though I knew he'd never call me on it. My death ended my career in the Saintsville PD too, leaving me no option but to move into the private sector.

Gordo grins at me as I set off, and I smile back, wishing I was as confident of success as I'd made out. Half an hour

The Case of the Saintsville Cattle Killers

later, I reenter the hustle and bustle of the city and return to my office in a rundown brownstone just off Saintsville's main drag. The wooden sign by the door has been vandalized again, and reads "OLOMON GRANGER, RIVATE VESTIGATOR" — more expense, for when the next payday comes. I begin to regret telling Gordo this job was gratis.

I can't do anything about his cattle until night falls, so I fill the time by developing the photographs. While they're drying, I mix up more doctored whiskey, recycling the developer fluid into it for a little extra kick. Just in case things go south later on, I add a handful of garlic cloves to the bourbon and rummage through my filing cabinet for the vial of holy water I got from Father O'Shaunessy. I accepted it as part payment when I'd helped one of his parishioners with a blackmail problem a few years ago, but that's a story for another time.

Once the whiskey's taken care of, I flick through the photographs. Fang marks on the neck of an exsanguinated cow — it's obvious who made them, and I don't need to spend any time looking more closely. I've got nothing left to do but pace back and forth across my threadbare carpet, worrying about the meeting to come.

When the sun disappears behind City Hall, I grab my fedora and set off for the vampire night spot at the edge of town — *Blood*, they call it. Real subtle.

The place is buzzing with pretty young things, foolhardy humans dressed in their flapper dresses and garish three-piece pinstripes, waiting to be granted entrance to the home of the undead. I shake my head at the kids' naïveté — once you get past their glamour, vampires ain't much to write home about. Several of the young and beautiful mutter as I muscle my way through the queue and speak to the goons manning the jazz club's door.

One of the goons — seven feet tall and almost as wide

— sticks his head inside the door and shouts something. A short, slick-haired human, most likely the queen's steward, comes out and asks me what I'm here for. I tell him I'm here to see the boss and hand him my card. He takes it and sniffs disdainfully before scuttling back inside. The goons fold their arms and scowl at me while the steward consults the queen.

They're also preventing anyone else from entering the venue, which earns me more than a few dirty looks from the queue. I nonchalantly tap out a Lucky and light up. I have time to puff my way through two cigarettes before the steward returns.

"Come, come!" The prissy little man gestures irritably, as if he's been the one forced to wait. He hurries me across the dance floor, where vamps and their chosen thralls are gyrating to the latest boogie-woogie tunes, then up stairs and along gradually quieting wood-paneled passages until we reach the inner sanctum.

The queen sits on a throne constructed from blackened bones. Some are probably human, but I don't want to look too closely. Her lieutenants stand like improbably handsome marble statues on her left and right. They turn their heads toward me, trying to savage me with their guard dog glares. The only reason I'm not perspiring under the pressure is because my sweat glands dried up ages ago.

"Your majesty." I touch the brim of my hat — no way am I going to bow. I'll get nothing from her if she doesn't believe I'm her equal, so I need to keep face and show that the PI who brokered a truce between her hive and O'Shaunessy's fanatical flock is not to be treated lightly. Truth is, the resolution of that particular feud was more a matter of luck than skill, but the queen doesn't need to know that.

The lieutenants' icy blue eyes narrow, but the queen

laughs. It's a light, tinkly sound, totally at odds with her gaunt appearance. She's rake-thin and bald-headed save for a few pale wisps, with cheek bones almost piercing her colorless skin.

"Solomon Granger, Private Investigator," she drawls, as if tasting each syllable before letting it roll off her tongue. "I'd hoped we'd never see you again."

"What I said, dollface, was our paths wouldn't cross as long as you stuck to your side of the bargain."

The queen's eyebrows rise, and her lieutenants actually hiss. "What are you talking about, Mr. Granger? We've done nothing."

I pull the photographs from my pocket. "How do you explain the punctures in Gordo's cows?"

The queen gestures to the left. The lieutenant on that side snatches the photographs and holds them up for her to inspect.

Her lips purse, then she breaks into a smile, letting her extended canines show. "Mr. Granger, we consume cattle only if there are no humans nearby, and we *never* stoop to killing them. In any case, if you think those marks were made by a vampire, you're sorely mistaken." Her voice drops, creaking like a rusty hinge. "Those wounds were created by no teeth, vampire or otherwise." She taps a long fingernail on one of the pictures. "Surely your dead eyes can see the charring at the edges. Something *burned* those creatures."

My shoulders fall. I hadn't believed the hive itself would be responsible since vampire are sticklers for rules and regulations, but I was certain the queen would spill the beans on some recently exiled rogue or an unwelcome newcomer. I should have looked at the wounds more closely instead of jumping to conclusions. Haste like that was what got me killed in the first place.

"Oh, come now, Mr. Granger, don't be so disappointed. They're only feedstock."

"They're Gordo's livelihood," I snap.

The queen's attack dogs take a step forward, but she holds up a hand. "Mr. Granger is leaving." Her gaze flicks over my shoulder. "Jacobs, see him out."

I jump when the prissy steward who escorted me in touches my arm. In the presence of the charismatic queen, I forgot he was there. To hide my embarrassment, I tap my hat brim and say, "See you around, doll."

With the queen's tinkling laughter echoing in my ears, I follow Jacobs to the front door, sighing as I step through it. I notice that the crowd of vampire-fawning wannabes outside has vanished — they must all be inside, getting drunk. In both senses of the word.

Jacobs coughs gently, and I turn to him.

"There's something you should know," he says, then stops, waiting for me to ask, but I just stand there, tapping another cigarette from the pack. Eventually he caves. "There have been strange lights in the woods the last few nights." He points across the car lot. "Over that way. I've mentioned them to the queen, but she's not concerned. I don't know what they are, but" — he glances at the goons before leaning forward to continue in a whisper — "I worry they might be more of a danger than she thinks. Odd things are appearing in the woods: eviscerated foxes and birds, churned up earth. . ."

"Why didn't you go to the police?" I ask. "This might have something to do with Gordo's cattle."

Jacobs blushes. "Ah, you must understand my situation. We human retainers can't do anything unless the queen ordains it. And — ah — the queen's not much of an admirer of the police."

I sometimes wonder why Saintsville has a police force,

for all the good they do in these situations like this. Still, it means more work for me.

I could wait until the morning to have a look around, but I've got nothing on my dance card for the night. I drive the three or so miles to Bakerfield woods, where I light another Lucky and prop myself against the car's wheel arch to watch and listen.

When I've just about emptied my hip flask with nothing happening beyond some small nocturnal predators chowing down on other nighttime critters, I decide to call it a night. I stub out my cigarette and get ready to drive back to Saintsville. As I reach for the starter, I hear a deep hum, and the ground begins to shake. Beams of blue light stab through the trees, as if there's a gang of people waving flashlights. Except they must be giants, since they're waving them from the treetops.

The lights descend to ground level and dim. The noise and vibrations stop, and the woods are silent. Even the chittering and rustling sounds of small wildlife that I heard in the undergrowth earlier have ceased.

I swallow the final mouthful of whiskey, the chili and mustard sediment tickling the back of my throat as it goes down, then quietly get out of the car. Even though it's dark, I can see fairly well — my shriveled eyeballs shouldn't be capable of sight at all, but they work fine whatever the light level.

After grabbing my snubnose from under the driver's seat and tucking it into my waistband, I creep toward the lights, wincing as my feet squelch through the leavings of some woodland animal.

I stop mid-step at the edge of a clearing to gawk at something from a Jules Verne yarn. Resting on the grass is a fat disk the size of a city tram car, perched on three articulated legs. Around it stand half a dozen short men wearing spherical helmets and formfitting rubber-like suits. I can make out narrow heads with bulbous eyes through the glass of the helmets.

The creatures turn to me, pointing ray guns straight out of the Flash Gordon funny pages. They warble something at me, gobbling like angry turkeys, then one shoots his gun.

My body goes rigid as its sizzling blue light hits me, then I fall flat on my back. I feel no pain, but can't move a muscle.

The guy — or gal, or whatever else they have on their planet — who shot me comes over for a look and gobbles some more. He shoots me again, then seems to look puzzled. Maybe he was expecting me to die, or at least fall unconscious. The whole group comes over then, peering at me and occasionally prodding my body with their boots. They have a long warbling conversation with a lot of head shaking and gesticulating in my direction.

Four of them pick me up and take me inside their flying saucer, boots clanging on metal walkways. They lay me on what, guessing by the sharp and pointy instruments on trays beside it, must be an operating table.

This isn't looking like it's going to be one of my better nights.

One of them stabs me in the arm with a syringe. It's got a heated end, and I smell my skin burn as the needle enters. He attempts to suck some blood into the syringe, but gets no more than a teaspoonful of dark grey sludge. Most likely bourbon with a dash of mustard, chili, Tabasco and photographic developer, not to mention garlic and holy water. After inspecting the syringe closely, he presses a button on the side of his helmet, opening it, and squeezes a drop of the liquid onto his tongue.

These critters are even more ugly out of their helmets

The Case of the Saintsville Cattle Killers

than in them. Purple skin with a hairless dome on top, huge protruding pupilless eyes, no nose or visible ears, and a thick-lipped mouth fixed in a sour expression.

The guy swirls my blood around his mouth and swallows, then his face goes red and he shrieks, spitting and pawing at his tongue as if it's on fire.

The corners of my lip curl up. Then I smile even more as the realization comes that the paralysis caused by the ray gun is wearing off.

The alien's companions hand him glasses of what looks like water, and he consumes close to a gallon before his face becomes purple again.

As he slumps to the floor gasping, one of the others picks up a small metal box and warbles into it. He presses a button, and a second later, a low moaning comes from the box, as the alien looks at me quizzically.

I sit up and swing my legs over the side of the bench. The critters take a step back. I guess they weren't expecting that I would be able to move, otherwise they'd have strapped me down.

The alien says something, and the box moans again, louder this time.

"Are you mooing at me?" I ask.

The alien's eyes bulge even further, and he fiddles with the box. After another warble, a voice comes from the box: "What. Is. Mooing?"

I wave an arm at the box. "That sound. It's what cows make. Now, who the hell are you?"

The box gobbles something — a translation of my words, I guess.

While the aliens form a huddle and have another conversation, I take a look around. They favor a minimalist style. Judging by the size of the spaceship, there's only a single chamber inside, with bunks on one wall and what must be the control console on the opposite side. There are no windows, and everything is metallic and grey, even the buttons on the console. I guess they don't have paint or wallpaper where they come from.

Eventually, the head alien speaks via his box. "We. Are. From. Planet. Far. Away. Seek. Conquest. Are. Cows. Leader?"

I laugh. "No, they're the poor creatures you've been stabbing and killing."

"They. Are. Not. Leader? Are. You. Leader? Need. Leader. Blood. To. Conquer."

Before I can answer, the two goons from the vampire dive crash through the door and take up fighting stances. I don't know if the queen told them to follow me or if it was Jacobs, but I'm pissed, so I say, "These jerks are our leaders. It's *their* blood you want."

The metal box has barely finished translating my words, when all the alien critters reach for their guns. The vampires act quickly and knock three of the aliens unconscious or dead. One of the little guys gets in a lucky shot, and vampire one falls to the floor, paralyzed. Vampire two seizes the closest alien and sinks his teeth into the critter's neck.

The goon's eyes shoot open, and he moans in ecstasy as he drains the alien. "This stuff is gooood," the vampire growls. He's drooling, and his skin is glowing. He tosses the deflated body aside and turns his attention to the remaining alien, who's trembling so much he can barely hold his ray gun. "You're next, buddy."

Before he can grab the unfortunate alien, blood starts to stream from his eyes and nose. He clutches at his throat and collapses.

The alien says, "You. Lie. They. Not. Leader. Is. You. Leader?"

The Case of the Saintsville Cattle Killers

"Damn straight, I'm the leader."

I get off the operating table and saunter across for a closer look at the controls.

"Not! Touch. Important." The alien points his ray gun at me, but I get my handgun up first. I pop him in the leg, and green blood spurts from his suit. As he drops to the floor, clutching his wound and screaming in alien warble, I take aim at the console. "I'll bet that if I shoot this, you ain't going home."

"No. Not. Shoot!"

Something clicks, and my brain switches into overdrive. "You saw the effect of my blood on that sad sap over there. All humans — all *leaders* — have the same blood, so you're getting nothing from us." I point at the vampires. "And you can see what our attack dogs will do to you. If you want to live, leave this planet and never return."

"We. Go. No. Shoot." He points to the damaged door. "You. Depart. Now."

After a short pause, he repeats, "You. Depart."

I amble out of the spaceship, as if I have not a care in the world. Just before the door closes, I tip my hat back and say, "I'll be watching the skies. I see you plugs again, you won't get off so easy."

The lights dotting the outer edge of the ship brighten, and the rumbling I heard before starts up. The ship wobbles on its legs, then slowly rises straight up, leaving behind the two vampire corpses. As soon as it reaches the top of the trees, it shoots into the sky. I'm not certain, but it looks like it's heading in the direction of Roswell.

I consider returning to *Blood* and telling them where the vampires are, but then figure it's not my problem. Besides, I don't want to be around to explain how they died. I stick another cigarette in my mouth and head back to the car. At least I can tell Gordo he'll be suffering no more livestock losses.

Despite my earlier promise, I might strong-arm him for expenses toward new loafers, though.

∽

L.N. Hunter's comic fantasy novel, The Feather and the Lamp *(Three Ravens Publishing)*, sits alongside works in anthologies such as Best of British Science Fiction 2022 *and* Hidden Villains: Arise, *among others, as well as several issues of* Short Édition's Short Circuit *and the* Horrifying Tales of Wonder *podcast, in which Solly Granger puts in an earlier appearance. There have also been papers in the IEEE Transactions on Neural Networks, which are probably somewhat less relevant and definitely less entertaining. When not writing, L.N. occasionally masquerades as a software developer or can be found unwinding in a disorganized home in Carlisle, UK, along with two cats and a soulmate.*

Get in touch via https://linktr.ee/l.n.hunter or https://www.facebook.com/L.N.Hunter.writer

Secret Family Recipe
Tracy Falenwolfe

The Pine Crest Mall was a one-story shopping center built back in 1972 when TV dinners came in little foil trays, appliances were avocado green, and the only men who cooked on television were the firemen of station 51 on *Emergency!*.

George Lesher was twelve that year, and had spent the summer working with his father's concrete business pouring the mall's foundation. His involvement made him a celebrity among his friends, because for the next fifteen years the mall was the place to be. After that, a newer, two-story mall with a glass elevator, a fountain, a double escalator, and an eight-screen movie theatre went in across the street, and most of the stores moved there.

Now, the Pine Crest Mall had forty-seven spaces, but only thirty-two tenants, most of them privately owned stores and start-up food franchises. A trip to the Pine Crest Mall, affectionately known as the old mall to those who still bothered to visit, was like grocery shopping at a place that only carried generic brands and day-old baked goods.

Still, when George bought his Gobble Gobble franchise

he'd chosen to locate it in the old mall for its sentimental value, as much as because he couldn't afford the rent across the street. And it was paying off. Gobble Gobble's business tripled after mall manager Sal Figuroa dismantled the food court and relocated the eating establishments into five spoke-like corridors with a drive-up window on either side of each spoke.

Now the parking lot smelled like a smorgasbord, but without the food court the inside of the mall reeked like a combination of forty-year-old mothballs, stale cigarette smoke, and regurgitated grape juice. The air was clean despite the smell though, everyone knew, because a new handler had been installed six years ago after the Legionnaires' outbreak.

George relieved his assistant manager, Dewey, at six a.m. on Thanksgiving morning. Dewey might have been a couple of slices short of a loaf, but he showed up on time, roasted the turkeys for Gobble Gobble's signature sandwich, and didn't complain about working overnight. George felt a little bad for leaving Beverly, his lead baker, alone with Dewey, but her job was to bake the 517 pumpkin pies that had to be ready for pick-up before noon, and the bread for the sandwiches, which needed to be cooled and sliced by the time the mall opened at three.

"Thank God," Beverly said when Dewey left for the day. "He's been giving me the willies all night."

"Did he harass you?" A lawsuit was all George needed.

"No," Bev said. "Nothing like that. He was jumping out of his skin, and kept saying something about death. Death is coming. Death is all around us. Death is coming. He splashed me with turkey blood and said it was for protection and that he was sorry if it didn't work because it was supposed to be chicken blood, but he didn't have any chickens."

"I'll talk to him," George said.

"Don't bother," Bev said. "He meant well."

"But he scared you."

"I'm not scared by a voodoo priest who can't be bothered to use the right fowl for his protection spell. Besides, chicken or turkey, I think he was supposed to be using a live bird, not a frozen one. It's how much he believed someone was about to die that freaked me out."

George made a mental note not to schedule Dewey and Bev alone together anymore.

"Yoo-hoo!" The call came from the mall entrance to the restaurant.

"Ugh." Bev rolled her eyes. "Already?"

A second later, the drive-up window chimed. It was open for pre-ordered pie pick up only at this time of the morning. "Saved by the bell," Bev said, reaching for a pie box. "You deal with her today."

George went out to the counter. He hadn't closed the gate all the way when he'd let Dewey out, so his visitor had ducked under it and was already standing at the register. "My mouth is just watering," she said. "I'm here to order my sandwich, and to make sure you don't run out of free pie before I get mine." She winked. "Don't tell anyone, but I'm eating the pie first, as soon as I get my coffee from JoJo."

Gobble Gobble's patented sandwich, The Thanksgiving Dinner, was six full ounces of thick-sliced, slow-roasted turkey in gravy, an ice cream scooper full of George's special recipe stuffing, and a slathering of cranberry mayonnaise, all squashed in between two fat slices of tangy homemade sourdough bread. The only person who could open their mouth wide enough to eat the monstrosity like a sandwich was Marge Shoemaker from The Hat Shack. Everyone else used a fork.

Mall employees got a twenty-percent discount on the sandwich 365 days a year, and on Thanksgiving Day only, a free slice of pumpkin pie to go with it.

"I'm not quite ready for customers, Marge," George said. "Bev hasn't sliced any bread yet."

Marge smiled brightly. "That's okay. I'll wait."

Of course she would. And she'd yak the whole time. Marge was a roly-poly 74 year old who wore orthopedic shoes, turtlenecks, and holiday-themed vests with pull-on corduroys. Sal Figuroa might have been the mall manager, but Marge was its mayor. Actually, mascot might have been a better word. Back at Saint Patrick's Day, Marge had worn head to toe lime green topped off with a baseball hat, and some little kid ran up behind her thinking she was the Phillie Phanatic. It had been an honest mistake.

Today she was wearing a pilgrim hat with a fan of turkey feathers sprouting from the back of her head. "Should be a great day for business, huh?" Marge's eyes twinkled in the emergency lighting of the darkened restaurant. Retail was in her blood, she'd always said. Busy days were her favorite.

Bev poked her head through the kitchen pass-through. "I sliced a loaf just for you, Marge."

George made another mental note as Marge chattered. This time to give Bev a raise. "One Thanksgiving Dinner, coming right up," he said to Marge, cutting off her steady stream of inane pleasantries. He made the sandwich and handed it to her in a paper boat lined with a sheet of waxed paper. The next time he saw her, the sandwich was clutched in her hand the same way Marge was clutched in the trash compactor.

∼

There was no use checking for a pulse. Only Marge's head, along with her left arm and right shoulder, was visible outside of the compactor's jaws. A foamy crimson ooze ran down the front of the massive machine. The turkey feather hat was still on Marge's head.

At first, George was stunned. It had taken him a second to process what he was seeing. Then he was confused. Even in her current state, it seemed impossible that Marge wasn't blathering on about something. By the time he accepted the finality of Marge's situation, his hands had begun to shake. He was dialing the first one of nine-one-one when a voice behind him said, "I wouldn't do that if I were you."

George spun around and faced Sal Figuroa. Sal had a face like a rat's, accentuated by his slicked back hair and a mustache that looked like it had been drawn on with a magic marker. Sal's hands were in the pockets of his pinstriped suit. He jingled his change.

"Why not?" George asked.

"Think about it." Sal took a step closer. "This is the biggest day of the year for all of us. If you call the police, they may not let us open. Think about the consequences."

George considered his three-hundred percent increase over last year. His 421 pies that had yet to be picked up at twelve dollars a pop. "We can't just leave her like this," he said to Sal. "As if she's a piece of garbage."

"That's not what I'm proposing at all," Sal said. "I was just thinking maybe we could figure out what happened before we call them. You know, speed things along."

"Figure out what happened?" George repeated. "I think it's pretty clear what happened. You don't think she crawled in there by herself, do you?"

"Of course not," Sal said. "What I think is that there are only a handful of us in the building and the doors are all locked. If we can figure out who did this, we can hand them over to the police along with Marge and get on with our day."

"How do we do that?"

Sal took a radio off his belt and keyed in a three-digit code. The piped-in music ceased and Sal made an announcement. "Your attention, please. Everyone in the building please report to the compactor room immediately. No exceptions."

The first to arrive was JoJo Minnich, proprietor of The Daily Grind coffee shop, who was in the mall so early because it was her policy to be there whenever anyone else was. JoJo was mid-forties, blonde, and stacked. Snooty with it, too. She barely gave George the time of day, but she made a hell of a cup of coffee, which was more than he got from a lot of women. "What's going on?" she asked, looking neither George nor Sal in the eye.

The men had stepped into the hall outside the compactor and Sal was blocking the doorway. "Let's just wait for the others so I only have to say it once."

JoJo fidgeted. The floor was sticky, so her shoes squeaked.

Bev arrived next. She had a bit of flour alongside of her nose and still wore her apron. "What's this?" She wiped her hands on a tea towel she had draped over her shoulder. "I have to get back to the oven in ten minutes for the second batch of bread. And nobody's manning the window now."

"We won't keep you long," Sal said. He blushed, and George wondered why.

Gaultier LeBeck, the manager of The Fashion Barn, a low-budget department store that was the Pine Crest

Mall's only remaining anchor, swept into the darkened hallway with an attitude. "I do not appreciate being summoned like a commoner. Unless there's a fire or an outbreak of the plague, I won't be staying for whatever this is." Gaultier was a thirty-something guy who wore black eyeliner and nail polish. He had a habit of holding his left elbow in his right hand when he spoke, which made him look like a ventriloquist who was missing his dummy.

"It's worse than that," Sal said. "I think this is all of us."

"Wait!" December Mansfield, a young girl who worked at Fantasies, a store that sold mostly leather and spandex, clopped down the hall in spiked heels. "I'm here."

Sal frowned. "I don't remember letting you in," he said.

"You didn't let me in either," George said.

"I let her in," Bev said. "Right before George." Technically, the mall manager or security officer were the only ones allowed to let people in before the doors were officially opened. But since Gobble Gobble was right next to the employee entrance, a lot of people waved to get Bev's or Dewey's attention rather than following the protocol, simply because Bev and Dewey got to the door faster than the authorized personnel did. "Sorry."

"What I mean is I don't recall seeing you on the list," Sal clarified. In order to avoid mistaking anyone for an intruder, Sal also required written notification when a tenant needed to be in the mall more than an hour prior to the start of business.

"I read my schedule wrong," December said. She blew a huge bubble with her ever-present wad of gum and then popped it. "I thought I worked at six a.m., but really it's six p.m."

Bev swiped at the flour on her nose. "So why didn't you go home?"

"Bus doesn't run this early. I'm waiting for my ride to come back, but he already left to go buy doorbuster stuff at the electronics store to return for full credit somewhere else."

JoJo scrunched up her brow. Bev shook her head, warning JoJo not to even ask.

"I have five minutes before my team arrives to set the sale," Gaultier said. "What is this about, please?"

"Okay, okay," Sal said. "We have bad news about Marge Shoemaker. And even worse news for one of you."

They were all quiet.

Finally, JoJo spoke up. "Is Marge okay? Has something happened?"

Sal jingled his change before he answered. "Marge has been murdered."

The response was a collective gasp.

"She's behind me. In the compactor," Sal said.

The gasp was louder this time, and accompanied by dramatic pearl clutching.

"We six are the only ones in the building," Sal said.

"So you're accusing one of us?" JoJo finally looked George in the eye.

"Hey." George held up his hands. "I wanted to call the police. This is Sal's idea."

"We *are* calling the police," Sal said. "As soon as we have something to tell them. Now, who was the last to see Marge?"

"She came in for a sandwich and a piece of pie right after George got here to relieve Dewey. That would have been around six," Bev said.

"I gave her the sandwich," George confirmed. "And

her free piece of pie. She told me she was headed to The Daily Grind for her coffee."

"She was," JoJo said. "I fixed her coffee around quarter after six. I know because I dump my pots out after they set for half an hour, so I looked at the clock before I poured. She was carrying the sandwich in one hand and the pie in the other, so I offered her a carrier." JoJo's breath hitched. "My God, she was so happy."

"Did anyone see her after that?" Sal asked.

"She had her coffee when I saw her," Gaultier offered. "That was at six-thirty. I had just punched in and I was running down to The Daily Grind for mine. She was heading to her store."

JoJo nodded, confirming the time she'd seen Gaultier.

"Anybody else?" Sal said.

Silence.

"Okay. How about before that." Sal shifted his weight from one foot to the other. "Bev, what time did you let her in?"

Bev's mouth dropped open. "Me?" She splayed her open hand across her chest. "I didn't."

"I didn't either," Sal said.

"Then who did?" If there'd have been a dummy on Gaultier's left arm it would have been swiveling its head to look at everyone.

"Who cares who let her in?" December blew and popped another bubble. "What was the crazy hat lady doing here so early anyway?" She swept her arm to encompass George and Bev and JoJo. "I mean, I get that you're all here to make food." She hiked a thumb toward Sal. "And you're like, in charge or whatever." She raised her chin toward Gaultier. "He's got the big important store to worry about. But the hat store is the size of a closet and she never rotates the stock, ever. So why was she here eight hours before we even open?"

It was a good question, but nobody had the answer.

"Maybe there's something in her store that could shed some light," JoJo said.

"Let's look," Sal said. "But all of us together, got it? No one goes off on their own."

~

December was right about The Hat Shack. The space was tiny and the stock was dusty and shopworn. The paper bags at the cash and wrap were from the 1980s. George wondered when she'd had her last sale.

The group learned nothing from the front of the store, but the back room was a different story. Like the rest of the retail spaces, the stockroom housed a small restroom for employees. Where most of the stores also had a table and one or two chairs for employee breaks, Marge had added a small refrigerator and a microwave to her space, along with an array of canned goods and powdered milk, and a lone African violet.

"Oh, no." Bev pointed to a sleeping bag and pillow on the floor in the corner alongside a rolling rack of Marge's beloved vests and turtlenecks. She clamped a hand to her mouth. "She was living here." Tears sprung to her eyes. "Poor Marge." She only cried for a second though, and then she cocked her head and frowned. Everyone else was frowning too. Above Marge's sleeping bag hung a huge poster of Engelbert Humperdinck signed, *Marge, thanks for the best two weeks of my life. EH.*

Gaultier said, "Huh," and the others agreed.

A curtain strung up in the middle of the room divided

the already small space. George pulled the curtain back, revealing a pop-up camping shower hooked up to the sink in the tiny restroom with a garden hose. Bev sobbed anew, and JoJo put an arm around her. Sal watched with interest. George noticed.

"Where did she get something like that?" December wondered aloud.

"Alan Dorsheimer carries showers like these in the sporting goods store. I bet she got it there," Gaultier said softly.

George drew the curtain back to its original position. He stooped to retrieve a leather-bound book that was lying on the floor next to Marge's pillow. "What's this?" He flipped a few pages and felt his eyebrows raise.

"What is that?" Sal asked. He reached for it, but George held it out of his reach.

"It's a journal." George thumbed through the pages.

"Read it," December said.

"No don't." Bev sounded offended. "It's private."

"Not really," George said. "It's about all of us."

"I'll take it," Sal said.

"No you won't." George kept hold of the book. "Look, let's cut to the chase. As far as I'm concerned, you are the number one suspect here."

"Me?" Sal took a step back and sunk his hands into his pockets. "How do you figure?"

"For starters, you wouldn't let me call the police." That drew nods of agreement.

"Then there's the whole Marge wanted to get you fired fiasco," Gaultier pointed out.

It was true; Marge was lobbying Alan Dorsheimer, the president of the mall merchants association, to petition the management company to fire Sal. Sal was the mastermind behind the food court renovation, and while it had been great for the food vendors, the drive-up windows made it so no one actually had to come inside the mall, and the merchants had suffered as a result. Most of them blamed Sal. As well they should have.

Sal jingled his change. "That's ridiculous," he said. "Now hand over that book."

"No." George opened it to a random page. "Here. Your name pops out on this page. Let's see what she has to say about you." He skimmed the first few lines and started reading toward the middle. "Sal Figuroa was leaving Gobble Gobble at seven p.m. on Friday night. His face was red. Probably because — "

"Stop! That's enough, George," Bev said.

"Bev, don't," Sal shook his head. "Don't."

December cracked her gum. "Don't what?"

"I don't care who knows," Bev said. "Sal and are in a relationship and have been for over a year," she announced. "There. Now I don't care what Marge wrote about me. Go ahead. Read it."

George kept his mouth shut.

"I'm serious," Bev said. "Go ahead."

"I don't think you want me to do that," George said.

"She asked you to read it," JoJo said. "I'm pretty sure we all knew about her and Sal anyway, right?"

The others muttered an agreement and took a sudden interest in their own shoes.

Fine. George read. "Probably because Bev finally told him she's been boffing Alan Dorsheimer behind his back."

Everyone's head flew up. Gaultier's mouth dropped open. "Girl," he said to Bev, "I had you pegged for a one man woman."

Bev was horrified. "How did she know?"

"You mean it's true?" Sal fumed. "For heaven's sake,

when did you have the time? You're all over me three times a day."

"Read some more." December rubbed her hands together. "This is getting good."

"I don't know if that's such a great idea," Gaultier said.

"Oh, it's a great idea," Sal said. "If I have to be humiliated by that nosy old biddy, why not everyone else?"

George and Gaultier involuntarily made the sign of the cross. George wasn't exactly a Catholic in good standing, but he still knew better than to speak ill of the dead. Bev spun around three times and spit on Sal's shoe. She chanted something that sounded like humina, humina, humina. As far as George knew, she was Lutheran, so it must have been something she learned from Dewey.

"It's possible if someone besides Sal has a motive it would be in the book, right?" JoJo said. "I think you should keep reading."

George turned a page. He looked at Gaultier. "It says here that you're a thief. Marge writes that you stole a hat from her store, and a pocket knife from Alan Dorsheimer."

Another collective gasp.

"You're the one who keeps stealing the wigs off Fantasies mannequins, aren't you?" December looked him up and down. "I knew it. You wear them, don't you?"

"Okay, okay. Enough." Gaultier waved off December's accusation. "Marge caught me stealing a hat from her, it's true. She didn't call the cops because she knew I was sick. It's an illness, you know. I can't help myself."

"Are you sure she didn't call the cops because you killed her before she got the chance to?" Sal accused.

"I did not. Marge was a sweet old lady." He looked at December. "And I only wear the wigs when I have a gig."

"She wasn't that sweet," George said. "She liked to spread gossip. So why did she keep your secret?"

"Yeah," Bev said. "And what kind of gigs are we talkin'?"

Gaultier ignored Bev and answered George. "Maybe I kept one of hers."

"Care to share?" Sal said.

Gaultier fixed a hoity-toity look on his face, then changed his mind about it and answered the question. "I had a hunch she was living here. I didn't know for sure. When she cornered me about the hat, I asked her about it. She backed off after that."

The group digested his story.

"Who else does she write about?" JoJo asked. She was back to fidgeting and avoiding eye contact.

George scanned a few pages and landed on an eye-opening entry. "It seems someone among us is not who she says she is."

December blew a bubble. Popped it. "That would be me, right?"

"Right. Marge says you're here spying on all of us for your doctorate in Behavioral Psychology."

"Not spying. Observing. I'm doing a cognitive study for my dissertation."

JoJo paled. "You're watching us?"

"You're in college?" Gaultier mumbled at the same time.

"I don't like the sound of that," Sal said. "You're doing what exactly?"

December got rid of her gum. "You all are an interesting bunch. You're all hanging on to this place as if it's worth something. What for? What are you getting out of it? Why do you choose to fight an uphill battle when you could go across the street and make tons more money? If you all left, this place would be sold and probably torn down."

"I guess you haven't been here long enough to have heard the stories." Bev chuckled. "Alan says the management company will never tear this place down. Rumor has it there are bodies buried under the mall and some interested parties want to make sure it stands forever."

George's eye twitched. Everybody else laughed at Bev's story.

December shrugged. "Deflect all you want. You're all holding on to something that doesn't matter anymore. The hat lady was too, but at least she admitted it."

"She talked to you about it?" Sal asked.

"Yeah. After she confronted me about what I was doing here, she seemed interested. She was observing you all, too. Granted, in her own way."

"What does she say about me?" JoJo asked.

George searched for an entry in the book. "I don't think I should read this out loud."

JoJo shook her head. "I have to know."

"But — "

"Please."

George felt uneasy spilling this secret over any of the others. "She says you're a protected federal witness."

JoJo fell to her knees. "How did she find out?"

"She lists your old name here," George said. "Along with the name of who you testified against."

"That's it," JoJo said. "It was nice knowing all of you. I was happy here, but I'll be gone by morning."

Bev comforted her.

George turned the page to see if there was more. "Crap."

"What?" Bev turned away from JoJo. "What's wrong?"

"She says Dewey is an ex-con. He was jailed for assault with a deadly weapon."

"He left right after you came in," Bev said. "He could have slipped back in and killed Marge."

"We need to call him back here," Sal said. "Alan Dorsheimer, too."

Bev was quick to defend Alan. "He hasn't been here since yesterday."

"That we know of," Sal said. "But his name comes up in that book an awful lot, and Marge's pop up shower came from his store. I think he should be here to answer a few questions."

"Alan wouldn't hurt a fly," Bev said. "I'll bet he's not even in Marge's book. Except for that part about me."

George thumbed through the rest of the pages. Marge had started a sentence about Alan, but the following page was ripped out of the book. He showed the rest of the group. "I think it's time to call the police," he said.

Everyone agreed.

"I'm just going to go back to Fantasies and get my purse," December said.

"No!" Sal stood in her path. "Everyone stays together until the police get here. No exceptions."

They all agreed it was for the best, and that they would all go to Gobble Gobble where there was seating for everyone and food, too.

When Sal called the police, he told them there was no rush. "Marge isn't going anywhere," was his reasoning. "And I'm sure they're not going to let us open."

With the six of them there, Gobble Gobble's dining room was busier than it had been all year. George made everyone a Thanksgiving Dinner sandwich, on the house.

"George," Bev said. "I hate to put you on the spot, but what did Marge say about you in her little book?"

"Yeah," everyone chimed in.

"It's only fair to tell us," Sal said.

Secret Family Recipe

"You're right." George nodded. "She revealed a secret family recipe."

"Not your secret stuffing mix!" Bev clapped a hand across her mouth. "If that got out you'd be ruined."

If that got out, everyone would know he used Stove Top. But George played along. "I have no idea how she found out about it." He shook his head. "No idea."

Gaultier made several attempts to take a bite of his sandwich. "This thing is so big I can't get it in my mouth."

"Marge was the only one who could," George said. That was the thing about Marge. She had such a big mouth. He closed his eyes and remembered her walking out of the restaurant not even two hours ago. She'd been balancing her sandwich in one hand and her free pie in the other. She'd been so focused on her food she hadn't even noticed it when the stupid book fell out of her vest as she ducked under the gate.

George almost chased after her to return it, but then it fell open to the page about him and he knew what he had to do.

He smiled at Gaultier and put his hand in his pocket to crumple up the pages he'd torn out of Marge's journal. He flashed back to the summer the mall was built. To one night when he'd tagged along to the site with his father. Some of his men had built a form during the day. Even though George's father had made him stay in the cab of the big cement truck that night, George had a clear view in the side mirror.

He watched two guys in suits throw three guys in tarps into the hole and then drive off. George's dad got back in the cab and pulled a lever sending cement down the chute into the hole. At first, George thought his father hadn't realized the rolled up tarps were people. But then he said, "you weren't looking, were you?" And George knew he had.

George shook his head. "No sir."

"Good." His father smiled and messed up George's hair. "Time to pour a little of the secret family recipe, son," he said.

George had never felt closer to his father than he had in that moment. All these years later he convinced himself he did what he did to Marge to preserve that feeling more than to cover up his father's crime. Later, when he visited his father at the nursing home and took him the Thanksgiving Dinner and a slice of pumpkin pie, he wouldn't even mention it.

Tracy Falenwolfe's stories have appeared in over a dozen publications including Black Cat Mystery Magazine, Spinetingler Magazine, Flash Bang Mysteries, Crimson Streets, All Due Respect *and several* Chicken Soup for the Soul *volumes. Tracy lives in Pennsylvania's Lehigh Valley. She is a member of Sisters in Crime, Mystery Writers of America, and the Short Mystery Fiction Society.*

Urban Swamp

Joe Giordano

I don't know my birthday. As an infant, my mother stuffed me into a turnstile at the Brooklyn Monastery of Our Lady of Mount Carmel, the nuns' main interface with the outside world. Maybe she gave the delivery bell a tug before she fled, or maybe the sisters heard a baby's sobs. All Mother Superior remembered was that it was raining.

Escaping the orphanage, I earned my living by doing tricks at a cheap motel. Millie rescued me from that life. Her warmth won me over, and she adopted me as her daughter, showing me what a loving mother could be — allowing me to change my destiny.

One of Millie's wealthy, recently widowed friends dropped into her Brooklyn restaurant between the lunch and dinner service. The bouquet of garlic lingered, but the guests from our busy midday meal had left. They greeted each other with a perfunctory hug, cheek pecks, and murmured salutations, until my mother's voice rose.

"Irene, anything you want to tell me, Valentina can hear."

I closed the laptop I used to earn my fee as a cyber-crime consultant for the FBI, browsing the Dark Web to sniff out sex trafficking rings, and joined them in the restaurant's private room decorated with landscapes of Italy. We sat around a small table.

Bleach-blonde Irene's heavily made-up brown eyes evaluated me skeptically. Wearing lots of dangling gold jewelry, she dressed flashy-expensive, what *cafone* think mimics sophisticated people's style.

Huffing acceptance of my presence, she opened her Gucci wallet to show me a picture of a young woman. Straight black hair, attractive, she sported a dragon neck tattoo and posed with an in-your-face stare radiating from blue eyes.

"My daughter Carlotta is being blackmailed."

"What's she done now?" Millie asked in a so-what-else-is-new tone.

Irene fidgeted uncomfortably, and I suspected she'd dreaded telling Millie, knowing she wasn't going to receive a tea and sympathy response.

Irene said, "She dealt drugs," then added quickly, "small amounts. But some bastard has threatened to go to the cops if we don't pay. If she's arrested as a dealer, her life will be destroyed."

"Sounds like you know the creep who's shaking her down."

"A former boyfriend, Chaz Lombardo. With my Salvatore gone, I would turn to Eva's husband Paul."

She showed me a second woman's photo. An attractive

brunette with a tight smile like she dreaded having her picture taken.

"My other daughter," she said. "But he's run off with another woman. I have nobody. . . Unless you help me."

I saw where this was going. Irene hadn't come to commiserate with my mother. Frank Provati, my biological father–a recent shocking revelation–was underboss in the Ruggiero crime family. He and Millie were old friends and was the impetus for her to adopt me. If you can't go to the police and a private investigator is too meek a response, the mob must've seemed a good option – although I would've warned Irene that they always extract a price. She'd come to ask Millie to intercede with Frank to take care of the blackmailer.

By the distasteful look on her face, I sensed Millie also understood Irene's trajectory. Frank wasn't the hired help, and he'd hate being approached for such a favor.

"Maybe you should just pay him off?" she asked.

Even under duress, Irene couldn't pass up the opportunity to remind us of her station. "He wants lots of money. I can afford to pay, but where does it stop?"

She was about to box my mother into the dilemma of either a relationship-damaging refusal or imposing on Frank, so I stepped in, saying to Millie, "Why don't Anthony and I visit Mr. Lombardo?"

Anthony Provati, my half-brother, was also floored when he learned that Frank fathered him during an affair with his mother.

Obviously annoyed that my interjection deflected her pitch, Irene threw cold water. "What could *you* do?"

I ignored the disrespect and continued to speak to Millie. "We'll let Lombardo know that Irene isn't alone."

My mother grimaced. "I don't want to put you two in danger."

"We'll take Basso." My huge other half-brother was also adopted by Millie and served as Frank's bodyguard.

Millie's face relaxed.

Irene said to her, "I was hoping you'd speak to Frank Provati for me."

Millie spoke pointedly. "Valentina has generously offered to help you."

Nonplussed, Irene said, "Yes. Well. Thank you, Valentina. I just don't know if you'll be effective."

Millie continued. "Frank would ask Basso to handle the situation, so you got what you came for."

She stood.

Understanding a dismissal, Irene rose, and we walked her outside.

I gave Irene my number. "Text me with Lombardo's address."

We all exchanged hugs and Millie said, "Great to see you, Irene."

A Mercedes with a driver waited for her at the curb.

When she'd driven away, Millie said, "Carlotta has always been a handful."

"I detected that from your reaction to hearing about her drug dealing."

"Selling small amounts is what she would tell Irene, but who knows? An ex-boyfriend could turn out to be a sinister character—even affiliated with a cartel."

An unsettling thought. "We'll tread carefully," I said in a tone of reassurance I didn't feel.

~

The next day, I called ahead before Ubering to Anghiari, Anthony's shoebox sized art gallery in Manhattan's West Village. The narrow space displayed paintings and sculpture on both side walls, and he sat at a counter beside an antique National Cash Register. After we hugged, he offered me a cappuccino from his Gaggia Accademia espresso machine.

While I drank the coffee, I outlined the substance of Irene's story.

"On the way over, I called Basso. He'll make himself available when we're ready to pay Chaz Lombardo a visit."

"You think this guy is a drug dealer?" Anthony asked.

"Don't know."

"Possibly connected with a gang or even a cartel?"

"Can't say until we confront him."

"Bringing Basso is a good idea."

The bell above Anghiari's entrance jingled, and I looked up to see Irene's older daughter Eva, who I recognized from her picture.

"Millie told me you'd be here."

We exchanged introductions.

"What can we do for you?" I asked.

"Did my mother want you to find my husband Paul?"

"Didn't Irene tell you why she visited us?"

"Not exactly."

I wondered why Irene hadn't confided in Eva, but as mother-daughter relationships are sometimes complicated, I shrugged that off.

"Your sister Carlotta is being blackmailed by Chaz Lombardo over some alleged drug dealing."

Oddly, Eva seemed relieved. "I see."

"Do you know him?"

"Carlotta brought him around once or twice."

"Do you know his business?"

"That was kept rather vague. With Carlotta, guys came and went. None long enough to know."

Did I hear jealousy in that statement? Sisters sometimes compete.

Eva had neared Anthony and directed her comments more to him than me. Not taking me seriously? Or being flirty? Her body language favored the second option.

Anthony was all smiles. He married Nori, a sweetheart, and a gifted artist. He was a good dad to Angelica their four-year-old, but when he was single, he'd been a bit of a dog, so when an attractive woman hit on him, I warily watched his reaction.

"Do you have someone looking for your husband?" he asked.

Eva stiffened, probably recalling a bad memory. "He ran off with Monica, the wife of a midtown nightclub owner who he met when we both frequented the place. I don't care where they went, and I don't want to know what they're doing."

A simple "yes" or "no" to Anthony's question would've sufficed. That Eva sounded scripted made me wonder. Probably just bitterness.

～

We headed for Chaz Lombardo's apartment at the north tip of Manhattan. Basso drove his vintage blue GTO with black leather seats and red trim. Anthony squeezed into the rear.

On the way, Basso groused about traffic. "This jamoke better be home or next time you're taking the subway alone."

Anthony asked, "What's the plan?"

I said, "Unless he wants another visit from a member of the Ruggiero mob, back off."

Lombardo's multi-story brick apartment building had fire escapes and a heavy front door that squeaked when opened. No elevator, we walked up three urine-smelling stone flights to reach the metal door of 3F.

Before we could knock, two gunshots rang out from inside.

We three instinctively jumped flat to the wall lest bullets were headed in our direction.

"Shit," Anthony said. "We should take off."

"Good idea," said Basso and he moved toward the stairs.

From inside, we heard a woman scream.

"Somebody needs our help," I said reaching for the door and finding it unlocked.

Stepping inside the studio apartment, a bleeding man lay crumpled on the floor. Naked on the bed next to him, I recognized Carlotta, her hand at her mouth. She spotted the three of us and recoiled. "Don't kill me."

"We're here to help you," I said.

She didn't look convinced.

A breeze rippled the curtain of the open window over the fire escape.

She didn't hold a weapon, and I didn't see a pistol anywhere.

"What happened?" I asked.

Her voice quivered. "Somebody shot Chaz."

"You don't know who?"

"I was stoned. Asleep."

I didn't buy that, but there was no point in disputing her.

Basso and Anthony had been watching the drama.

Anthony said, "A neighbor probably called the cops."

She started to dress. "I need to get out of here."

Carlotta slipped on her shoes as she headed for the door.

The guys looked like they might block her, but I said, "Let her go."

She fled down the stairs.

We heard police sirens approaching.

Anthony asked, "What now?"

"We might as well wait for the cops. Otherwise, we become their prime suspects."

Basso said, "We'll be suspects anyway."

I said, "Frank will get us an attorney. Let's coordinate our stories. We arrived, heard gunshots, opened the door, and found Lombardo on the floor. We don't need to mention Carlotta. A favor to Irene."

Anthony asked, "You think she shot him?"

"I didn't see a weapon. The window is open. Maybe the killer left by the fire escape."

Basso said, "She could've thrown a pistol out the window. They'll find her DNA on those sheets."

"If we're confronted with the fact, we'll admit her presence. For now, silence is golden."

We stepped outside the apartment and held our hands high as the police came up the stairs. They cuffed us and we were hauled to the station.

Jack Slade with his baby blue eyes and tousled dirty-blond hair showed up in the gray interrogation room where I sat with my attorney. My nose crinkled at the stress-sweat odor that pervaded the space. Jack was a boyfriend. Anthony's buddy since their time at City

College, he joined the NYPD and progressed to become a gold-shield detective.

"Valentina, you were at the scene of a murder with the son of a mob underboss and his bodyguard." He sighed. "What have you gotten yourself into?"

I tilted my head at him. "Do your superiors know we date?"

"They're aware about a possible conflict of interest. We hope that you'll be forthright with me."

I huffed at his posturing for whoever stood behind the two-way mirror in the room. "You've known Anthony for years. He and Basso are both my half-brothers, and as you apparently have forgotten, I'm the daughter of the same underboss, Frank Provati."

"Those connections raise people's suspicions."

"Yeah, well, as I told your colleague, we were at the wrong place at the wrong time. We heard gunshots inside an apartment, opened the door and spotted a man crumpled on the floor. We didn't touch the body. You didn't find gunshot residue on our hands, and if any of us had a gun, it was registered and clean–certainly not the murder weapon."

I knew Basso carried and was certain that ballistics tested his pistol.

"It's not so much, Valentina, what the three of you are telling us. It's what you're not telling us."

"We didn't witness the murder."

"The victim, Chaz Lombardo, was a drug dealer. Did the Ruggiero mob have a beef with him, and you went to straighten him out?"

"None of us knew Chaz Lombardo."

"Then, why were you there?"

"I'm finished answering questions."

My attorney piped up. "Detective Slade, my clients are

innocent and didn't witness the murder. You have zero evidence to the contrary. Please, either charge or release them."

Jack taught me to fire a pistol, which saved my life. I liked him, but ever since my birth mother abandoned me, I worried that like her, I was incapable of love. Hopefully Jack understood that I was treating him like a cop not a boyfriend, and this incident wouldn't ruin our relationship.

Fortunately, nobody witnessed Carlotta leave the building. If questioned directly by the cops, we wouldn't deny her presence as lying gets you charged with obstruction of justice. Saving that, with Lombardo dead, I presumed matters with Irene were closed. As things turned out, I was wrong.

~

Millie received an urgent call from Irene. She put her on speaker so I could hear.

"Another blackmailer has shown up. Will this nightmare never end?"

"When can Valentina speak to Carlotta?"

"I'm out, but she's home now. I'll phone her you're coming."

I called Anthony and he met me at the Manhattan Fifth Avenue brownstone. Carlotta opened the door dressed in a skimpy yellow bikini.

Anthony's eyes widened.

She struck a pose, saying to him, "You'll have to forgive me for being overdressed. The last time you saw me, I was naked. Have you come from that cute art gallery Eva told me about?"

Anthony croaked out. "Yes."

Smiling coyly, she said, "Come in. I'll get you a drink." She turned and gave us a rearview catwalk strut.

From a vaulted entranceway, we were led to the bar past expensive looking paintings and statuary.

She said, "I'm having an Aperol Spritz. But I'll make you anything you want."

"Nothing for me," I said.

"Same," said Anthony, still sounding raspy.

We took a leather sofa, she an armchair opposite. Carlotta parted her knees. She knew what she was doing.

I glanced at Anthony. He was keeping his eyes on hers. Good boy.

I asked, "Why were you at Chaz Lombardo's apartment?"

She tore her eyes from him. "I expected sex and drugs to relight the flame and end the threats. Would've worked, but someone shot him."

"You don't know who."

"I'd passed out. The gunshots woke me, but by the time I focused, the room was empty."

"The police don't know you were there. When they find out, you might consider coming up with a better story."

Carlotta shrugged that away.

"Tell us about this new blackmail threat."

"Nicky Granger. He has a nightclub in midtown."

Anthony and I exchanged glances. "You know this guy."

She sounded bored. "He wants money. What's new?"

"You don't seem concerned."

She stood and approached Anthony coming nearly knees to knees, saying, "Why don't you tell her to take a hike. We can spend the rest of the afternoon together. You won't regret it."

Anthony cleared his throat and stood, sliding away from her, saying to me, "We need to get going."

As we left the apartment, Carlotta displayed a look of pouty disappointment sprinkled with a tinge of hate.

~

On the street, Anthony said, "Please don't tell Nori about her."

"A fantasy nightmare, I would imagine. She certainly didn't like you leaving."

"Do you think she lied about being passed out at Lombardo's murder?"

"She seemed strung out, but who knows."

"What do you want to do about Granger?"

"Millie feels obligated to help Irene."

Anthony said, "Drugs, sex, Carlotta acts any way she damn well pleases. Her mother will need to constantly bail her out of trouble."

"Sounds right, but we owe Granger the conversation we intended for Lombardo. I'll call Basso."

That evening, we three dropped in at Granger's nightclub, Love Triangle. The huge room had floor to ceiling windows with a view of New York's skyline. Chic in velvet and wood, a DJ spun beats for a well-dressed crowd.

Granger, in his forties, handsome, wearing a blue designer suit held court at the far end of a leather-accented bar. A tall, thick dude with a flaming skull neck tattoo stood behind him scanning the room. To my surprise, Eva nursed a cocktail at Granger's side.

We approached. Basso and the neck tattoo exchanged malevolent stares.

Eva looked surprised and a little uncomfortable to see us. I took note that the check in front of her had sufficient zeros to cover a round for the house. I concluded that she was making a payoff and Granger used the club to launder money. Eva had been roped into the blackmail scheme.

Granger's eyes lit up. "Eva, who do we have here? A friend of yours. Where have you been hiding such a beauty?"

His repulsive leer flashed me back to my sex-worker life, and I said in a rude tone, "I'm Valentina. This is Anthony and Basso. He's bodyguard to Frank Provati of the Ruggiero crime mob. Heard of them?"

Granger lost his smile. "What do you want?"

I gazed around the room before saying, "Let me guess. You concoct ways to compromise rich marks, then blackmail them for your silence."

The flaming neck tattoo took a step forward. Basso blocked his path. Granger held up a hand to halt the confrontation. "Kurt, we're having a friendly conversation. No need for a ruckus."

Granger asked, "What do you want?"

"The blackmail of Carlotta over her drug dealing ends now."

Unexpectedly, Granger grinned at me. He took some moments before saying, "Carlotta laced drugs with fentanyl. At least one of the kids she dealt to died from an overdose. She had to pay, one way or the other."

A penny dropped for me. "Your wife Monica ran off with Eva's husband Paul."

Granger displayed no anger. "I'm not complaining, just getting even. Irene can afford the tariff."

"Paying you is over," I said.

Granger protested. "Suddenly the mob that makes a ton from illegal activities will begrudge me an income?"

"Ply your trade elsewhere."

Granger grimaced.

I voiced a hunch. "Your creature, Kurt, killed Chaz Lombardo because he muscled in on your scam?"

Granger shifted uncomfortably.

"As revenge, did Kurt kill Paul too?"

Eva was listening to our conversation. At that question, she shuddered.

Granger huffed. "If he's been murdered, I would be the obvious suspect. I'm not that stupid."

I nodded, then demanded. "Are we done here?"

Granger spoke with mock sincerity. "Cross my heart, I won't tell the cops about Carlotta's drug dealing. Goodbye."

I crumpled Eva's check in my fist and threw it in the trash. Granger didn't protest. I gestured to the guys, and we headed out of the club.

Basso asked, "You think that finishes it?"

I let out a long sigh. "It went just a bit too easy."

Anthony asked, "Granger has another angle?"

I agreed. "Something's not right."

I called Jack about Granger. I judged from his cool tone, that he was still processing how he felt about our interaction at the interrogation.

I said, "Granger is a blackmailer who uses Love Triangle to identify and trap potential marks. His henchman, Kurt, probably murdered Chaz Lombardo for encroaching on his turf."

"He has an impressive beach home in the Hamptons that suggests dough from illegal activities, but ever since the FBI nabbed Al Capone for tax evasion, smart crooks have found a way to launder their money."

I thought for a moment before asking, "Do you have the Hamptons address?"

～

Basso wanted to drive me to Long Island, but I saw no need.

He said, "You've stirred up some dangerous jamokes."

"I rented a car and I'm ready to leave. I'll be fine."

He was still protesting when I hung up.

I pulled up to a wood-slatted house of gray and white with three fireplaces. Granger's Hamptons home fronted a beige beach with waves rolling in like wood shavings. Out back, I found a blonde reclining on a chaise lounge.

"Monica Granger?"

Surprised, the woman sat up. "Who are you?"

"Where's Paul?"

She grimaced. "You don't look like the police."

"Why would the police want to know about Paul?"

"Go away or *I* will call the police."

"I don't think so," I said. "But I might contact them if you don't answer my questions."

Monica shrank back.

"Well?"

Reluctantly, Monica responded. "I don't know Paul's whereabouts."

"I was told you and he were an item."

"An ugly rumor. Now, please go away."

I contemplated a moment before asking, "Will you be returning to Manhattan soon?"

"My husband told me he'd join me, but he hasn't shown up. If he has another woman, I don't want to know, because then I'll need to do something about it."

I nodded at the odd logic of what she said and walked away.

When I rounded the house, almost to my car, Kurt strode from the shadows, revolver raised.

I reeled backwards and raised my hands. He closed the distance - the muzzle just a few feet from my face. The barrel drew my eyes like a magnet. Should I run? No chance of escape. My gut sickened.

My voice was hoarse. "You don't need to do this."

He cocked the revolver. "You had to stick your nose where it didn't belong." His eyes were like a cobra before the strike.

I heard seagulls, the roll of waves, and the sound of my short breaths. Sweat rose on my face.

Leering, he enjoyed my fear. "Time to die."

I sensed his finger tightening on the trigger.

Behind me, tires squealed as a car skidded. Three shots rang out in rapid succession.

As he was hit, Kurt's revolver discharged. The bullet whizzed past my left ear.

Basso had fired his Glock through the driver's side window of the GTO, and his slugs plowed into Kurt's chest. The impact collapsed him, and his dead legs folded under his body.

Basso lumbered from the car.

My feet felt rooted to the ground. My heart galloped.

He gave me a wry smile. "Mama would never forgive me if I let anything happen to you."

I found my breath. "You're my rock," and collapsed in his arms.

B ack in Anghiari, as I described my near-death experience, Anthony's face became grave.

"Jesus," he said and gave me a warm hug.

"Please don't tell Millie. There's nothing she can do about what happened except to get herself upset."

"Who imagined," he said shaking his head, "that when we tried to scare off a blackmailer, we'd be putting your life in danger."

"Yeah," I said. "Unintended consequences."

Our discussion turned to the implications of my finding Monica alone in the Hamptons.

"Why are Eva and Granger pushing the idea that Monica ran off with her husband Paul?"

I shrugged.

"Can a person just disappear?"

"If you're an orphan," I said, wincing at my abandonment, "or if you're estranged from your family, some bastard can off you, dispose of your body, and nobody is looking for you."

"If he's not run off with a woman, why isn't Eva trying to find him?"

Suddenly, Anghiari's door flew open, and Carlotta stormed toward Anthony with a pistol in hand. "You bastard." Her finger curled around the trigger.

My stomach twisted into a knot.

Anthony threw up his palms, and his voice betrayed fear. "What do you want?"

"Nobody spurns me," she said raising the pistol.

"I'm married. I didn't mean any disrespect."

She growled. "Bullshit."

I was too far away to leap on her. My head spun, trying to think of something so she wouldn't shoot.

Focused on the gun, I didn't detect Eva entering the gallery.

From behind Carlotta, Eva shouted, "Don't."

Just momentarily, Carlotta flinched.

Anthony jumped forward and grabbed the pistol, twisting it out of her hand. Carlotta punched at him, but he held her off.

I almost collapsed in relief.

Carlotta began to sob. Eva took her into her arms.

"Please," Eva begged, "don't call the police."

I looked at Anthony. He was shaken, but he didn't pull out his phone.

"She's in need of serious psychological help," I said.

Carlotta sneered at me.

Soothing Carlotta's face, Eva said, "I promised my dying father I'd look after her."

"It's only a matter of time before you won't be able to save her."

"Then it won't be my fault."

I played a hunch. "Did she murder your husband Paul for rejecting her?"

Carlotta hissed at me.

Eva recoiled. "I won't allow my sister to be locked away in an institution or worse, a penitentiary."

Still in each other's arms, they left the gallery.

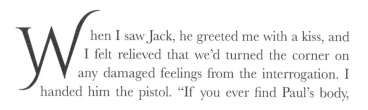

When I saw Jack, he greeted me with a kiss, and I felt relieved that we'd turned the corner on any damaged feelings from the interrogation. I handed him the pistol. "If you ever find Paul's body, and he has a gunshot wound, you need to test the ballistics of this gun for a match. No proof, just speculation."

"Where did you get it?"

"Carlotta Rosso."

"She threatened you?"

"Anthony. Considering Irene's relationship with Millie, he won't be pursuing charges."

Jack gave me a dubious frown. "If she's a murderer, you're not doing the world any favors."

Sitting together in Anghiari, Anthony's face was clouded, and I asked him how he was doing.

"I've stared down a killer's gun barrel before." He let out a sigh. "But you never get used to it."

I flashed to the fear I felt when Kurt held a revolver in my face. "Yeah. I get it."

"Shit," he said. "You and I came close to adding to the body count in this caper."

I gave him a hug. Contemplating that we both faced death was a scary thought.

"Carlotta, Eva, and Granger created a mirage," he said. "You put it all together."

I took a moment before responding. "Carlotta murdered Paul, because he rejected her advances."

"I almost followed his fate," Anthony said ruefully.

"Granger kept Carlotta's secret but was shaking down Eva. They concocted the story about Paul running off with Monica to cover Paul's absence."

Anthony mused. "Obligation to her sister trumped wanting revenge for her husband."

"That's why when we confronted Granger at the Love

Triangle, he was snide about the drug dealing blackmail. He was pleased we hadn't yet discovered their real secret."

"How do you think he knew about Paul's murder?"

"Given the recklessness Carlotta showed coming after you, I'd guess that, in a fit of rage, she shot Paul at the club."

"When Irene approached Millie, we had no idea of the swamp we'd enter."

I nodded, sadly. "Millie agreed that she'd be the one to tell Irene." I looked at my watch. "They're together at the restaurant now."

"Do you think Irene and Millie will remain friends?"

I shrugged with doubt. "Tough to forgive someone for telling you the hard truth about your daughters."

∼

Joe Giordano was born in Brooklyn. He and his wife Jane now live in Texas.

Joe's stories have appeared in more than one hundred magazines including The Saturday Evening Post, and Shenandoah, *and his short story collection,* Stories and Places I Remember. *His novels include,* Birds of Passage, An Italian Immigrant Coming of Age Story, *and* the Anthony Provati thriller series: Appointment with ISIL, Drone Strike, and The Art of Revenge.

Visit Joe's website at https://joe-giordano.com/

Shagra the Untangler
Kay Hanifen

She called upon me in the late evening, just as I was about to retire for the night. The notes from my most recent case were scattered about, and although it was resolved rather happily for all parties, I hadn't yet had the chance to file it away among my other cases.

The knock echoed through my small apartment, and my curiosity piqued as to who would be calling at this time of night. I'd already settled the matter of the stolen dragon's egg with the city guards, so they weren't there for any attempted entrapment poorly disguised as additional questions. I stretched, the vertebrae in my spine crackling like a campfire. Hunching in an apartment built for much smaller people was murder on my back. I opened the door. A woman stood before me on a dark and mostly empty street. Most vendors had packed up for the day, but a few stragglers headed home, watched over by a police constable at the end of the street.

Though a portion of her face was hidden by a cloak whose embroidery shifted in patterns that made me wish to avert my eyes and forget I saw her, I could make out the honey-brown skin and delicate features of someone with elvish ancestry. "May I speak to the detective who lives here?"

I stepped aside, letting her in. The white-haired woman pulled back the hood of the invisibility cloak, looking around with confused eyes the prettiest shade of violet I'd ever seen. "Am I to wait until he comes out or..."

"You're speaking to her," I said, holding out a hand to shake.

Her eyes widened in shock. "I — I'm so sorry. I didn't expect you to be, uh..."

"An orc," I said, taking a seat on a wingback chair by the stove and gesturing for her to do the same, "My name is Shagra the Untangler. And to what do I owe the honor of the king's own sorceress coming to visit, Mage Rhonwen."

If possible, her eyes widened even further, and her jaw dropped. I knew how I must have looked to her as a seven-foot tall, green skinned and muscular orcish woman who hadn't bothered filing down her tusks when she moved into Arabon City. I looked like a stupid brute barely able to string together a series of grunts into a coherent sentence. And here I was, correctly deducing the identity of one of the king's more mysterious advisors.

Sometimes it was fun to play with my wealthy and powerful clientele. I was so far outside of their expectations, I might as well have descended from the heavens, but because I was growing tired and didn't care much for the king, I decided to keep the torture short and nodded to the cloak still on her shoulders. "The embroidery on your cloak. Invisibility cloaks are rare enough, but this one is powerful. It plays with the minds of all who surround it, averting their awareness of your presence and making them forget you if they did happen to see you. The runes embroidered into it are unique to the Valenor Academy of Magic, which is where the king's personal sorceress attended school. So, what royal errand are you on?"

She sat for a moment in stunned silence, fiddling with the threads of her cloak. Rhonwen looked young, barely in her mid-twenties, when most of the king's personal mages were more than triple that age. In my wingback chair, she looked rather small, like a rabbit hiding among hungry wolves. Finally, she seemed to come to a decision, straightening and raising her gaze to meet mine to say, "Shagra the Untangler, forgive my rudeness and the lateness of the hour, but I'm in need of your services and your discretion."

I leaned forward, resting my elbows on my knees. "With all due respect, what does King Elio need from a lowly orc? I thought we were no better than the pigs he slaughters for dinner."

She winced, which brought me a degree of satisfaction. I'd always wanted to give King Elio a piece of my mind. Every year, his knights venture further into our ancestral lands, and every year, we lose more brothers and sisters, husbands and wives. They call us savages while they slaughter us. "That's why I came here," she said.

And now, I was listening. "Go on."

"I know I shouldn't be his personal sorceress. I'm talented, but not *that* good, not like Mage Bonnard, the previous sorcerer. He wanted someone to manipulate, someone who would make a beautiful martyr, and thought that, because I'm young, I wouldn't question his choice. But I'm no fool. I know why I'm there."

"And what do you want from me?"

"I've begun to believe that he wants to stage an attempted orcish revolution, killing me in the process to use as an excuse to go to war."

My heart stuttered. For the past few years, our peoples

had been living in an uneasy peace. The kingdom pushed its boundaries, and we'd fight back, but we have no magic of our own. In a total war, we'd be slaughtered. "And you want me to prevent that from happening. How do you expect me to do that?"

"If there's a way to sabotage the coup, to prevent the attack before it even starts. . ."

"And then what? Forgive my bluntness, but he'll just try again. He's the king, and his power is absolute. If he wants you dead, I suppose I can help you escape with your life, but I have no idea how I alone can prevent him from creating an excuse to go to war."

Her shoulders sagged in dejection, but she nodded. "I understand your concerns. Thank you for your time." She got to her feet, and I held up a hand.

"Wait."

She stopped, turning to look at me with a quiet hope.

I sighed, fearing that I'd regret this. "I'll help in any way I can. Perhaps if we leak this conspiracy to the press, we can enrage the public enough that he'd be forced to abandon the plot."

Her eyes glistened as she gave me a grateful smile. "Thank you. I am in your debt."

"You can repay me by protecting my people from his tyranny."

"Of course." She stood, taking her leave.

I never did get the chance to send the story to the paper because the headline that dominated the news the next day changed everything about the case. "King's Sorceress Kidnapped! Orc Separatists Suspected."

They must have grabbed her on her way back from my home, a theory confirmed when Constable Bartholomew Scrubb came knocking at my door. He looked down at me from his handlebar mustache, an impressive feat considering that I was a good foot taller than him.

"What can I help you with, Constable?" I asked, gesturing for him to take a seat. As he pushed past, I caught a waft of Elder Lilly, a distinct scent found in only one establishment in town. His shoes were scuffed with the type of red clay found in the red-light district. I had it on good authority that they mixed the clay cobblestones poorly on purpose so that it would stain the shoes of anyone who frequented its establishments, marking the constables that chose to break the law by partaking in these activities as a means of fighting corruption. Unfortunately, because the area was also heavily policed, it became impossible to tell the corrupt constables from the ones doing their jobs. The measure was deemed a failure, but the city never bothered to properly repave the roads in the district, so the red clay remained. I suspected that Constable Scrubb was among the police officers that partook in illicit activities, rather than a cop doing honest work.

"I believe you've seen the papers. Mage Rhonwen has gone missing, and your home was her last known location. What have you done with her?"

I arched an eyebrow. "She came to me in secret. How do *you* know I was her last known location?"

"Answer the question, orc."

"I agreed to take her as my client. Now answer mine."

His mustache twitched in disdain. "This is police business. You don't need to know. Now, why did she go to you instead of the police? What could she possibly want with a brute who fancies herself to be a detective?"

"I'd be careful with comments like that, Constable Scrubb. A brute who fancies themselves a detective applies to at least half your men." I laid back in my chair, letting him fume for a moment before continuing. "And I'm afraid that information is between me and my client. Confidentiality laws, you know. But I can tell you for certain that she wasn't afraid of orc separatists." This was a little bit of a gamble, but if the most powerful people in the kingdom were in on this conspiracy, then the police would be useless at best and dangerous at worst. I watched his face redden, vein bulging in his forehead as he waited for me to elaborate further, and I kept mum. It's a common tactic for interrogation. If you stay quiet long enough, the suspect will eventually open up to fill the silence. Unfortunately for him, I didn't mind a bit of silence.

Our staring contest ended when he blinked, averting his eyes in the guise of straightening his already rigid tie. "Did you see anything suspicious? Anything that might indicate *who* exactly took her?"

I thought back, picturing the streets last night. It had appeared that she came alone, with no one tailing her. The few people on the street were caught up in their own lives, ignoring the sorceress at my door. No one had even glanced in our direction. "I don't know. We parted once I agreed to take her on and I saw nothing unusual when I showed her to the door."

"You claim to see everything, noticing every small detail, and yet you saw nothing. You see how I find that odd, Shagra the Untangler."

"Perhaps they took her after she was out of sight of my house. I have an eye for detail, but I'm not omnipotent. For example, I can deduce you went to the red-light district from the clay on your shoe, and judging by the perfume still on you, I'd say you went to the Waltzing Wastrel. The ladies there are lovely, aren't they, Constable? I helped the Madame resolve a delicate matter once and enjoy dropping by from time to time. As only a friendly face, of course."

Shagra the Untangler

"Of course," he replied through gritted teeth, "now if you're done wasting my time. . ."

"By all means. Don't let me detain you." I showed him the door with my most cordial smile before returning to the stove and brooding over my next steps. There was so much I didn't know, and the stakes higher than any other case I'd worked. If she died, King Elio would use her name to start a war, but I had no idea where to begin. If there were witnesses to her kidnapping, the cloak she wore would have prevented them from remembering her. I didn't know the route she took back to the castle, so finding clues as to what happened or where she was taken was like trying to find a single dryad in a densely packed forest.

Picking up the newspaper, I read the article again carefully. Apparently, an anonymous witness recognized her as she was walking down the street only to see a band of five orcs grab her and drag her away. There were several problems that stood out to me. First, the cloak would have prevented the witness from remembering her, so how would they know that it was the royal sorceress? Second, court mages were among the most secretive group, operating from the shadows as they decided the fates of kingdoms. Mage Rhonwen had garnered some attention because of her youth, but not enough to make her immediately recognizable. Third, like my question to the constable, how did the newspaper know about this and break the story so quickly?

My thoughts returned to the constabulary. I had seen a constable when I let her in. At the time, I didn't think much of it because it wasn't unusual for them to police the area, but if she was being watched by the powers that be, what better way than through the people so familiar that they practically fade into the scenery but with enough authority that you could get in trouble for resisting them?

Putting my hair up and donning a City Cleaner's uniform, I slipped out the back of my apartment because the front was likely being watched. I pushed a cart in front of me full of cleaning supplies as I headed in the direction of the constabulary. The secretary let me in without a glance. Why would she? I was an orc in her proper place. Eyes downcast and listening carefully, I mopped the floors until I reached a small, empty conference room. When it was clear no one was watching, I slipped inside.

The work of a janitor is only noticeable in its absence. When they're there and the halls are clean, no one looks in their direction, but when they're gone, the garbage piles up and people start to complain about the laziness of the person who's been thanklessly cleaning up their messes. I knew for a fact that if it wasn't for the donuts always in the break room, the constabulary's resident brownie would have been offended and left long ago, not that anyone would notice until the trash started piling up.

I removed the false bottom of the cart and pulled out my stash of sweets. Setting down a number of sugary delights, I sat and waited, but not for long. A small creature literally came out of the woodwork, sniffing the air and making a beeline for the candies.

When Pip the Brownie spotted me, they smiled and waved. "Shagra, what are you doing here? If Constable Scrubb finds you. . ."

"Then I shall do my best to be quick. I have a favor to ask of you."

They took their seat on the table, diminutive legs swinging from the chair. "Of course you do. You only bring me sweets when you need something, so out with it. What do you need?"

"Your eyes and ears," I said, "The king's sorceress has

been taken and I suspect that the constabulary is behind it. If you overhear anything unusual, please let me know."

They took a bite of a stroopwafel, chewing thoughtfully. "There's been a lot of coming and going from the red-light district. I thought maybe they were planning another raid because they've been talking a lot with the station in that district, but maybe it has something to do with your missing sorceress."

"Thank you," I said, knowing my next stop, "If you hear anything else. . ."

"I'll let you know. Be careful, Shagra. The constabulary is powerful, and they really don't like you."

I patted the top of their head with my finger. The whole hand would probably flatten them. "You know me. I'm always careful." I pulled another stroopwafel from my cart, setting their favorite treat next to them before bidding the brownie adieu.

In the daylight, the Waltzing Wastrel could almost be mistaken for an inn. It was two stories, with an entertainment room on the main floor and its less than savory business done in the bedrooms upstairs. The whole building smelled of Elder Lilly, an aphrodisiac of Madame Vox's own creation. I wrinkled my nose at the powerful floral scent. We orcs have sensitive noses. We can smell blood from almost a mile away, so any powerful aromas quickly become overwhelming.

The girl at the bar, Namia, smiled when she saw me, pouring my usual tankard of honey mead. "Good day and well met, Shagra, you're not usually in until nightfall."

"I'm afraid I'm here on business," I said, cradling my drink, "Is Madame Vox around?"

"Of course. I'll be right back." She disappeared behind the bar. Moments later, Madame Vox came striding in.

The succubus was tall — her head coming up to my

shoulder — and imposing, wearing a fine gown, and having perfectly coiffed hair. Of course, I was among the few people aware she was a succubus. It was how we met, actually. Because all forms of vampirism are generally frowned upon, she kept it a secret. A former lover had found out through one of her employees and blackmailed her, threatening to expose her to the police. I managed to get the evidence back from him without much issue and she's been trying to repay the debt ever since.

When she smiled, it was tighter than usual around the lines of her mouth. Underneath the makeup, I could see bags under her eyes. She patted my shoulder once, twice, three times, a warning we'd devised to signal when someone was listening in. "Namia told me you have something you'd like to discuss. I'm afraid I don't know how much help I'll be. With tax season coming up, I've been toiling away like a troll in a cave. I swear, if accountants weren't mostly vampires, I'd say they were magicians."

I arched an eyebrow but decided not to press when it clearly wasn't safe. "Toiling away like a troll in a cave? Can't say I've heard that one before, but I know what you mean," I said, "It's why I'm here too. I'm chasing down the invoice for the case I took on for you. I wanted to see how much you owed me."

She laughed, a high, musical sound meant to distract any eavesdroppers with a sudden feeling of lust and desire to hear it again. "Not as much as I owe the government. I can tell you that much. Let me see if I can find it in my records," she said, disappearing to the back once more while I pondered our veiled conversation. Had she been roped in on the plot? Elder Lilly's effects in high enough doses could make people vulnerable to suggestion — far more than what the workers here wore. But she knew how to synthesize the perfume into a drug like that. If the constabulary was behind the kidnapping — and that seemed more likely by the second — they might have been leveraging their police powers to force her to cooperate.

Madame Vox returned, and there was something off about her smell. It was sickly sweet, almost as though. . .I leapt to my feet, backing away from her. She paused, tilting her head. "Shagra, whatever is the matter?"

"You've never been one to mince words with me, and I shall give you the courtesy of doing the same. I know of your involvement with the kidnapping and that it wasn't of your own volition. I can help you, but I need you to work with me, and not use that perfume to make me do what you want."

"I was going to tell you to just go home, get some sleep, and forget you ever met Mage Rhonwen. I'm sure you've figured out by now that they want to lump you in with the 'orc separatists.' It would be better for you if you dropped this and let what happens happen."

"Would it be?" I replied, "Her death means all out war with my kind. A war based on a lie that will lead to the slaughter of my people. You understand why I have to find her."

She sighed, suddenly looking exhausted and far worse than I'd ever seen her. "I don't know where she is. Constable Scrubb and his goons came in here a week ago and threatened to expose me as a succubus to the city council if I didn't do as they asked. I had no idea what they planned to do with it."

I can't say I was surprised by this revelation. He made the mistake of going to one of the few people in the city whose respect and friendship I had earned. Remembering earlier that day, I winced. Perhaps I made the mistake of showing my hand too early, but in all fairness, I didn't know the Waltzing Wastrel was involved. "I understand,

and I'll do my best to keep your name out of this when I find her. I do suggest that you take a vacation to the seaside for some time. Just until it gets sorted one way or another."

She chewed her lip as she considered my words. "Probably for the best. I do hope you find her. For the sake of everyone."

I nodded. "Take care and stay safe."

At that, she smirked. "I think you stole my line."

"What can I say? I got tired of hearing people say it to me and thought I'd make someone else hear it for a change." I waved goodbye and left. The sun was rapidly going down, the gods painting the sky in brilliant reds, purples, and oranges. The day was just ending, with merchants packing up their wares and staring twitchy eyed at the straggling customers as they agonized over final purchases, oblivious to the fact that everyone else was packing up for the day.

A few blocks from my home, I felt a pebble hit my back shoulder accompanied by a *psst*. I turned to find Pip standing in the alley, eyes wide in alarm. I hadn't sensed anyone watching me, but I made sure no one was looking anyway as I ducked into the alleyway. Taking a knee, I whispered, "Did you hear anything?"

"Don't go home," they said, "They're waiting to arrest you for treason, saying that you took her as a political statement."

"Did you hear anything about where they took her?"

They shook their head. "Constable Scrubb has been acting odd. He tells his fellow officers to toil like a troll in a cave to find her, whatever that means. Trolls don't toil in caves. They don't toil at all! They just sit all day and eat livestock."

I didn't feel like correcting them and pointing out that trolls did, in fact, have a unique and varied culture across the kingdom and only earned that reputation because they were nocturnal creatures. Instead, I was thinking about that phrase because it was unusual. I hadn't heard that expression until today, and this was the second time. This could have been just frequency bias, but I suspected it was a code of some sort. "Pip, do you know of any cave systems in the city?"

They scratched their chin. "There's the old smuggler's caves, but the constabulary had flooded it a long time ago."

"All of it?"

They glanced around, and opened their mouth, but no sound came out. They tried again. And again, before sighing. "Sorry, being the Brownie for the constabulary means I'm under a geas for certain state secrets. I can't tell you where it is."

I fiddled with my tusks, an old nervous habit from when I was a child preparing to spar with the older orclings. "Can you tell me where it isn't?"

The Library of Aeldor was as much a holy site as any temple or cathedral. It was open to all who claimed sanctuary on its doorstep at all hours of the night, which was how I found myself with a Brownie sitting on my shoulder as I studied maps of the city's old smuggler cave system.

"It's not here," Pip said, pointing to one entrance and then to another, "or here." Geasa were tough things to bend or break, but because Pip was a lowly Brownie, the constabulary hadn't been careful about wording the specifics of the taboo spell. Through hours of pointing and crossing out, we had slowly narrowed down the entrance the constabulary was using to three possible locations.

"It's not here," they said, pointing to one in the red-light district, "Nor is it here." And with a map of almost completely crossed out locations, I finally found my entrance. And of course, it was the most dangerous of them all. Siren's Cave was halfway down the cliff face on which the castle sat. Down below were jagged rocks, and rumor had it that the only way to safely enter was to know the password to reveal the path.

I stifled a yawn, rubbing my heavy eyelids. "Thank you, Pip. I can take it from here."

"Oh no you don't," they said, leaping from my shoulder and on top of the map with their arms crossed, "It's the middle of the night and you're exhausted."

"If I wait much longer, she could die."

"And if you go now to scale that cliff tired and in the dark, you'll die and that's not useful to anyone. The constabulary doesn't know what you know, so you can spare a few hours rest." They had a point. I'd had a very long day and probably shouldn't attempt anything death-defying in the middle of the night. As much as I burned to move, I knew I had to wait, at least for now.

With a sigh, I replied, "Fine. I'll get some rest. You should probably head back to the constabulary too before anyone realizes you're gone."

They saluted and vanished into the woodwork while I laid down on one of the reading couches. It was too short for me, leaving my legs dangling off the side, but things are rarely made with an orc's size in mind. Although unintentional, every too-small couch and park bench and too-low ceiling was a reminder of how unwelcome I was in public life. Even a sanctuary for those in need of help or guidance wasn't built to accommodate me. After staring at the vaulted ceilings for a long time, I eventually drifted off into an uneasy sleep.

And then I was standing in a cage. Mage Rhonwen laid on a dirt floor, shivering in the damp cold, her white hair turned brown with dirt. She was covered in cuts and bruises, one arm bent at an awkward angle. Her calf had a piece of broken iron in it, making me wince. For beings with strong magic, iron was a slow poison that nullified their ability to tap into the secret forces of the universe. I stared over her with a mixture of sadness and misplaced guilt. I couldn't have known what would happen when I bade her farewell, but a part of me wondered if I could have done anything differently. When she saw me, her lashes fluttered as though surprised and she struggled to sit up. "It's you. You're here."

"And you're in the Siren's Cave," I said, "Is this a dream, or are you making this happen?"

"An astral projection," she said, "I've been trying to call to you, but I couldn't reach you until you went to sleep."

"Orcs are a bit more resistant to magic than most," I said, taking in her squalid surroundings. The hallway outside the cell was lit by a single lightbulb casting heavy shadows across the room. I could hear the crash of ocean waves, but they were muffled, indicating that we were relatively deep in the cave system. The taste of saltwater hung in the air, the chill sapping the warmth from my body.

"The broken iron I've been beaten with doesn't help," she said, "I've tried to get most of it out of me, but if I remove some of the bigger pieces, I'll bleed out."

"Do you know the spell to reveal the safest way to enter the cave?"

"Yes. It's an old high elvish word. M'threadir. It means safe passage."

"Thank you," I said, half expecting to wake up when she gave it to me, but I remained. "Shall I. . .wake up now?"

"No, stay," she exclaimed, before schooling her panicked features into something more stoic, "Please. Just for a little while longer. It's — it's nice to have a friendly face. The constabulary want to make the orcish crimes convincing, and. . .I just would like some conversation that doesn't end in pain."

I sat down cross-legged beside her, leaning against the wall. "We've only met once. What makes my face so friendly?"

"You're not a member of the royal court, or their guards, or even their servant. My headmistress warned me that I would be a mouse in a den of snakes when I took the position, and she was right. I've yet to find any allies, anyone who listens when I argue against war and King Elio's overreach. I tried winning over the people, but that just made things worse, because now I was a threat to their power. You were the first in a long time to listen to my concerns, to believe me and treat me with respect when you had every reason to turn your back on me."

I propped my elbows on my knees and rested my chin in my hands. "I suppose you're wondering how an orc of all creatures became a detective."

"I thought it wasn't my place to ask," she said.

"As a child, I lived among my people. Things were tense between humans and orcs, but not quite as bad as they are now. My family took me to a festival in the city where I saw so many beings living together in harmony. I played games with a human, a witch, and an elf. They were nervous at first, but when I played the three-shell game and proved myself adept at keeping track of the pebble no matter how quickly the game maker moved it and even catching the sleight of hand when he would slip it from one cup to another, I earned their respect. When it was time to go, a man stopped us, and accused us of polluting the festival with our very presence. We're known for our fighting ability, but my father. . .he was a pacifist. He believed that our minds were the greatest weapon of all, so he taught me to think, to see what others did not. It didn't save him in the end. One angry human? Easily dealt with, even if it meant bending his pacifist beliefs. But two? Three? Four? Five? He was overwhelmed, and Mama joined the fray. A gunshot rang out, and Papa dropped dead. The fight froze as the constabulary arrived. They arrested the woman wailing over her dead husband and the sobbing child, but let his murderers go."

"That's — I don't know what to say," Rhonwen said, wincing as she pulled her knees in towards her chest.

"A part of me cried out for justice, screamed for it, but knew I'd never find it through normal legal means. For years, the anger that simmered inside told me to hunt down every one of them and kill them, but then I'd hear my father's words. 'Anger is like a fire, Shagra. It can be a tool to drive you, but let it burn without controlling the blaze and it consumes everything else.' So, I decided to use it, to direct it into action. If I couldn't find justice for his death, then I would stand up for those that the constabulary ignores or would hurt."

"Have you? I mean, do you really think you can change things?"

I smiled at her with a shrug. "I like to think I can. Not a lot, but when I think about that festival, I don't just think about my father. I think about the human and elven children I befriended. It won't fix centuries of oppression and propaganda, but when I ran into one of those kids years later, they told me that I'd changed their life. Because they met an orc completely different from what they'd believed, they decided to research us, discovering the history the king doesn't want you to think about, and was advocating for our rights."

"I wish I had as much optimism as you," she said, studying the ground, "I'm in one of the most powerful positions in the land, and I can't help anyone. If I'm being honest, I don't think I ever could. Valenor Academy was all mages stabbing each other in the back to try to get ahead. I...I don't think I had a true friend in that place. Even the people I believed might have cared for me would have slit my throat in a second if it was convenient for them. It prepared me well for the courts, where everyone double-crosses one another. But I had to speak my mind, to speak out against war and the powers of the constabulary. It was foolish of me, but he seemed to listen at first, placing me further and further into the spotlight. Then one night, I overheard him talking with his court officials about plans to make a martyr of me. Two birds, one stone, right? If I'm dead, then I can't speak my mind and the people will want the head of whoever killed their beloved sorceress. I want to say I felt shocked and betrayed, but I wasn't even surprised. Not really. I just heard it and thought to myself *sounds about right*."

I went to pat her shoulder, but my hand went through as though it was made of fog. She saw me trying and cracked a small smile. "Astral projection, remember? You're not really here." With a slow breath, she closed her eyes. When she opened them, she said, "You should go now. I'll wait for you."

"Rhonwen — " I began, but the dream ended abruptly. I sat up stretching the stiffness from my spine. I missed my custom-made bed, something long enough that I wouldn't have to contort into awkward positions just to sleep, but sanctuary seekers can't be choosers, I suppose.

While I waited for evening to come, I spent the day avoiding windows and studying the cave system. The library only protected people inside and I didn't want to risk arrest by venturing out for supplies. I had no idea what state Mage Rhonwen would be in, but I would have to move fast to get in and get her out of her cell without anyone noticing. Wounds like that broken arm I saw would slow us down, something potentially deadly when you're being pursued by police.

I stayed in the library until the evening, reading up on a fascinating book about the history of the Mer Kingdoms, a group that, because I was a landlubber, knew very little about. As the sun began to sink below the horizon, I embarked upon my journey to the cliffs.

It was a breathtaking sight once I got there — the skies painted in hues of orange, red, and purple against the backdrop of foamy waves crashing against the shore. I stopped and cleared my throat. "M'threadir." The grinding of rock against rock below me set my teeth on edge, but I looked over the uncomfortably high ledge to see a staircase emerge from the stone. With a growing pit in my stomach, I hugged the wall as I took my first steps down. My heart pounded in my ears, but I ignored it, ignored the terror gripping my soul with every strong gust of wind. Said wind was also carrying the moisture of the water into the air, making the stone steps slippery. I briefly wondered if I should just go, turn my back on her and my people and mind my own business, but that wasn't me. The day that happened would be the day the world stopped spinning and flipped upside down.

I paused just outside the mouth of the cave, listening for any movements. Given the secrecy and danger of the location, security could go one of two ways: either they would let the environment do most of the guarding, or men would be posted everywhere. Massive conspiracies were rare because it's only natural to talk, and all it takes is a little drunken bragging for government misdeeds to be revealed. It was better that only a privileged few know about something like this. That, and posting few guards probably saved money on the annual budget for maintaining the secret site.

With no sign of movement, I poked my head in. The immediate hall was empty, so I stepped inside and away from the precarious ledge. No cells lined the walls here, but I could see torchlight around the corner up ahead, and slowly crept in its direction.

The thing about orcs is that people assume because we're big and strong, we're lumbering oafs, but that's far from the case. We've lived off the land for millennia, and in that time, learned how to walk so quietly we don't even alert the rabbits we hunt.

Reaching the bend, I paused once again, listening for any signs of life. I heard a faint shuffling, a quiet snore, and the crackle of torchlight. Apparently, the electric grid didn't yet extend to secret police prisons. Peeking around the corner, I saw the single guard asleep at his post. The faint smell of Elder Lilly reached my nose, likely a dose to make Rhonwen compliant. With the stealth of a cat, I crept towards the dimly lit cell.

When she saw me, the sorceress picked up her head, opening her mouth to speak and thinking better of it when she glanced at the sleeping guard. Priority one: get her out of the cell. I brought with me a lockpick, but that could take several minutes, enough for the guard to wake up. Or I could lift the keys from his belt. It would be faster but risked waking him as well. Taking my chances with the more time-consuming option, I pulled out my lockpick, but felt a shock when I tried to set them inside. Biting back a yelp, I looked back to the guard to see if he stirred. Enchanted. Of course, the locks were enchanted. The key was likely the only thing to open it.

Pressing a finger to my lips, I looked to the guard and then the lock, hoping she'd get my meaning. She must have, because she nodded, and I reached slowly for the key ring clipped to his belt. One disadvantage to being big is that no matter how dexterous I was, my large fingers made finer actions like sleight of hand and pickpocketing more of a challenge. Scarcely daring to breathe, I unclipped the ring, gently wrapping my fingers around the keys so they wouldn't make noise and I pulled back. Bracing myself, I picked a key labeled with the number one into the lock. It turned without shocking me, and we both sighed in relief.

The cell door opened with a shriek louder than a banshee in a hospice ward, startling the guard awake.

Perfect. Just perfect. I threw open her door while he reached into the inside of his jacket. For a moment, I thought he was pulling out a gun, but instead, it was a perfume bottle. If he sprayed us, he could force her back into the cell and me to take the shorter path to the bottom of the cliffs. I punched him in the stomach, taking advantage of his momentary surprise to grab the perfume bottle. Spraying it in his face, I commanded, "Sleep."

His eyelids drooped, and he dropped to the ground like a puppet without strings. I turned to Rhonwen, who was struggling to get her legs under her. "Can you walk?"

"I can try," she said, and I pulled her close, scooping her up with one arm. Perhaps it was just the cold, but her cheeks flushed red, and I found mine warming as well.

"I hope you don't mind, but expedience is key here."

She looked away. "Yes. Uh, thank you."

"Thank me once we're out of this cave." The staircase was still there when we returned, and she wrapped her arms around my neck, clinging to me as we slowly made our way back up to the earth. I don't think I fully let out a breath until I was at the top.

"What next?" she asked.

I looked her up and down, staring at the mottled

bruises marring her skin. "We take you to a hospital. Even if you can use magic to heal yourself, it's important to go somewhere with witnesses."

She considered my words, nodding and shifting as though trying to get down. I let her get her feet, but still held her steady. Her breath came out in short hisses. "The optics of an orc bridal carrying a wounded maiden in town. . .it won't look good for you, especially with the constabulary wanting to blame you for my kidnapping."

"If you're sure," I said.

She nodded, taking a few tentative steps in the direction of the nearest hospital. "I need them to see that they didn't break me."

"You and I, we're diamonds, I think." I supported her as we made our slow trek into the bustling streets, "No matter the weight, the pressure, or the blows, we don't break."

People stopped to stare at the two of us, parting as we reached the front of the hospital building. Near the entrance was the newsstand. The paper's headline read, "Royal Sorceress Slain! King Readies Army!"

"You weren't a moment too soon with my rescue," she said as the doctors and nurses took notice of her and leapt into action. Her legs gave out under her, and I caught her in her dead faint. Lifting her up, I gently deposited her onto the wheelchair brought by one of the nurses. While the others tended to her, a nurse pulled me aside.

"Can I speak with you for a moment, er, ma'am?" I nodded and she led me into a small exam room. The nurse fidgeted, looking for all the world like she wanted to be anywhere but in a confined space with an orc. She kept glancing towards the entrance as though expecting someone to come through the door at any moment. Gesturing to the chair, she said, "Please sit. I would like to know a little more about her condition. If there's anything we should look out for, or. . ."

"That's not why you wanted to talk with me," I said, not unkindly, "You're stalling to give time for the police to arrive and arrest me."

Eyes wide with panic, she looked again to the door as though she was about to bolt at the first sign of movement. Raising my hands slowly, I took a seat on the exam chair. "It's okay. I have nothing to hide. I'm not the one who took her, and when she's coherent again, she can vouch for me. I'm not sure how much is safe to say yet, but I promise that all is not as they said it was."

A knock at the door, and a different nurse poked her head in. "Mage Rhonwen requests the orc's presence at her bedside."

The other nurse shot me an incredulous look but led me to the VIP ward. Rhonwen's arm was in a splint, and doctors busied themselves around her, magic sparking from their fingers as they healed superficial cuts and bruises. When she saw me, she gave a tired smile and gestured to the chair at her bedside. "I thought it best if we stayed together for the time being," she said as I took my seat.

"Probably wise," I replied as the room emptied of doctors. I trusted the constabulary like I would trust a fox to guard a henhouse. If we were alone, they could more easily arrest me and spin the narrative. I was an orc separatist who grew a conscience and let her go, but died resisting arrest or some nonsense story like that. They could also quietly suffocate her with a pillow, so she'd never tell of the plot and say that she died of her wounds. Alone, we were vulnerable, but they wouldn't dare attempt something when we were together.

"What now?" I asked, "We won't exactly be able to accuse the king of this conspiracy."

"I'll name the men who took me. The constabulary will probably say they worked alone, and King Elio will side with them rather than admit a part in this conspiracy. I don't have any proof that it wasn't just this small group, but I'll be sure to emphasize that you were the one who rescued me in all conversations with reporters."

The look she gave me was so affectionate that I couldn't help but avert my eyes, my cheeks warming. "That's probably as close to the truth as we can get for now," I said.

As if on cue, the door slammed open, and Constable Scrubb lead the charge into the room. "Shagra the Untangler, by order of King Elio of Arabon, you're under arrest for the kidnapping of Mage Rhonwen."

Rhonwen gave him a flat, unamused look. "No, she's not. I refuse to allow you to arrest my rescuer, especially when we all know she's innocent."

He bowed with a flourish. "My lady, I am so glad to see you've escaped the brutes with your life, but you must be confused."

Head held high, she shot him a glare so cold that the temperature in the room literally lowered. His breath came out in puffs of white steam. Her hair rose as she gathered her power. "No, Scrubb, I am not. And I'll not be silenced. You leave now, and I'll give you and your co-conspirators a ten-minute head start before I summon the Royal Guards and order your arrest. A rather generous gift, is it not, Shagra?"

I smiled, showing off my tusks. Normally, I didn't play on my more orcish traits to intimidate others — it gave them more of an excuse to fear creatures like me — but it was well worth it to watch Constable Scrubb and his men blanche in terror. "Far too generous after what they put you through, my lady."

"Then go, before I change my mind."

I jerked as though about to get up and pursue them, and they fled like children hiding behind their mother's skirts. Our eyes met and she snickered, making me laugh, and before we knew it, we'd broken down into nigh hysterical guffaws.

She winced, grabbing at her ribs and without thinking, I took her hand. "Should I get a doctor? They clearly haven't finished healing you."

Glancing down at my hand and back up at me, she stammered, "I — uh — "

"Sorry," I said, taking it back.

She snatched my wrist. "I didn't say it was an unwanted touch, Shagra." Moving her hand up so her much smaller and softer fingers intertwined with mine, she laid back on the bed, eyelids half closed. "We'll have to call upon a reporter. Let's get ahead of whatever narrative they put out."

"But first, you should rest," I said, "I can summon a friend at the paper for you to tell your story to. I owe him one, anyway."

"Stay?" she asked, her words slurring from exhaustion.

"For as long as you need," I answered, giving her hand a squeeze and watching as her eyelids closed and she drifted off into a peaceful slumber.

Kay Hanifen *was born on a Friday the 13th and once lived for three months in a haunted castle. So, obviously, she had to become a horror writer. Her work has appeared in over fifty anthologies and magazines. When she's not consuming pop culture with the voraciousness of a vampire at a 24-hour blood bank,*

you can usually find her with her two black cats or at kayhanifenauthor.wordpress.com.

Twitter: https://twitter.com/TheUnicornComi1

Instagram: https://www.instagram.com/katharinehanifen/

What Can I Getcha

Cassondra Windwalker

This forest is not a place, it is a predator. Patiently it waits for its prey, for any unwary interlopers to trespass its verges. An unwitting eye might imagine these ferns and mosses, these mushrooms and vines and blooming carpets, evidence of boundless life, but I who sit here waiting to be eaten know otherwise. The forest is an open grave, and I merely a woman becoming bones.

Only a few hours ago, a lifetime ago, a possibility ago, I was the hunter.

I pulled off the highway, rubbing blearily at my gritty eyes. I was pretty sure the last of my mascara had flaked off about a hundred miles ago. Two days of driving had my legs wobbly and my head pounding. Empty energy drink cans and peanut butter cup wrappers littered the floorboard of my car. Despair had begun creeping in around the edges of my vision like a dark cloud, but then I'd spotted it.

Her little purple jalopy, its paint chipped, its sides dented, her dad's cowboy hat in the rear window, sat in the corner of a diner parking lot. My heart kicked into gear like an organ grinder's monkey, banging and jerking. I'd finally found her.

I tried the doors, of course, half-expecting to see her sleeping in the back seat, but they were locked and the car was empty. Mostly empty, anyway. I saw her coffee tumbler in the console, a crumpled paper bag on the passenger seat, a blanket and pillow on the floorboard. My head snapped up, my gaze narrowing on the grimy windows of the low-slung diner whose formerly neon lettering proclaimed *Maddie's* in a font straight out of the 1960's. She had to be in there. So close. Maybe even watching me through that glass that, to my eyes, only reflected the tall, dark trees lining the other side of the highway.

But when I walked in and set the door bells jangling, Amalie was nowhere to be seen. At a glance, I took in the single row of booths and the counter bar that comprised the whole place. One old guy, so gray all over from his hair to the gnarled hands clutching his coffee cup that the original color of his skin was indeterminate, was the only other occupant I could see. He squinted briefly in my direction, and as quickly lost interest, returning his focus to the remains of a cherry pie on a plate in front of him. The clatter of dishes from the kitchen assured me there was at least one other person here, but I doubted Amalie was playing chef.

The bathrooms.

I checked them both, banging open stall doors, but they were empty. I even peeked in the trash cans, as if I might find some detritus that spoke of her passing by. Nothing. Faded posters with sex trafficking statistics and domestic abuse hotlines were plastered beside a condom dispenser and a safe needle disposal. How very progressive of this hole-in-the-wall of Armpit, British Columbia.

I opened the bathroom door and nearly ran slap into a woman with spiked green and black hair with little silver skulls dangling from her earlobes. She wiped her hands on an incongruously flowered apron and grinned at me, all her crooked teeth on full display.

"Seat yourself," she said, and it was an order, not an invitation. "Menus are on the table. I'll be right over."

Impatience crawled up the back of my neck, but I'd been in this business long enough to know I had to let people come around in their own way if I wanted to get anything out of them. So I trudged over to a booth and turned the plastic sheet over in my hands, trying to get my eyes to focus on the menu items long enough to pick something out.

She didn't have a notebook in her hand when she returned, and I wasn't surprised. I didn't think this place was ever busy. An unmanned gas station and a post office almost lost in the shade of the trees across the street were the only other evidence of civilization that I'd seen for miles. Amalie's car was the only one in the lot—I couldn't fathom where that old man had come from. Maybe he was only a ghost.

"Chicken club with fries," I said. "And a coffee. But first — have you seen this woman?"

I pulled a battered photo of a laughing young woman with shoulder-length blonde hair and impossibly dark eyes from my wallet. My server held it out like maybe she was farsighted and gave it a careful once-over.

"Can't say as I have. She your sister? She don't look much like you."

"Are you sure? Her car is parked in your lot."

She handed me back the photo, sticking her fists on her

hips and leaning over the table to peer out the window. "Well, would you look at that. I wonder how long that's been there."

"There's nowhere else for her to go but here."

"I don't know what to tell you, hon. I admit I don't pay much attention to faces in here. It's nonstop strangers, don't you know, pulling off the Al-Can, all on their way somewheres else. Maybe she came in and I don't remember her. Maybe she met somebody in the parking lot and went off in their car. Why you looking for her?"

I tried to keep the disbelief off my face and the irritation out of my voice. Nonstop strangers in this place? There was actual dust on the counter bar. I could see it from here. But it wouldn't do to alienate this woman just yet.

"Her name's Amalie Richardson. She went missing three days ago. Out of Kansas."

"Aw, shame. And her family's got you looking for her?"

"They're real worried. She's in danger."

"One of those bad relationships?"

I nodded.

"And here you are looking for her up on the Trail of Tears or the Highway of the Damned or whatever it is they call it. True enough women disappear along this road all the time. A travesty, what it is. I sure hope you find her. Meantime, I'll be right back with your lunch."

I watched her walk away, my appetite suddenly and unexpectedly sharp. I hadn't had a hot meal in days, and I realized I was starving. The other woman's ample hips rolled like sea breakers, but her waist was comparatively small and her arms wiry as a wrestler's. She was a study in contradictions, this woman, half-repulsive, half-compelling, and all sensual. I found myself wondering what her palms felt like, if they were soft like pillowed bread dough or calloused and sandpaper rough.

By habit, I started to run my hand through my hair and remembered too late I'd braided it back to keep it from tangling. Oh, well. A few more straggling hairs would hardly detract from my already less-than glamorous look.

Ten minutes later, a plate piled high with greasy potatoes and a burgeoning club sandwich slid onto my table. Much too fast to offer any reassurances about the quality of the cooking, but my stomach made no complaint. My server–who I was beginning to suspect was also the cook and the owner of this fine establishment–leaned a hand on the table and cocked her head at me. I noticed her nametag read *Jane*. Who was named Jane anymore? That wasn't a real name, was it? More of a placeholder for the unknown and unidentifiable.

"So, this gal went missing in Kansas and you're up in British Columbia?"

I didn't want to discourage her talking in case it turned out she did have anything helpful to say, either by accident or on purpose, but I didn't intend to waste time either. I shrugged around a big bite of my sandwich and shot a plop of ketchup into my plastic food basket. "Had reason to believe she was headed this way."

"Of her own volition? Maybe she just wanted to get away. Maybe she's leaving that bad boyfriend behind."

I hesitated, making time with a couple of fries, before deciding on tact. "She's got a delicate constitution, you could say. Even if she did leave on her own–and I'm not saying she did–she's vulnerable. It's not safe for her to be out here on the run by herself, with no resources. No plan."

"Let me see her picture again."

I dug in my pocket and handed it over. She looked at it, as intently as she had done last time.

"It's funny, ain't it. She looks so happy here. Strong. The shadows just don't show. I guess we never really know what people are struggling with. What they're hiding."

She handed it back.

"She's lucky she's got you on her trail. To make it up here this fast, with her just missing three days ago, her folks must've set you after her pretty quick. With that car out there, I bet you just missed her. I guess you've already talked to the Mounties, huh? I can call them for you, let them know her car is here. I imagine they'll want to check it out. Forensics and all that."

I shook my head. "It's a tricky situation. She's not officially a missing person. But is it okay if I leave her car there for now? It won't get towed or anything?"

Jane threw her head back and laughed, a full-belly cackle if I ever heard one. "Does it look to you like tow trucks come through here often? You don't have to worry on that score. As long as it doesn't stay out there so long the tires sink into the gravel, I guess I can leave it."

"Hopefully it won't be long. You're right—I must have just missed her. I aim to find her quick and get her back where she belongs. And I don't think she meant to abandon it—her dad's hat is still in the back, and I know she wouldn't leave that behind."

"You do, eh?" Jane gave me a long look, but her lips still smiled. "Well, I reckon I'll let you finish eating in peace."

"Wait." I held out my hand. "You mentioned maybe she met up with somebody, left with them. Did you notice anyone that might have been in here in the last day? Somebody who caught your eye? A truck driver or somebody ordering food for two to go?"

Jane shrugged, her face scrunched with uncertainty. "I really couldn't say. Nobody made an impression. People order food, I make food, they leave. I spend more time counting potatoes than memorizing faces. And almost everybody orders some food to go, even if they eat in. Next place to snag some grub is far, far down the road."

A thought gave me hope. "What about security cameras? In the restaurant, or at least in the parking lot?"

"Oh, honey. You can't be serious."

"Everybody at least has one of those Ring systems or a doorbell camera anymore."

"Everybody but Maddie's. This ain't exactly a high-risk establishment."

I sighed. "All right. Thanks for your help, anyway. I really appreciate it. My name's Dana, by the way. Dana Farmer."

"Nice to meet you, Dana. I'm Jane Doe," she said, without so much as batting an eye. I struggled not to choke. What kind of cruel joke was that for parents to play on a baby, I wondered. Takes all sorts, I suppose.

I snuck a look over my shoulder at the old man I'd spotted at the counter when I first came in. Looked like he'd eaten maybe three more crumbs of his crust since I'd come in. No reason to be in a rush, I figured. Where else could he be going? Still, I decided to talk to him now in case he surprised me and made for a quick exit.

I slid my photo of Amalie onto the counter by his coffee cup. "Hey, mister. I don't suppose you saw this woman recently, maybe yesterday?"

He barely flicked a glance at the picture. "Nope."

"Are you sure? She's missing, and her car is parked outside. Anything you might have seen would be awfully helpful."

This time he didn't even pretend to look. "I'm sure."

Grouchy old ass. What kind of person couldn't drum up a moment's compassion for a missing woman out in the middle of this godforsaken wilderness?

"Thanks," I said, unable to keep the sarcasm from dripping off the word.

"Some missing folks don't want to be found."

"And some missing folks show up dead. I'm just trying to save somebody here."

"Regular hero you are. Hero*ine.*"

I shook my head in disgust and stomped back to my booth, not trusting myself to say anything remotely helpful to the situation. Sexist grouchy old ass, I amended my earlier thought. I barely tasted the last third of my sandwich. I sucked down the last dregs of my now-tepid coffee and left forty Canadian dollars on the table. Generosity never went amiss, in my experience.

I quickened my steps when I saw a pickup truck parked at the gas pumps, but they pulled away before I could cross the street. So, I changed direction and went into the post office instead. This was for sure a long shot–it wasn't as if Amalie would have been sending a package on her way through town–but who knew? Maybe a bored clerk had been looking at the window or had crossed paths with her at the diner after work.

No dice. The bleak-faced young man behind the counter hadn't seen a thing. He possessed none of the reticence of the old man across the street, though. Poor thing was practically starved for human interaction. It took me three tries to finally get back out the door. I wondered where all the people lived whose mailboxes were lined up in neat, numbered rows in there. Must be hidden away deep in the woods that lined the narrow highway. What a lonely, desolate place this was. Beautiful, but forbidding. At least to a Kansas girl. I was used to being able to see the horizon for miles around. Here leaves and limbs crowded the sky. It was suffocating.

Amalie's car was my first real clue, and it was also a dead end. Heading this direction had been more hunch than anything, and I'd been about ready to give up and turn around by the time I made it this far. Now I finally had concrete proof I was on the right track, and no idea where to go from here.

Amalie could have hitched a ride with a complete stranger. She could have met up with someone I didn't know about, maybe someone she'd met online. Or she could have made it safely all this way only to be abducted in that parking lot. Maybe before she'd even had a chance to go in the diner, which would explain why Jane didn't recognize her. No matter what she said, I had a hard time believing anybody in the service industry could be quite as oblivious as Jane claimed to be. Once upon a time, in another life, I'd waited tables myself. Servers lived for tips, and tips came from reading people. You couldn't very well do that without ever looking at their faces. And Amalie–I dug in my pocket and pulled out her photo, tilting it to catch the dying sunlight. Amalie was memorable. She was beautiful. She shone.

I walked back over to her poor old purple beater and circled it again, looking more closely this time. I needn't have bothered. It gave up no secrets, told no tales. I even squatted down and examined the gravel as if I could decipher footprints and somehow figure out where Amalie had gone and with whom. The gravel just looked like gravel, though.

I leaned against the hood of my own car and pondered for a minute. The only real course of action I could take was to drive farther down the road to whatever came next and show Amalie's photo around there. That was an even slimmer chance than the one that had brought me this far. If Amalie had met up with someone as part of a plan, there was no reason to believe she'd have kept to the highway from here. She could be anywhere out in this wild country, down any of a hundred little backroads winding away from the Al-Can. If she'd been abducted by somebody, odds were even worse. He'd have probably done whatever he intended to do and then disposed of what was left of her, and that I'd never find in these woods.

My only real hope from here would be that for some reason she had abandoned her car and struck up with a truck driver, somebody with a reason to keep driving straight. Somebody I might find at a gas station or a truck stop along the way.

It didn't seem likely. Maybe there was something wrong with her vehicle; maybe it wouldn't start, but I was sure she'd have grabbed her dad's hat out of the back before she threw in her lot with a stranger. Her dad had died when she was ten, and she dragged that cowboy hat with her everywhere she went since. Besides a few photos, it was all she really had of him. My gut told me Amalie hadn't gone anywhere. She was still here.

And if that was the case, odds were good that friendly Jane and the crotchety geezer were lying about not having seen her. I didn't know why they would. I didn't much care, either. But I was sure they were.

I climbed back in my car, pushed my seat back, and pulled a blanket from the back seat over myself. Sleep would be no problem. I was exhausted. The sign on the door said the diner closed at eight. Seemed early, but it didn't look like they'd be exactly turning away business. Once the place shut down, I'd do some serious snooping. In the meantime, I could grab a little shuteye.

I underestimated my fatigue, as it turned out. By the

time I woke up, it was ten o'clock at night, and the parking lot's one dim yellow light barely diminished the utter blackness. Across the street, I could see a bulb lighting up the Canadian flag in front of the post office, and the canopy over the gas pumps next door was illuminated, too. But rather than quelling my unease, the false lights only heightened it. The solitude, the loneliness, was inescapable.

I made sure my interior lights were shut off and crept out of my car, closing the door as quietly as possible. Not a breath of wind stirred. I winced as every step I took on the gravel parking lot sounded like popcorn going off.

As I made my way to the back of the restaurant, I saw light oozing under the back door and heard low, feminine voices. I froze, straining, but I couldn't make them out. I inched closer, nearly falling over myself when the door swung open without warning.

It all happened so fast.

The light from the kitchen shone full on my face, nearly blinding my night-adjusted eyes. I caught a glimpse of Jane's face, a flash of furious movement, and then a crashing pain in my head brought all the darkness tumbling down.

I woke up hogtied in the backseat of a vehicle that tore over ruts and bumps at top speed. My head was pounding, and it took me an unreasonable amount of time to realize the vehicle was my own. No gag. No blindfold. For which I was momentarily grateful, but that certainly didn't bode well for my survival chances.

"Jane?" I forced out, my mouth all cottony with the sudden dehydration of real terror.

She shot me a quick look before redirecting her attention to the road.

"That's right, Dana. I'd say I'm sorry it's come to this, but that's not really true."

None of the good cheer and charm I'd heard in her voice earlier today. The woman actually sounded like she *hated* me. I couldn't fathom why. My brain scrambled to make sense of what was happening.

The passenger seat was empty, but I was sure there had been another woman with Jane when I'd surprised her. Or when she'd surprised me, I wasn't sure which. And I was almost certain Amalie had been that other woman. If only I'd been able to focus a tiny bit clearer. . .

"Why?" I asked. "What did I do to you? And where's Amalie?"

Jane laughed, but this time the sound chilled me to my bones. "Don't you worry about her. She's behind us in her own car. You won't be seeing her again, though."

"What is happening? I'm trying to help her. To save her. To bring her home."

"You think you're pretty smart with your detective schtick, don't you? But honey, you're just one more abuser. Nothing special about you. And I've dispatched plenty of your type over the years. I admit, they've almost all been men, but I'm equal opportunity."

"Amalie is sick," I tried. "She needs her medication. She needs help."

"You mean she needs you. You can't play me, Dana Farmer. I've been doing this a long, long time. I made you from the minute you walked into my diner."

The car jerked to a stop. Jane opened the back door and pulled me out by my feet. I tried to keep my head elevated, but it banged agonizingly on the jamb of the door and then on the ground. The pain muddied my thoughts. She dragged me across the ground. A second set of headlights shone into the forest where she'd brought me, and I heard the familiar chugga-chugging of the little purple car.

"Amalie!" I yelled at the top of my lungs. "Amalie! I love you! Baby, I'm not going to hurt you. I just wanted to tell you I'm sorry. Amalie!"

"She's not going to listen to you," Jane said, untroubled. "She's been out from under your spell much longer than you realize. It just took her a while to actually leave."

I squirmed as best I could, but the ropes only cut more tightly, and it was hard to breathe. Jane stopped and went behind me. I could feel her working with the ropes, but they didn't loosen. Then she disappeared a few yards into the dark. She was humming as she did something in the brush.

She returned quickly enough, and a quick downward motion released my ankles from my wrists. I shot my legs straight out, the relief immense and followed quickly by agony as blood poured freely back down through my veins. I gritted my teeth and tried to caterpillar over the ground. Rationally, I knew there was no getting away, but the body can't help but fight. Immediately, I realized what she'd been doing. My bound feet were now tied fast to some tree trunk I couldn't see. She seized my wrists still twisted behind my back and hauled me over to a second tree where she propped me up into a sitting position, my legs now stretched taut in front of me.

"Amalie! Amalie! I love you. Don't let her do this. You know I love you. She doesn't even know you. Not like I do."

Jane stuck her face in mine and shook her head. "Oh, Dana. You've got the wrong end of the stick. This isn't some love affair. I run a sort of underground railroad for battered women. Where better for an abused woman to disappear than along the most dangerous highway for women on the continent? And on the off chance some abuser follows—well, the woods take care of them for us."

I didn't know what she meant then, but I do now. In that moment, though, I quit trying to make sense of what she said. Pure panic bubbled through every cell in my body. All my energy was focused on Amalie. God only knows what I said or cried or screamed. Meanwhile, Jane kept at her task, undeterred by my noise or my struggles. There was no doubt she spoke true: she'd done this before.

Then, through the panic, a single thought shone through like salvation. "That old man," I wheezed. "He saw me. He'll tell the cops I was here."

Jane snickered. "Old Man Pete? His sister was murdered by her husband fifty years ago. He runs the salvage yard where we trade out vehicles so my girls can disappear. You just happened to show up a little earlier than we were expecting. But no fear on that account. He won't say a word. The cops never did his sister no good."

Once she had me fully tied to the tree behind me, my arms splayed, she crouched down beside me. "This next part will seem kinda cruel," she warned me. "But from my point of view, it helps hurry things along. These woods are practically a rainforest, you know. Lush. In no time at all, you'll be part of it. And I admit, I'm not merciful by nature."

She took that long, wicked sharp blade and slit me open like sausages. My arms. My legs. My belly. Screaming, choking, blind with pain and shock, I prayed she'd slit my throat next, but she didn't.

She'd been right. I didn't see Amalie again. Jane disappeared into the headlights. A car door closed. The engine whined as Amalie turned her vehicle around, and then it was just me and my car and the woods and the pain.

I'm not alone now, though. All sorts of insects have

joined me. Some strange little mammals that look like fat round mice. Magpies and crows. My only hope is that a bear or a wolf will come and end this swiftly. How the eater longs to be eaten.

∽

Cassondra Windwalker is an award-winning poet, essayist, and novelist who has lived across the US from Oklahoma to Alaska and written in the cafes of Paris and Vietnam and on the beaches of Madagascar. Her favorite writing companions are cats, but she accepts visits from wandering ghosts and anyone who will bring her coffee. Her work includes two full-length poetry collections, THE ALMOST-CHILDREN *and* TIDE TABLES AND TEA WITH GOD, *as well as the award-winning collection on social justice amid the pandemic*, THE BENCH. *She's also the author of seven novels*: PARABLE OF PRONOUNS, BURY THE LEAD, PREACHER SAM, IDLE HANDS, HOLD MY PLACE, LOVE LIKE A CEPHALOPOD, *and* WHAT HIDES IN THE CUPBOARDS. *She enjoys interacting with readers and generally decent humans across social media.*

When the Evidence Leads Upstate

Michelle Kaseler

I was on my third cup of coffee when she came into the station: early thirties, salon highlights, and the same style of Lululemon yoga pants I wore on my days off. She had the look of a badge bunny, but not the demeanor. When she took a seat across from my partner, Higgins, I couldn't help but listen.

"So, let me get this straight." Higgins stroked his beard. It had been salt and pepper when I'd started eight years ago — now it was more salt and sugar. "You're here because some guy you hooked up with didn't call you back?"

"He wasn't some random hookup." She met his pointed gaze without flinching. "We've been chatting at the park for the last couple of months. Every weekday morning, like clockwork. Our sons enjoy playing together."

"But then you go out for dinner, end up back at his place, and when he doesn't show up at the swing set for a couple days, somehow it's a police matter?"

She folded her arms across her chest. "We had a nice time."

Higgins leaned back in his chair. "You wouldn't be the first woman who got blown off by a guy who said he had 'a nice time.'"

"Look, he hasn't answered my calls or my texts. I even knocked on his door."

Higgins raised an eyebrow.

"My son wanted to see Ralphie. That's his boy's name." She twisted her blonde hair, pulling her ponytail askew. "He's some kind of day trader, so he's home most of the time. But today he wasn't, even though his car was there."

"He went for a walk. He was in the shower. Or *maybe*," — Higgins drew out the words — "he wanted to be left alone. Unless you can give me some reason to suspect foul play, it's not the job of the department to hunt down every guy who disappears after a one-night stand."

Higgins offered her his card, but she didn't take it.

"I won't take up any more of your time, but if something happens that you could have prevented, maybe you'll end up needing my services." She tossed a card of her own on his desk and walked away.

Higgins picked up her card and shook his head. "Shrinks."

Most of the folks who came in were sobbing, cursing, or some combination of both. My gut told me she wasn't the kind of woman to worry for no reason.

I rose from my chair and hurried after her. "Ma'am?"

"Yes?" She had a china doll smile: smooth, cool, and fragile.

"Brynne Nixon." I extended my hand.

"Lara Peterson."

"I know my partner has all the warmth of a Russian winter, but there isn't a better detective in Los Angeles. If something happened to your friend, he'll get to the bottom of it."

"Happened. Past tense." Her lower lip quivered. "I just know something's not right."

"Don't assume anything yet. I'll ask patrol to drive by his house, knock on the door."

"Thank you," Lara said with a loud exhale. "This may be the first time in my life I've wanted to be wrong."

~

A trio of gang bangers occupied my attention for the next couple hours. I had just started to update the case file when the patrol officer called.

"Nixon? It's Davies. Something's definitely not right. After we knocked, and no one answered, Johnson noticed the Luigi's Pizza flyer stuck on the door. Their flyers always come out on Tuesdays, so we figure the guy hasn't been home in at least a day. The Camry's sitting out front, like the lady said. When we knocked harder, I noticed it kind of rattled around, like it wasn't locked." He paused. "I was right."

"Go on." I rapped my fingers on the desk. Higgins and I called Davies "The Farmer" for his ability to milk a story.

"So, we go in and find two bowls of soggy cornflakes on the kitchen table and one of the chairs flipped over. The one with the booster seat is pulled back just a little. On the ground, there's a broken glass and half-dried puddle of tomato juice. We check all the rooms, and the rest of the house is like my mother-in-law."

"Reeking of gin and freesia?"

"No, Nixon," he chides. "Lights are on, but there ain't nobody home."

When the Evidence Leads Upstate

I cover the phone's mouthpiece and groan. "Did anything else seem strange?"

"Other than the kitchen, the house is immaculate. We're locking the scene now."

Higgins and I drove right over. Upon arrival, we examined the windows and doors.

"No sign of forced entry," he said.

"He either knew the perps, or they were pros." I furrowed my brow. "Or both."

I entered the master bedroom. A leather wallet filled with cash and credit cards lay on the dresser. I studied the man's driver's license: Jordan Baylor, thirty-two, five-eleven and one eighty-five. Not a bad photo either. Much nicer than my last few dates. Maybe I should start hanging out at the playground.

I handed the license to the patrol officer and continued searching for evidence. Pictures of a chubby, brown-eyed, smiling toddler cluttered the hallway, but they all appeared to have been taken within the last year. There wasn't a single baby photo.

The kid's bedroom was decorated in a safari motif. A stuffed lion sat on the perfectly made bed and books filled the shelves. There was also a separate playroom containing a climbable plastic castle, complete with a slide, a toddler-friendly laptop, and half a dozen musical instruments. Both rooms were worthy of an HGTV pictorial.

Higgins entered the room. "Something weird here, Nix. I ran that name and DOB and all that came up was a woman who died six years ago."

"Identity theft?" Even though we were iffy on the how, where, and why, I'd thought we at least knew *who* we were looking for. "Davies," I called the patrol officer over, "I'm going to need you to run his prints."

My phone rang. Lara. "They found Ralphie, but he's

not Ralphie. He's Dennis. *Dennis Carlton.* It's all over the news."

I almost dropped the phone. Just over a year ago, Dennis Carlton, the two-year-old son of Silicon Valley millionaires, had been snatched from a park while his teenage brother flirted with a girl. That case had never gotten as much airplay as JonBenet Ramsey or Elizabeth Smart, but there had been a couple of months where my true crime-obsessed Mom wouldn't shut up about it.

I found the Carlton press conference on my smartphone. They'd aged since the kidnapping, but there was no mistaking those patrician features and ice-blue eyes.

The neatly coiffed matriarch held the boy on her hip while the father stood next to her, resting a hand on her shoulder. Lester, the older son, stood off to the side, looking dazed. Barely even twenty, he had the scabbed and droopy skin of a long-term addict.

"I never gave up." Tears trickled down Mrs. Carlton's face as she kissed the top of Dennis's head. "Everyone told me it was hopeless, friends, family, police, but I hired the best private investigators money could buy. And today we got our Denny back."

"Lester" — a reporter shoved the microphone under the older son's fidgety lips — "tell us how you're feeling."

"I. . . I was sure he was gone forever." Lester's voice trembled.

Mrs. Carlton shifted and handed Dennis to her husband. Mr. Carlton's face tightened as he took the boy.

"No!" Dennis tried to wriggle away.

"There, there." Mrs. Carlton took her son back. He quickly burrowed under her jacket. "I'm going to have to cut this short. Dennis is exhausted and so are we."

The screen cut back to the newsroom where the

When the Evidence Leads Upstate

anchors interviewed the private investigator who found Dennis.

". . .gas leak and he let me right in. I point out the birthmark on the kid's arm, and he starts getting twitchy. Once I mention who really sent me, he split."

"Do you have any idea what happened to the alleged kidnapper?" The anchor asked.

"Nah. My job was to get the kid, so I wasn't going to leave him. I called Mrs. C. right away, and she sent a private jet to pick us up. That's some ritzy" — network bleep — "right there."

I turned to Higgins. "Dennis couldn't wait to get away from his father. Mr. Carlton didn't exactly look comfortable with his boy, either."

"A rich man like that might not spend much time at home." Higgins shrugged. "Maybe he never bonded with the kid."

My phone rang. The station. "Jordan Baylor is really Joshua Markham. No record, but he had prints taken when he volunteered with Big Brothers Big Sisters."

"It looks like being a big brother was no longer enough," Higgins said.

~

Back at the precinct, we learned Joshua Markham had been a self-employed geek-for-hire in San Francisco: setting up Wi-Fi, removing viruses, that sort of thing.

"Jordan Baylor opened his investment account with half a million dollars," Higgins said.

I whistled. "That's a lot of cash for a freelancer."

Higgins' phone rang. "San Francisco area code."

He didn't say much in the two minutes on the phone,

but his eyes alternated between wide open and suspiciously narrowed.

When he hung up, he turned to me. "The Carltons aren't interested in pursuing the kidnapper. There was never a ransom request, the kid was healthy, well-fed, and there were no signs of abuse. They're just happy to have him back and want to put this whole thing behind them. The family has ties to the commish, and we've been told to drop it."

I arched my eyebrows. "Oh really?"

"While I have nothing but admiration for our counterparts up north," Higgins said, "Markham lived in *our* jurisdiction when he was reported missing by one of *our* concerned citizens. I'm going where the evidence leads."

"Even if it leads to a commissioner's buddy?"

"Especially if it leads to a commissioner's buddy." Higgins grinned as he picked up his sport coat. "I think we need to revisit the crime scene."

I grinned back. "I like how you're now referring to the reporting party as a 'concerned citizen.'"

"I'm wrong exactly once a year, Nix," he said as we walked toward the parking lot. "You can question my judgment again in January."

"Something obviously went down." Brian, one of the CSU guys, briefed us as we stood around the kitchen table. "Still, there's no sign anyone was hurt, and the chair and glass could have fallen over when the PI confronted Markham."

"But why did he leave his car?" Higgins asked.

I shrugged. "We're close to a bus station."

"Point taken." Higgins scratched his beard as he looked

around the room. "That glass of tomato juice flew pretty far. Also, it made a nice, round puddle, where I'd expect the edges to be more... spidery."

I snapped my fingers and pointed at him. "Like it was spilled after the fact to cover something up?"

"Would luminol pick up blood mixed with tomato juice?" Higgins asked.

"Yes. Although, if it's a Bloody Mary," Brian said, "it won't necessarily mean anything because luminol also reacts strongly to horseradish."

"Don't we all," Higgins murmured as he crouched down and sniffed. "Definitely not a Bloody Mary."

But it was, we soon discovered, definitely bloody.

After CSU bagged and tagged the evidence, we all headed back to the station. It would take a while to run DNA, but since the kid and the PI appeared to be fine, my money said the blood was Markham's.

"It would be understandable if Markham fought back after being confronted by the PI," Higgins said while driving, "and it would explain the blood. It's not a crime to defend yourself, so why would the PI lie if everything was above board?"

"He also seemed like the type who would enjoy bragging about besting someone in a fight."

"I agree." Higgin sighed. "But it's still not enough to call San Fran."

"Don't forget the Carltons, who would have reason to rough up or even kill the person who ran off with their child, don't seem like the type to get their own hands dirty," I said. "But we still don't know why Joshua

Markham kidnapped Dennis in the first place. Or how he got that half million."

Higgins' phone rang. "The Carltons paid Joshua Markham several times while he was in their employ, but just a few hundred bucks a pop. He had twenty Gs in the bank before the kidnapping went down."

"I'd like to get my hands on the Carlton's financials," I said.

Sighing, Higgins scratched the back of his neck. "I've dealt with these kinds of people before. You can't get within ten feet of them without evidence, and in order to get evidence. . ."

"So, let's focus on finding Joshua Markham," I said.

"For all we know, he's already assumed a new identity." Higgins yawned. "Sorry."

"It's getting late, and you're not as young as you used to be. What do you say we contact the local hospitals and call it a night?"

"I'd love to argue with you, Nix, but — " Higgins' phone rang. "The precinct."

"No rest for the wrinkled."

He glared at me before answering his phone. "*What?* We're on our way."

My pulse quickened. "What's going on?"

"Joshua Markham's mother is at the precinct."

Ellen Markham was waiting in one of the interrogation rooms. Her dark brown eyes, the same shade as her son's, were puffy and bloodshot. A microcassette answering machine, the likes of which I hadn't seen in a decade, sat on the table in front of her.

"He called yesterday," she said. "I was on a cruise with some girlfriends and didn't get the message until about an hour ago. Then I turned on the news. . ." She choked on a sob as she pressed play.

Mom, it's Josh.

We strained to hear his voice over the rumbles.

I think. . . I'm in. . . trunk. . . not gonna make it, but. . . I had to tell you. . . I love you. And I'm sorry. There's a letter. . .

His words became slower and more garbled.

Home. . . net. . . were. . . you. . . it's. . . inside.

We listened to another minute of what sounded like engine noise before the machine cut the message off.

"We haven't been close," Ellen sniffed. "When I remarried, I had a daughter with special needs who took up most of my time. I know he was resentful, but Josh was always so smart and able to take care of himself. Not to mention, my second husband could be demanding, and Josh got angry that I didn't take his side more often. We've long since split up, but Josh never forgave me."

I offered her a tissue.

After she wiped her eyes, she continued, "He moved out as soon as he turned eighteen and we've barely spoken since. I know I sound like a terrible mother, but I had my hands full with his sister and going back to work."

Talking to grieving loved ones was the hardest part of the job, and since Higgins was about as soothing as a chemical peel, I broke the silence. "We're very sorry about your son and are doing everything in our power to figure out what happened."

"Thank you." She broke down again. "Lord knows there's nothing else I can do for him."

I stared at the notepad on my desk.

Letter. Home. Net.

I'd underlined the words half a dozen times in an attempt to jump-start my tired brain. "He hid a letter, but where?"

"I didn't notice any nets in the home." Higgins played the tape again.

home. . . net. . . were. . .

"Were is past tense," he said. "Maybe the net isn't there anymore."

"What if he wasn't saying were, but work?" I asked "Network. He was an IT guy after all."

"One of the techs is already working on the computer."

"But he didn't say computer. Granted, he was struggling to say anything, but maybe there's a hard drive or some other device hooked up to the network at the house."

"Let's go back," Higgins said. "It beats sitting around here."

∼

A search of the office and master bedroom produced a Kindle tablet. I swiped the screen. Damn. Password protected.

"Maybe the IT guys can do something with it," Higgins said. "I don't see anything else in here."

"We still haven't checked the kid's room or the playroom."

We looked under the bed and in the closet. Higgins couldn't squeeze into the castle playset, so I crawled inside. I fit. Barely. No electronics, though.

When the Evidence Leads Upstate

Higgins had to pull me out. Leaning against it, I examined the bookshelf. It contained a mix of classics like *Cat in the Hat* and newer books I'd never heard of like *Seahorses Send Selfies*. On top of the shelf, far beyond a child's reach, was *Home Networks: A Professional's Guide.*

"Home Networks. Seems out of place in a toddler's room, doesn't it?" I picked it off the shelf.

"Especially for a neat freak like Markham."

I opened the book and found a letter.

To whom it may concern:

My name is Joshua Markham, but I have been living as Jordan Baylor since Dennis Carlton went missing. During the five years I worked for the family, Mrs. Carlton and I had an affair. She wanted to stay with her husband, and that suited me just fine. I eventually became her son Lester's private tutor.

Dennis was born during this time, but since we were always careful, I didn't think anything of it. But when Lester and I started studying genetics, we realized that brown-eyed Dennis probably wasn't the child of his blue-eyed parents. A paternity test confirmed it.

I started dropping in on Dennis during my visits. He was such a happy baby. Clever, too. While I started falling in love with my boy, Lester grew resentful about splitting his inheritance with a half-brother. I don't even remember who came up with the idea to stage a kidnapping. He offered me seed money to start a new life, but when he tried milking his trust fund, his father found out. Rather than punish his son, he gave me half a million dollars and a new identity on the condition I moved far away and never contacted them again.

I've kept my end of the bargain, but I'm not sure I trust them to uphold theirs.

We sat silently, absorbing his words.

"It looks like Joshua Markham and the Carlton men forgot one thing," I said.

"What's that?" Higgins asked.

"That a mother will never stop looking for her child," I said.

"I think we finally have enough to call San Francisco."

∽

Michelle Kaseler *is a software engineer by trade, but can be whatever she wants to be when she reads and writes. She enjoys funky shoes, hot sauces, and long runs. Her short fiction has been published by* Flame Tree, Daily Science Fiction, *and* NewMyths.com. *Stop by* www.storycobbler.com *to learn more.*

Angelita's Night Out
Robert Richter

I

Mostly, it was just a matter of timing. Ten minutes before he walked into Juan Carlos' Iguana Bar, I had been thinking of drifting down toward Old Town just to see if anything was left of it under the booming pressure of new high-rise construction going on. Had I left, he still would have died, only my life would have gone on as usual – if I have such a thing as a usual life.

Bored as I was, I let Juan Carlos point out my booth in the back that was still making do as my informal office in Puerto Vallarta. He was a kid on Spring Break. It didn't take much imagination to know his trouble would be about a woman, a girl, from my aging perspective. He sat down across the table from me with a cat-who-ate-the-canary grin and blue eyes lit up like he knew that what he was doing was foolish and wild. He had freckles, for God's sake. With the strawberry blond hair trimmed and styled, he looked as Kansan as a cornfield.

He said, "You're this guy named Algo?" A question with a doubt in the tone that any such thing could exist.

I said, "Okay."

"Someone tells me you can help find people."

"Who tells you such things?"

"A bartender down in Old Town?" Another question.

"For whatever it says, I know a lot of bartenders in Old Town. You get a name?"

He named a name I trusted. Later, when the jam got sticky, I backtracked and asked. It would turn out that the kid never got my name from him. But I took his reference on faith at that first and only meeting and never double-checked. My mistake. Sometimes I get caught up in that sleepy time Vallarta, nothing-much-happens-here mentality, and I get careless.

He gave me that aw, shucks, hayseed grin with a good dose of self-mockery and said, "I know it's like totally crazy, but basically last year about this time I met this woman, this incredibly beautiful Latina. You know, at some bar downtown, and we hit it off, I thought. Hell! I know we did! We hung out all night and nothing, you know, happened of *that* kind, partly because this fairly big guy — her cousin — was always hanging around us and discouraging things.

"Well, the short of it is, time is up, but we promised to meet again this year. Same time, same place, same thing. – I know, I know, sounds hokey as shit, movie shit! But I thought it was real."

I could fill in the appropriate lines: he showed up this year, and of course, she didn't. He wasn't surprised. He knew from the start it was a definite possibility, but she had even given him a picture with her own promises.

"A lot can change in a year in Mexico, friend. Especially these days. If she wasn't there, it's because she didn't

Angelita's Night Out

want to be. Maybe it was real for her too, at the time, but things look different in tomorrow's light, or in a month or two, or a year later." Maybe she was even doing him a favor, I thought. I tried to discourage him, but in a nice way. I've mellowed. Twenty years earlier and hearing a version of the same story, I would have just laughed at him, bought him a beer, and maybe even shown him where someone just as fine and alluring could be found this year. Nowadays, I try to be a little more sympathetic, yet tell it like it is in a fatherly way. This kid wasn't even half my age. It was like letting him know there wasn't any Santa Claus.

But his story – he called himself Elijah Connors – veered from the usual inane cliché right here, with her picture. When the señorita didn't appear – she called herself Angelita – Eli from Kansas showed the picture of Angelita – from north of the Nayarit, she said – to the bartender who he recognized as having worked there the year before and being on friendly, conversational terms with Angelita's cousin. The bartender had gotten really testy, had snatched the picture and ripped it up, and had the bouncer throw him out with the warning not to return.

Elijah Connors showed me a couple of abrasions on his arms, a puffy red place on his left cheek where he said the bartender had punched him. The hayseed wasn't that roughed up. Maybe a couple of bruises passed as violence in Kansas. In PV that would pass as a friendly pat on the back in some circles. On the other hand, the beating wasn't the usual response to the lead-in, "I'm looking for this girl. . ."

Connors showed me her photo then. He had copies. Made me think that he had already prepared for a search. And the girl in the photo? Okay. No doubt any guy worth his *cajones* would make an effort to find this beauty. Mayan long hair and Spanish green eyes, the slight twist of a colonial and pre-possessing half-smile, the tilt of her sharp chin, proud and haughty. Her pose was a turning toward the camera, her hair flaring out with the motion of her twist and a mischievous grin showing as if the photographer was in on a surprise or a joke about to be sprung. She was framed from the breasts up. Nice breasts. In the background beyond her shoulder, in the upper left part of the six-by-four picture, were the out of focus profiles of others in the room holding drinks and talking, suggesting that it was snapped at some party. There was nothing giving a clue as to where the photo had been taken.

"Did you take the picture?" I asked.

"No," the kid said. "She gave it to me, kind of slipped it to me like a memento to remember her by. I don't think she wanted her cousin to know that she gave it to me. You know what I mean?"

I gave it to him in straight terms as it looked to me. There are a lot of different social and economic strata in Mexico, from actual destitute begging mothers to some of the richest women in the world. Even in resort towns like PV, the strata coexist and collide. Social and financial and political pecking orders work their way through day-to-day life.

I said, "There are some well-to-do businessmen and their families who hold and demand of their members strict social guidelines. I was once — in my youth — apologized to by a young Tepic socialite I had chanced to get to know one wild weekend. She told me she couldn't take me into her house, even though I was gringo, because of the way I was dressed, in the white muslin pants and *huarache* sandals of the Nayarit peasant. Even if her parents weren't home, the maids would know and tell them." I told him that his Angelita was probably the daughter of a very rich

Jalisco businessman or *politico,* or both. That she was probably forbidden anything like she pulled by going out to a PV Old Town nightclub on her own. She somehow got a family member to take her, though he didn't like the idea at all. She had some inside family leverage on him, probably.

"So, like I said before, she probably came to her senses, or her parents found out anyway and put a stop to it, or maybe she's doing the same thing some other place to some other gullible guy."

Connors replied that he felt sure she had been serious, that she wanted to change her life. "We talked," he said as if this were something taboo or rare. "She really wanted to be with me. We spent a lot of time whispering about ways to ditch her cousin."

I just sat back and smiled at his eager, apple pie look of faith. What more could I say? I suppose true love happens in Vallarta once in a century or so, but this scenario wasn't coming close to a hint of such a thing. I didn't, and still don't, believe in movies.

Then he said, "Look, you don't have to believe what I believe. Just help me locate her, and I'll find out for myself."

I was just shaking my head.

Then he said, "I'll give you five hundred bucks if you'll look for a couple of days."

Well, like I said, he seemed like a nice enough boy at the time.

II

Roxy's was a too dark, too loud, too crowded pickup palace in those days, frequented by the Spring Break mob, recent divorcees and their Mexican gigolo pursuers, and the nightly walk-in tourist trade. If you wanted to let loose and dance, to see and be seen, to do the tequila tangle on the

PV night scene, Roxy's was one of the hotspots. The management sometimes brought in name bands to keep the place crowded and buzzing with party possibilities, the dance floor full, and the hookup game moving to the tropical beat and mood.

Never my kind of place, even when I wasn't aging into the look of Mister Silver-Haired Retired Dentist in the loud shirt and gawky jewelry set, working the nightclub on the prowl for anything he can get, still believing he can and that it's not the money they smell. There were a few of those guys around too, drifting through the crowd, sizing up the possible partners for the last chance primal meeting dance. In the mixed crowd were the dressed-to-the-nines young Mexican couples, eager to show off their money in resort style. It was a regular Old Town barroom crowd working hard at having fun.

I had gotten in by showing an ID at the door to the bouncer who had punched Connors a few times and thrown him out on his ass the night before. A tattoo of a spider on his left-side jugular made his ID easy. He was big for a Mexican, but that's a job requirement. Size is a looming warning in a bouncer, but his bulk was mostly taco soft, prone to luxury. As tall as me and a hundred pounds heavier, he could damage a few drunk college kids, but no one who was really ready for him. He dismissed me with a nod toward the open room.

The silhouetted band writhed on the bandstand above a dance floor that seemed to move en masse like kelp under dark water. Beyond the bodies, bunched tables and occupied chairs faded back into the dimness. To the left in an alcove was the bar itself, the only well-lit area of the place. Two fine-looking Latinas with their breasts bulging from black halter tops and a guy with sideburns and Zorro's pencil mustache scrambled behind the counter, mixing margaritas and opening Coronas. He had good upper body tone that he showed off under a tight black T-shirt. The bar stools were all full, and I ordered a Modelo from one of the waitresses shouldering by me. I watched the bartenders work while I decided how to play it.

The kid had wanted to be straightforward. I would be his local "adult" reference. I'd explain how the kid was sincere and give the bartender a letter to give to the cousin to give to Angelita. Connors had connected the cousin and the bartender as friends, and maybe that was why Roxy's had been chosen as her field of play. The cousin had mostly sat at the far end of the bar that night the year before, talking to the barman when he drifted over during his breaks. I was for shadowing the barkeeper, following him after work and being a little more persuasive in a private way. Roxy's was his territory. He could easily have me taken care of, or have the bouncer try. I'd make a scene bouncing the bouncer, and we wouldn't be any farther along toward reaching Connors' true love. A dark Vallarta alcove or a deserted street is more my territory, or at least neutral territory, some place where a sincere conversation can take place. Or I could do both. I kind of wanted to bounce the bouncer. Sometimes there is an opportunity to teach someone the error of his expectations. And creating a real scene might be something serious enough to bring the cousin back into the drama to stem the growing collateral damage.

Finally, I got the vacated stool at the end of the bar where the cousin had sat – Angelita had called her escort "Romano," when addressing him, but always in a taunting kind of way. At least it had seemed that way to Connors when he heard any exchange of words between them during the night he had met them. I had made Connors tell me in as minute detail as possible what had happened that evening and what exact words had been exchanged, so I could listen for clues to who Angelita might be, or where she might be from. The name of a town, or a street, or a bar would likely mean a lot more to me than to him. I didn't just saunter into the saloon like a Texas president talking trash and guns blasting. I prepared.

So, the cousin is Romano, or maybe not, and the bartender is Beto, who looks down the bar for Romano's okay each time before handing Angelita her next Margarita. After one such exchange Angelita had leaned in with a smile and snickered, "Beto knows he shouldn't be letting me get drunk, but Beto is Romano's little burro."

She had thought that funny and giggled and said loud enough for Beto to hear, "Beto, el burrito." He didn't do anything but move and go on mixing his drinks farther down the bar. And then she whispered, "And Romano is my burrito."

Connors asked, "Isn't a burrito something you eat?" She had laughed and patted his cheek. He asked, "Well, how does this bartender know he shouldn't let you drink?"

Angelita had told him that the bartender had once worked for her father and that his sister still did. "Little burros," she said. "Burritos. They are the ones who carry a load both ways. Beto thinks if he doesn't serve me, I will have his sister fired. But if my father ever finds out, they'll probably both lose their jobs." Connors was rightly amazed. She confided, "That's why I must be so careful. I can't tell you anything more."

Beto was the weak link. Whatever happened now, he was going to lose something. I nursed a Corona that wasn't cold when I got it and watched him work a while. It was before midnight and the dance floor was still full, but around the bar and tables, the loners and curious had begun to drift out. When Beto was ducking into a cooler behind the bar and just below me, I said, "This is where Romano sits when he comes in, isn't it?" He paused a beat too long before he raised a blank face to look at me.

"Excuse me, señor?"

I spat it out in Spanish then. "You know, Romano with the beautiful cousin. If you give me his name or just get him to meet me somewhere, you still may not lose your job."

He growled back, "Who the fuck are you, man?"

"Just a guy wanting to see true love run its course."

"You need to get out of here fast, old man, or you'll get hurt."

"You're not going to raise hell with customers two nights in a row, are you? Management won't like that." On my periphery I could sense the bouncer's bulk pushing through the crowd toward me. He had been silently signaled.

"Just give her cousin a message to meet me in the lobby of the Oro Verde Hotel any time tomorrow."

"There ain't no cousin, man. You don't know what the fuck you're talking about." The bouncer was five steps away, shoving people to the side.

"Just give him the message."

"Oh, he got the first message, amigo." He looked past my shoulder at what was coming on. I pirouetted inside the bouncer's first reach and drove my elbow up against his scowling jaw. His teeth clanked like a slammed steel door, and his eyes rolled up in their sockets as he staggered back. The crowd drew back and let him drop into a growing puddle. I turned back to the bar, but Beto was long gone out the back, a flung open door still swinging behind the bar.

Time to go. I jumped the bar and followed Beto through a hallway, another door, then a long galley kitchen, dodging two cooks in clouds of greasy steam and a waitress with a tray of empty glasses that didn't survive the rush. The last open door led out to an open-air alcove were Beto was crawling up an eight-foot wooden fence. He was halfway over when I caught his legs in a two-armed lock and dragged him down as he screamed and kicked, hung up on the fence top.

"Come on, Beto, give me something."

"We're dead men, *whey*. We're both dead men," he screamed down at me.

"Give me a name, Beto. Who is the girl?" He was still struggling, but I was dragging him down. "Who's the guy who isn't her cousin, amigo. Let's trade."

He yelled, "Ask him yourself. He went after your friend."

I let him go and was over the fence before he was, running a dark street for the Hotel Oro Verde on Amapas, seven or eight blocks away.

III

Calle Amapas is at the far end of Old Town, a narrow-cobbled lane perpendicular to Los Muertos Beach a hundred yards beyond the Hotel Oro Verde. An older, four-star, five-story whitewashed resort hotel, it catered to the college crowd with package deals, but was moving toward the rainbow crowd with more money to spend and fewer destructive tendencies. Quiet couples, heads down, were fleeing a noisy reality when I arrived. The red and blue flashes of a city patrol car whirled against the shadows and glass street fronts. A couple of drunks jabbered with wild gestures in front of friends. There was a sense of somber reality slapping drunks sober as I moved into the lobby against the exiting crowd. A siren could be heard now in the distance. I saw cops and hotel staff across the lobby and in the swimming pool patio area. The hotel's interior loomed up around the poolside scene, each floor with a balustraded aisle accessing the room doors where still other partiers gazed down in mesmerized awe. I caught the gist of it from the snippet of voices I pushed through. A drunken kid had fallen from the fifth floor balcony, where there wasn't even a party going on, and speared himself on the pole of an umbrella table next to the pool, injuring one of the persons who had been sitting there.

I didn't go out onto the patio to identify the body. I went out looking for someone who didn't belong there, but I was half an hour too late. Shock had set in. Nobody was even sure yet who Connors was, or who he had been with. Cops were talking to tequila-puffed faces and beer glazed eyes. I didn't see anything that made a difference. I turned and left, hitting the street just as a screaming ambulance slid to a stop, followed by another police car that completely blocked the narrow street. I turned right, striding hard toward the beach, and never looked back.

Any sensible businessman would say that I had done my job in good faith and was paid. The client met his demise, rest of the story no longer pertinent. Walk away, keep walking. But ten hours before, I had taken a hayseed's five hundred dollars to help him play out a TV Love Boat fantasy. Elijah Connors may have needed a strong dose of life's hard knocks to dent his romantic view of life, but he didn't deserve to be thrown off the fifth floor hotel balcony just for wanting to know the name of a girl who had picked him up one star-filled night in an Old Town Vallarta bar. There would be no other resolution of the death scene at the Oro Verde because it conveniently fit expectations and answers, obligating no one but the victim. Happens all the time to binge-drinking fools. The Vallarta fine life rolls on, but the kid deserved more justice than that in the cosmic scheme of things. Of course, nowhere in the cosmos, especially in Mexico, does such a thing exist — God's justice or man's.

Or maybe I was just acting now on a need-to-know basis. I had made a scene at Roxy's Bar too. Maybe I needed to know more about who might be coming after me, just to ensure my survival. I found myself headed back to the bar uptown. Beto the bartender was still the weak link, and he was long gone. I would only find him through the bouncer now, and he would probably have some idea of who was after his coworker anyway. I would just have to find some way to convince him to have a nice chat, probably after a little more pain to show him it wasn't just luck the first time this gray-bearded gringo dropped his ass on the barroom floor.

It was after midnight as I walked the streets back to Roxy's. Revelers still staggered around, looking for something that would never happen. The clubs I passed sounded louder with the late hour. Taxis, buses, and cars still rumbled over the cobblestones and the Río Cuale bridge. Old Town wouldn't shut down till nearly dawn. I could walk past Roxy's on the opposite side of the street and scope the scene without being noticed. If the bouncer — easy to spot because of his size, shape, and Michelin Man softness — was still at the door, I would wait till after two a.m. when the bar closed and confront him when he came out. I planned to move around, have a drink here and there, and check back now and then. After all, I realized it didn't matter now when I got to him. Tomorrow night would work just as well, but I didn't want to be hiding like a refugee till then.

The first time around the block I caught a glimpse of

him through the open door, behind his little box stand where he checked IDs. There was no line waiting to get in now. The music was muted and dragged with the band's own fatigue. I moved on, had a beer at an all-night taco stand a couple of blocks deeper into the barrio, circled back. As I turned the corner a block away from Roxy's, the street was empty of moving traffic. A car here and there was parked for the night. As I moved through the shadows on the opposite side of the street again, I saw a pair of brake lights and the dark back end of a car pulled up in front of Roxy's. The bouncer stepped down into the street to talk at the window. As I neared and slowed, I could make out a taxi's light atop the car. Then there was a flash and a pop and the squeal of tires peeling out. I saw the bouncer's head tilted back, and he melted into a puddle for the second and last time that night. I U-turned and forced myself to walk calmly away in the dark. At the first corner, I turned and ran. On Calle Insurgentes I leaped into the open door of a moving commuter bus. I paid my pesos, moved to the back, slinked to the corner, and rode it as far out of Old Town as it would take me.

IV

Over the years, I have found it occasionally convenient, even life-saving, to have several different kinds of places around Vallarta, and the Nayarit and Jalisco region in general, to escape what particular problems might be pursuing me at any given time. There are social and geographic varieties in my hiding places to confound a range of possible pursuers. For instance, a Nayarit fisherman with a grudge just isn't going to get anywhere near me in a gringo's penthouse apartment overlooking Mismaloya Beach, and neither is the Mexican army. A well-heeled gringo, no matter who he hires, will not find me in a Huichol village in the high sierras, or probably even in one of Juan Carlos' bedrooms on the second floor of the Iguana Bar. And no bureaucrat or *federale* is going to find me in a walk-up bedroom in the worst part of Guadalajara in a place that's kept just for me because I once found someone's daughter still alive. Just simple examples. There are all kinds of people hiding out in all kinds of places all over Mexico, both native and foreigner, like old Nazis or Butch Cassidy, like insurance defrauders and abused spouses, deposed politicians and drug lords.

I still wasn't sure I was even being pursued. It depended on if Elijah Connors had been questioned before being thrown off the balcony of the hotel. I had made my appearance at Roxy's at the same time someone was going after Connors. The killer or killers might have heard afterward that an old tourist gringo had been there and knew about things too, but other than that I was anonymous. Yet Connors might have been questioned. Seemed logical. And if so, someone I knew at Juan Carlos' Iguana Bar might be dead, too. Nothing personal, just more collateral damage.

At the beginning, I had tried to persuade Connors to wait at the Iguana Bar while I looked for his girl. But he had left his hotel room number at Roxy's, and he wanted to be there if she did try to contact him. He had been contacted all right. I wasn't going back to my booth at Iguana Bar to wait and see if I would be contacted too. I had no names, but I had been sure of who I was dealing with since hearing the terror in Beto the bartender's voice. He hadn't been afraid of anything an aging gringo would do to him. And I was just as afraid now as he had been. So just before dawn, I was holed up somewhere around Banderas Bay. My main worry was folks and friends at

Juan Carlos' bar. Later that afternoon, I made a call and on pickup my first word was a code for "Beware."

After a breath, Juan Carlos said, "Yes, may I help you?"

"Are you safe there? Can you talk?"

"Sí, señor."

"Have there been any visitors? Anyone staking out the bar?"

"I don't know."

"Send Noemi's son out around the streets to check. Very, very careful. Narcos, probably."

"Ay, que la madre de Dios."

"I'll call back."

Then I called Pamela Kirksen, a woman with grandmother gray curls, grandmother dresses, and broad straw hats. She shuffles around Vallarta's streets with a cane and uses taxis to get around otherwise. She chases what news there is in Puerto Vallarta as the beat reporter for the *Guadalajara Reporter*, Jalisco's major English-language newspaper. The editors liked her to limit her stories to convention events, regatta news, and municipal business, but she also knew a lot of the news that didn't get printed, a lot of it gossip and rumor from taxi drivers, hotel maids, and other service providers.

"Well, what are you up to these days," she asked after I identified myself.

"Just checking up on PV News."

"I thought you might have some for me."

"Do you need more? I hear there were a couple of deaths last night."

"Are you the ambulance chaser, or what caused the ambulance call in the first place?"

"You hurt me."

"I know you."

"I knew the kid who died at the Oro Verde last night. I

don't think it was an accident. And I witnessed the shooting in front of Roxy's Bar a couple of hours after that too."

"Jesus, Algo. You're next if anyone knows about this."

I told her about my night.

When I finished, she said. "Then you must know about the other murder, too."

"Another?"

"You don't know? I'm shocked. The bartender at Roxy's too."

"Well, yeah. He told me himself before it happened."

"Jesus, Algo."

"I may need Him, His mother, and all His friends. I really called to ask you to get next of kin information on Connors so I can at least write them a letter and tell them that their kid wasn't just a stupid drunk who fell off a balcony."

"Well, there's an interesting thing. More interesting now. The police are still trying to figure out who he was with, so they can get all that figured out. But no one knew him in the hotel. He wasn't with friends. He didn't even seem to have luggage in his room or anything other than his passport. The consulate has been called in to take care of it. You are dealing with narcos here, Algo, you know that. Maybe he was DEA."

"He was a kid. He didn't make this up. He believed it. And if he were, would he have set himself up for a fall like that?"

"Algo, you don't have to answer this, but... Can you identify anyone? Can anyone identify you?"

"No, no, but the kid had a picture of the girl. With out-of-focus faces in the background. He showed it to Roxy's barman, and the whole thing exploded."

"Did you see the picture?"

Angelita's Night Out

"No," I lied. Narcos could get to Pamela, too. They got to everybody. "I really think I'm out of the loop. Anyone I dealt with is already dead."

"Doesn't say much good about knowing you, does it?"

"I really need to know who I'm dealing with, Pamela, even if it is over and cleared up. I just feel the need to cover my back. I think there's a way to find out if you do me a favor."

"The more you know, the more dangerous it is."

"Someone once told me that it's what you don't know that gets you killed."

"You're a fool."

"I know."

"What do you want?"

∨

Four days later, I was still in my safe-house with a fine view of Banderas Bay, bored and impatient, but happy to still be alive and with the death purge probably over. The true test of that would come when I stepped out into the public world again, but I was still waiting on information from Pamela Kirksen and made daily check-in calls.

This call she finally said, "Some things are finally coming into focus. I told you how the consulate was stonewalling on identifying Connors. It seems a brother has come to claim the body, and that brother" – she had accented the word – "just happens to work for the FBI."

"Then I was wrong about Connors being a hayseed. He fooled me."

"Not exactly," she said. "You were right, too. The agent wants to talk to you, of course. Same setup. I'll give you the number he gave me and a time, and you call from wherever you are, both of you on public phones."

"He's probably being tailed or targeted already."

"He knows that. He's no hayseed, this one." She passed on other information about Beto and the bouncer at Roxy's, and I hung up. Sometime later, I made the requested call. A very measured, businesslike voice answered. "Yes, Mr. Waters. Thank you for calling. First let me assure you that the agency is here to –"

"Save your bullshit, Mr. Connors. I haven't believed those fairytales for thirty years. Why don't you just tell me about your deceased brother, you know, as one grieving relative to a grieving friend."

He took a breath. "Yeah. Sorry. He really is – was – my brother. I didn't know you knew him."

"I didn't. Did you?"

"I guess not. But he didn't come down here for us – for me. He came despite what he knew, what I told him."

Elijah Connors had come home to Lawrence, Kansas after Spring Break the year before with the wild love story and a picture of a beautiful Mexicana. He was sure she wanted him to whisk her away from her life of constraint in Mexico. By summer, the whole Connors family knew about the affair, and Eli was the good-natured butt of most of the season's jokes around barbecue pits and boat docks. His brother, Agent Connors here on the phone, claimed to have been happy for his younger brother, but dubious like all but the most romantic-minded relatives – his mother and his aunt. The girl's mysterious background, of course, came into question. Eli's older brother, with "ins" in The Company, offered to try having her picture identified.

"Checking against U.S. criminal files?" I asked.

"Well, no, not necessarily. The Company keeps all kinds of records on all kinds of people, it seems, but then we're all coming to realize that, aren't we? Maybe the picture might be compared with a Mexican passport, for instance."

"Uh huh, sure."

Like a good idealist, the kid refused to go along with that, but his amoral, for-his-own-good-and-ours brother did it anyway like the paranoid, self-righteous Company man that he is. Well, he was sure he had saved his brother's life when he — reluctantly, of course — confronted brother Eli with what he had turned up. It had not been a picture match of the girl that was found, but a match for two of the men in the out-of-focus background of the picture, two brothers of the most powerful cartel family north of Mazatlan.

Elijah had been enraged at his brother's going behind his back. He demanded the picture back, and they had a falling out. Elijah brooded into his junior year at KU, but the incident was never mentioned again. In fact, he refused to come home that year for Christmas. He kept in touch with family, but he was distant. Then he returned to Puerto Vallarta on his own to find the girl and prove everyone wrong and bring her back. Or if she was what his brother claimed, he was sure she wanted out and could be turned to the good side like Darth Vader's sister. He had left a note with a roommate, stating as much, to be opened in the event, etc. etc. Way too many Hollywood movies make up middle-class dreams. When he had gotten beat up outside Roxy's Bar, Elijah Connors finally got the idea that he was in over his head.

"I don't know how he found me," I said. "He couldn't have known me from Adam."

After a breath, Agent Connors said, "I gave him your name."

"What!"

"After he got beat up, he called me in a panic. We

don't–the DEA doesn't, the NSA doesn't — have anyone down here close enough or anyone who could. . ."

"Break cover? Where did my name come from, grieving brother?"

Another breath. "There's an informal list of –"

"I'm off the list, brother." I hung up on the creature that crawls through the shadows.

The next day I rode second-class stop-and-go buses into Sinaloa to attend a double funeral scheduled for the following day in the Pueblo of Agua Punta, a town of dusty narrow streets and no trees. Once its own place, by '96 it had been engulfed by the agricultural and drug trading city of Culiacán, a scene of major consequence in Mexico's narco wars and a drug family's home territory. People bus and drive through and around Culiacán all the time. A gringo stopping for a funeral is another thing altogether.

But I wouldn't attend the funeral in person. My old friend, Cuate, he of the six-toed feet, sexagenarian and jungle scrounger, bodyguard and lifesaver for going on some twenty-five years, would attend for me. His hair was silver white now, swept back from his high forehead and behind his ears. Deep wrinkles line his eyes and mouth. The old J-shaped scar on his lower lip, a reminder of our very first adventure, is barely visible now. In creased black pants and a new white shirt with a tie loose at the open collar, Cuate looked like a distinguished old señor and never less like an old, laughing Nayarit jungle scrounger. And he wasn't laughing now. He knew the situation and would be my eyes and voice (I hoped) at the Rosary that night and maybe at the actual funeral the next day. From the way Elijah Connors had told me the story of his night with Angelita, I had guessed that all three Mexicans covering for her knew one another well. Maybe even

Angelita's Night Out

Angelita knew all three well. That's what had made Roxy's Rock Bar a safe place for her escapade. Pamela Kirksen had gotten the police reports and funeral arrangements, and sure enough, Beto and the bouncer, Enrique Murillo, had grown up in Agua Punta together. They had gotten into the local booming business and tried to move up in life, like anyone anywhere, going where the jobs are. The pay and the circumstances might have been good, but in their business, getting fired for messing up takes on a whole different meaning.

And the thing was, Beto and the bouncer really hadn't messed up. They were just "little burros" carrying someone else's load both ways. I wondered what their mothers and sisters thought about the recent deaths of their sons and brothers, how much they knew or even if they wanted to know. In Mexico blood runs hot and thick, passions deep.

Once in Agua Punta and settled in a hotel room that Cuate had gone in and rented alone – as few people as possible were going to see this gringo on this turf, we found the church where the Rosary would be said that night and funeral held the next day. Then we found a nearby café with sidewalk tables on a fairly busy intersection that would serve for what I had in mind.

When the Rosary recital began Cuate went back to the church and joined in. Maybe he was risking his life for me again, but a parish church in large towns is often full of local members engaged in their own services, regardless of Rosaries or funerals, weddings or baptisms. Cuate's job was to identify the victim's family, his mother and a sister, at least, that would be about Beto's age. Angelita had told Connors offhand in her own little drama that Beto had a sister, that they both once worked for her father, and that the sister still did. Cuate would make his own decision. If he could approach them without endangering himself, he would whisper to the sister that a man had "the truth" about what had happened to her brother, if she cared to come with him and hear it. He also carried a note to that effect that he could slip into her hand in a gesture of bereavement if he couldn't speak to her. And if the sister pointed him out to elders and he was questioned, he was no one from Nayarit, paid by a stranger to deliver a message, nothing more. I didn't think there would be anyone there to threaten Cuate's acts. There would be no armed guards, no sunglasses hiding a drug lord's eyes, no limos and no tinted windows hiding a capo's army. The dead boys were merely soldiers themselves, the expendable ones. Generals and presidents don't attend those funerals; only the truly grieving attend these ceremonies for the nameless sons.

From safe shadows I saw Cuate's sign for a green light, and I returned to the café at the corner and sat at one of two tables I had reserved, keeping the restaurant wall to my right shoulder and giving me a view down the sidewalk paralleling the busy four-lane street. I could sense Cuate and his guest approach the table next to me and just over my left shoulder. He had her take the chair facing out toward the street, her shoulder almost touching mine but facing the opposite direction. Cuate took the chair on the other side, putting his back to the intersection. A waitress quickly came and took orders for coffee and disappeared.

The woman leaned toward Cuate and asked, "When is the gentleman coming?"

"He's there at your shoulder, señorita. Please don't turn around. We will just enjoy our coffee and our view," Cuate answered, and he moved his chair around the table slightly to sit facing the same way as she, while blocking a view of me from the street. From the corner of my eye, I could see a sliver of woman dressed in black, with a hat and veil, probably bought long ago for some first death, probably to be worn many times more. Under the black veil her profile was delicate and pretty.

I leaned slightly toward her and said, "I am truly sorry for your loss, señorita. I saw your brother the night he died and I know what happened. If you want the information, I will tell you."

Her voice trembled in a harsh, edgy whisper. "What do you want?"

"I want not to die like your brother did. And if I am being hunted because of what I might know, I want to know who it might be coming after me."

"It's family business," she said. She named them.

"Sí, señorita, but why? Do you know?"

After a pause, she said, "Tell me what you know."

"This has to do with a girl named Angelita."

I felt a flaming intensity suddenly ignited beside me, but her voice lost its wariness. She echoed, "Angelita, *por supuesto*. Angelita."

I told her what I knew of what had happened a year ago and what I thought had gone down the night of her brother's death. Her face was stony except for a slight smile when I mentioned the name Romano, Angelita's so-called cousin and escort. She corrected my story. Romano wasn't her cousin, the girl had said. "He's our cousin, Beto's and mine. He is her bodyguard. She calls all her bodyguards centurions, Romanos. We all went to the same Catholic boarding school. Mario, that's his name. Mario Joaquin Bustamonte. Mario was in love with her forever. Like all of them. They do whatever she wants them to do, and someone dies for it later. This is the third time, then. At least three. Angelita must have her "normal" night out. No one knows about this one yet."

"Well, your cousin, her bodyguard, covered up the trail

fast."

"By killing his own family."

I let that hang in the silence.

Finally, I said, "if he is your cousin, perhaps better for me. Please tell him, if he is looking for another gringo who might know something, that I know nothing more than I've told you, or that you have told me. I've never even seen your cousin, and I didn't know his name until you told me. *Nada.*"

The woman sipped her coffee in a black silence, then said, "I will deal with my cousin. Thank you."

Then I made the pitch. I didn't have to, but something in the sound of her voice brought it out of me. I said, "You can escape this. There are people who would help you, who could help you. I have a number that you can call."

"Help to kill more people?"

I let that hang, too.

After another silence she said, "What number?"

I gave it to her. "Just say, 'Angelita,' and whoever answers will know who you want to talk to."

There was nothing else to say after that. I watched Cuate escort the woman across the intersection and back toward the church. She was tall and lean in her mourning dress, but stepped through traffic with certainty, shoulders back. Cuate met me at the hotel, and since we had accomplished the goal without having to wait until the funeral, we abandoned the room and Culiacán altogether by midnight bus, seeking the safety again of our Nayarit coastal home.

VI

I felt sure Beto's sister — Adriana, Cuate told me later — would at least get her cousin to give me up as a target. But that didn't mean he would personally agree or that he had a choice. I felt sure, but I didn't sleep well for two weeks, couldn't make myself stay in one place more than three nights in a row, whether it was at home on the cliff north of Lo De Marco or at the Iguana Bar or holing up at a friend's place. The cartel trade wars were in full fury and their territorial and leadership skirmishes spilled over sometimes even into fantasyland places like Puerto Vallarta and Acapulco, spreading their collateral damage into all parts of Mexican life. The soldiers fall in battle or friendly fire just like in other wars, innocent bystanders too, and the families move in to drag their loved ones from the battlefield to the cemetery. The ripple from a rock thrown into a calm pool spreads, widens.

It was more than two weeks before Pamela Kirksen left a message for me at the Iguana Bar. She was sending a boy over with a copy of an obituary she had received by post from Culiacán. It had been sent anonymously to her as the bay area correspondent. It was just another ripple on the pond. The obit was for Mario Joaquin Bustamante from Agua Punta, twenty-five years of age, who had worked as a family bodyguard in Sinaloa. It didn't say for what family. He had been stabbed to death by a fifty-six-year-old woman, the sister of his own mother, who had accused him of killing her son, his cousin.

The tragedy was front-page horror and gore in several other country's supermarket magazines a couple months later — family vendetta, deep secrets, spreading family feud. Some of it was even true. The victim's aunt and mother were both placed in a mental asylum in Guadalajara. I never heard word if a woman named Angelita ever went to any of the funerals or visited those mothers in their recuperation.

Pretty soon, there was another horrible killing in Juarez

and another and soon after, a couple in Zacatecas in Zeta territory. The trade war continued. The drugs continued flowing north, no matter who died and who didn't. Life, as they say, got back to normal in North America.

Nine months later, another event made national news. The wedding of the niece of a man reputed to be one of Mexico's most powerful drug kingpins was raided at a ranch in Sinaloa by twenty-six units of the new Mexican Army antidrug force along with judicial *federales*. Three people died, including the groom, and twenty-six people were arrested. The kingpin, who had warning, escaped. The bride, named Angela, was wounded in the shootout. There was no word on when she might be well and up for another night on the town.

∽

The author of ten books, including poetry, fiction, and regional history, Robert Richter has a fifty-year relationship with Latin America, and that cultural geography inspires his work. In 2000 Richter won the Nebraska Arts Council's Literary Achievement Award for nonfiction, and in 2007, he was a Fulbright Research Fellow in Buenos Aires. Richter has also been a wheat farmer, substitute teacher, and tour guide in Latin America. Besides the "Something" series, Richter's other books on Mexico include Search for the Camino Real: a history of San Blas and the Road to get there; Cuauhtémoc Cárdenas and the Roots of Mexico's New Democracy; *and* Sayulita: Mexico's Lost Coastal Village Culture, *which received the Silver Award in the multicultural division of the Kopps-Fetherling International Book Awards in 2020.*

A Corpse in the Martian Sand

J.F. Benedetto

Standing next to the hovering recorder-bot, I checked my space suit's readout. The air in the pressurized portion of the unfinished monorail tunnel stood at 50 degrees below zero — about what you'd expect at this depth beneath the Martian surface. Ahead of me was what the recbot was filming: at the end of the pressurized tunnel, three *AresRail* "sandhogs" in yellow space suits were entering the vacuum-caisson airlock. The digger had jammed near the cutting face, and they were going in to clear it.

To be honest, I'm glad it jammed. Working for the revolutionary government in the Police Oversight Ministry, I've been hip-deep in greed and hatred and murder for so long that I had forgotten my past life as an engineer for *AresRail*, when a simple problem like this was the worst thing that could happen in a dig site. I had to get away from murder and dead bodies, so I was taking a week off, spending it with a team of *AresRail* sandhogs, trying to shake off the darkness smothering me. Martian Police Corps detectives talk about this feeling, about how when you see too much of man's inhumanity you begin to die inside, one piece at a time.

I've already lost a lot of pieces. And I was losing more every day.

Enough was enough. I'd been at peace for three days now, caught up in the old routine of working an *AresRail* tunnel dig, work familiar enough for me to do it in my sleep. No blood, no dead bodies, nothing but robots, machinery, and pressure suits. And my mind was made up. I'd spent this morning's trip out to the dig site composing my resignation letter, not only from the Ministry of Police Oversight, but also from the Bureau of Social Responsibility itself. I needed to find a silent haven, and this was it. Here, wearing a space suit in the pressurized section of the tunnel just behind a boring machine out in the middle of nowhere, I was at peace, far away from all of man's cruelty.

I could not have been more wrong.

The indicator above the airlock leading to the unpressurized caisson went amber; someone was coming back out. But the sandhogs had just gone in; why would they turn around and come right back out again? The airlock door slid opened and the three space-suited sandhogs came tumbling out, frantically shoving and clawing each other out of the way. I made the *AresRail* hand sign for STOP at the one lumbering frantically in my direction in the two-fifths Martian gravity. "What is it?" I asked over the commlink. "What's wrong?"

"There's a woman in there!" the sandhog cried, pointing back at the caisson. "A nude woman! And she's dead!"

A Corpse in the Martian Sand

It took the Martian Police Corps the better part of three hours to get a team in space suits from Kamenev Station down into the dig, and then travel all the way to the unfinished end of the tunnel. I stood waiting as they cycled through the airlock in their khaki and blue police space suits, carrying vacuum-rigged cameras and evidence kits.

The caisson is essentially just a long metal tube, currently half-filled with orange sand and, for no explainable reason, the desiccated body of a very nude, and very dead, woman. The space-suited police officers paused at the sight of the body — or rather at the sight of me standing there next to it. One of them — the head officer, given the traditional red "commander's stripe" painted across the top of her helmet — stared questioningly at me, waiting. I switched on my commlink. "Special Agent Granitski, Bureau of Social Responsibility, Ministry of Police Oversight."

The Chinese MPC officer spoke, her voice over the commlink carrying the clipped tones of someone raised in the domes of the Martian capitol, Draper City. "Lieutenant Tung Jinghua, Ministry of Public Security," she said, telling me the name of the ministry she worked for, rather than saying she was a police officer.

This was not good; when an official greets you by announcing which Ministry controls her department, it means she's not-so-subtly questioning your presence in her territory. I'd worked police oversight long enough to know her type: open schooling probably, then trained for the Police Corps at the Mars Services Academy: *Service means Sacrifice*. She served the Corps cleanly enough that after the Martian Revolution two years ago, she got promoted to senior lieutenant to fill a space left by a cop who had not been that clean, then an assignment to an out of the way place like Kamenev Station. The Police Corps needed a trustworthy officer for a small posting, and she drew the short straw. Day in and day out doing nothing but routine work, keeping the peace, seeing the laws were obeyed. Probably been holding just short of making captain for some time now. No reason to promote her. And then today came a report of a dead body found over a hundred kilometers away, inside a subsurface tunnel under construction. Completely nude. A case noteworthy enough that solving it would bring her official recognition, promotion to captain, assignment to the big city-domes. She would have spent the hours in transit from Kamenev Station looking at this case as her ticket to bigger and better things, only to discover an agent of the Police Oversight Ministry was on the scene ahead of her.

And if there's one thing every single cop on Mars hates, it's having an agent of the POM standing there watching them, just waiting for them to slip up.

Lt. Tung's questioning gaze went from me to the dead body, and then came back to me.

I answered her unspoken question. "Before the Revolution I was an *AresRail* engineer. I'm on mandatory vacation time from the POM, decided to spend it sandhogging with a work crew in a tunnel dig. I'm not here in any official capacity. It's just pure chance my being here when the DB was turned."

"Ah."

First the silent treatment, and now one-word answers. *Great.*

With the question of who had jurisdiction settled, she got to work and set the crime scene investigators to holo-imaging the dead woman. Caucasian, most likely; age indeterminate due to extreme desiccation of the remains, but height suggested an adult female. She might even have been pretty once.

Lt. Tung took up the station alongside me and proved that she was smart enough to run a check on me. "You've worked as a special observer on a number of civilian police investigations in Tharsis, and in the Capitol. Reports say you were instrumental in helping crack the Nasr murder case. So tell me: how was the body discovered?"

First she tried to pull rank on me, now she was checking to see if I was an idiot. *Terrific.*

I sent her the footage from the recbot to cover my irritation. "The caisson was pushing forward, cutting the tunnel bore. The rotating teeth — "

"Rotating teeth? Why wasn't the body ripped to shreds?"

"Because they weren't using a full-face tunnel boring machine," I explained, adjusting the volume on my commlink. "Those are used to excavate through solid rock strata. Because of the extremely loose fill here, the area behind a full-face cutter would continuously fill up with falling sand before the plate crew could shore up the tunnel walls. So we use hydraulic pistons to push an open-faced cylinder — the caisson we're standing in right now — forward one meter at a time through the loose fill. The front of the cylinder is open, with cutting teeth only on the rotating outer edge, to break up any solid debris and scoop it into the caisson."

"Sort of like pushing a cup sideways through sand," Lt. Tung suggested.

"Exactly. The sand at the caisson face is removed by a screw-conveyor," I said, pointing at the auger partially visible in the sand at our feet. "We only send workers into the caisson if the screw removing the sand jams. As a safety feature, a sensor package makes sure no one accidentally gets drawn into it. What happened here was the sensor scanned something that appeared to be the size and shape of a human being about to be scooped up and shut down the conveyor. Of course, the work crew knew no one could be in the caisson, so they came in to correct the false shutdown signal."

"And instead found a dead body." She strode off through the loose sand, leaving me behind like a discarded food wrapper.

I probably should have kept my mouth shut, but that's not my style. "Did you notice something odd about your victim?"

She stopped, half turned in her suit to look at me, then glanced instead at the DB. "What?"

I pointed a gloved finger. "She was exposed to vacuum only *after* she died. Notice the lack of bloodstains around the mouth. There'd be some if she had tried to hold her breath. That suggests she was killed under inside pressure, and only after death got dumped out into vacuum. There's so little sand abrasion of the skin that she was either buried by the killer, which seems unlikely given the depth of her grave, or else she was dumped in a crevasse, where the corpse was covered naturally by windblown sand falling in."

Tung stared hard at me. "You seem to know a lot about what happens to murdered people when they're dumped outside."

"No," I said, correcting her. "Not *murdered* people; just dead ones. *AresRail* lost an entire work crew in a surface blowout back in '31. I was one of the recovery team that brought their bodies back the following year. I got to see firsthand what a year on the surface does to a human corpse. Since there's no scouring of the body by windblown sand, I'd say your victim must have been covered over pretty quickly, probably by a fairly large sandstorm."

The CSI team moved the body and began sifting for clues. *Literally* sifting, given all the sand we stood on. They got nothing for their troubles: none of her clothing or belongings had been dumped with her.

The Medical Examiner's voice came over the commlink. "My initial diagnosis," she said, "would be blunt force trauma to the back of the skull as the cause of death. Pretty savage blow, too. And I concur with our Bureau friend there that the body was placed here postmortem; there are no obvious signs that the lungs expanded and ruptured, which there would be if the victim had been vacced out an airlock while still breathing."

I patched my datalink to Lt. Tung's. "I ran the current orbital map scan and layered in all of the previous scans. The tunnel we're in is being pushed through a crevasse that half filled with sand about 18 months ago, during the planetwide dust storm we had in January that year. Before that, it was open all the way to the surface. It's my guess that the killer chose the open crevasse as a hiding spot for the DB. We're more than 100 kilometers from the nearest settlement; the chances of anyone stumbling on a body way out here are so remote as to be infinitesimal."

Lt. Tung made an appraising grunt. "Yet *AresRail* dug a tunnel right up to where she was buried. And people say there is no God."

I frowned at the idea of divine intervention being introduced into a criminal investigation, but let it pass. "There's no way to reach this spot short of a floater or a crawler. If the murderer brought the body here that way, there'll be a record of it on Planetary GPS Tracking."

Lt. Tung turned toward one of her team. "Feed in our

location to PGT and call up all ground and low-float transits within 30 kilometers."

"How recently?"

"Just roll backward until you find one."

The search didn't take long, but then again, how many such trips would have passed right over the spot where we were standing? "Got it. A floater surface-crashed within 10 meters of the crevasse just over two years ago."

About the time of the Revolution? That was interesting, with a capital I. "Who was aboard?"

The Tech glanced questioningly at Lt. Tung; I might have been Police Oversight, but I also had no jurisdiction here, remember? When she said nothing, he reluctantly answered me. "One passenger. Dhiren O'Connor of Draper City. He was alone, according to the flight log he filed with Draper City Outport Control."

"Which doesn't mean that there wasn't anyone else aboard the floater with him," Lt. Tung pointed out. "What do the files have on O'Connor?"

"He was a corporate security chief working for Butler Trans-Stellar Provisions in Draper City. Last official entries on him are dated the morning of the Revolution."

His official record ended the morning of the Revolution? Given that he was one of the chief corporate bastards sending guards with chainsaws against the protesters, the rioting mobs surely had killed him — although he might still be alive, hiding under an assumed identity. "What was the last entry in regard to?"

"Uh — he was questioned in the disappearance of one Nadezhda Sergeyovna Lukashenko. Female. 25. Missing Person's report filed two days before the Revolution broke."

I stared at the desiccated corpse. "Status on her case?"

"Unresolved. It might have been one of the investigations that fell through the cracks during the Revolution. What with everything that was happening. . ."

Lt. Tung grunted. "The case got lost in the upheaval when the old government fell. A cold case now." She looked down at the dead woman's corpse and then gave me a very Chinese smile through the faceplate of her helmet. "I'd say this case just got hot again, wouldn't you, Agent Granitski?"

∽

Unfortunately for Lt. Tung, the heat generated by our discovery turned out to only be a momentary spark of warmth. Former BTSF security chief Dhiren O'Connor had vanished, as so many of the smartest corporates had, during the upheaval that overthrew the corrupt megacorporations and gave Mars its first taste of freedom in over a century. There was no actual record that O'Connor had been killed during the riots, nor any evidence that he had left Mars. But as to where he was now — assuming he was still alive — we had nothing to go on.

I spent the next three days of my mandatory vacation time alongside Lt. Tung, combing through what was left of the corporate records not destroyed during the riots. The other Martian Police Corps officers who worked beside her made it quite clear that they were less than thrilled to have an agent of the Ministry of Police Oversight present. Not that I blamed them, really. *Quis custodiet ipsos custodes*. *"Who watches the watchmen?" I do, comrades. Remember that.*

And that was something else that was slowly killing me. If I wasn't hunting people who were murderers, I was hunting cops who were crooked. It had reached the point where I stared at every person I met and wondered what they were guilty of. *There is no such thing as innocence, just degrees of guilt.*

How had I ended up here? I was top of my class in the Engineering School at the Services Academy, an *AresRail* engineer whose duty to the people of Mars was to keep the system working, keep the people and goods of Mars moving. Yet after the Revolution, I'd taken on the mantle of a political commissar in Police Oversight, shadowing police officers and judging them on how they chose to uphold the Law: by the letter, by the spirit, or not at all. Oh yes, I'd helped solve criminal cases, but only because I stuck my nose in where it wasn't wanted. Results be damned; the police hated me more than they did the criminals they fought against.

And two years of this had taken their toll on me. These days I got my breakfast and my dinner both from a bottle of spiced rum. That was the deciding factor in my decision to quit and return to AresRail. At the rate I was going, my career in the Ministry of Police Oversight would end with the words *And then he turned the gun on himself.*

With a heavy sigh, I popped an energy tab and entered the MPC station, ignored the hate-filled stares the officers threw at me, and went to Lt. Tung's office.

We managed to locate O'Connor's former secretary, one Ms. Nila Pandit, an import from New Delhi on Earth. He'd had a serious fling with her, but then had her transferred out of his department after she turned up with an unwanted pregnancy, a major violation on corporate Mars with our limited air, water and living space. When she tried to protest the transfer, she lost her job, with the corporation forcibly terminating her unregistered pregnancy.

Hell hath no fury like a woman scorned. Ms. Pandit all but spit at the mention of O'Connor. "I hear of discovery

Nadezhda's body in morning news. They not mention Dhiren, but I know he is man who kill her. This I cannot prove, but Nadezhda say to me she discover he embezzle company money. She say she go to confront him — and next day, she vanish. You not need be genius to figure out he one who killed her."

Lt. Tung squinted at her. "You don't happen to know where O'Connor is now, do you?"

A dangerous, icy smile filled Pandit's face, the kind that actually gave me the chills. "I saw him one month past, in Candor City. He change name, but it Dhiren. I trail him back his apartment block. He hides in cheapest warren under south dome. But that Dhiren for sure; he so cheap, he would take rupees off dead man's eyes." She linked a short note to our wrist comms. "He now call self Erich Bowes. This address his."

A quick security check via the Candor City Office of the Ministry of Public Safety revealed one Erich Bowes currently living at the address Pandit had given us. I accompanied Lt. Tung on the night express monorail to Candor City, and we took a team of the city's Martian Police Corps troops into the rundown underground apartment complex where "Bowes" lived.

Tung and her khaki blues stormed his apartment with guns drawn. We found O'Connor standing at the kitchen sink eating a microwaved bowl of kibble, his packed bags sitting on the floor beside him. In his pocket was a spacer ticket out to the distant colony world of Ulander. He'd seen the news article on the discovery of Lukashenko's body and was just five minutes away from leaving for the starport when we burst in on him. Of all the Outer World colonies, Ulander is the most primitive: a corporate retreat world, it had been largely settled by Amish, Mennonite and other Luddite "back to nature" groups living on the land without access to modern tech, with a million places for a new arrival to go to ground, unseen and untraceable. Had O'Connor gotten to Ulander, there would have been no hope of ever finding him again.

He had the nerve to look outraged when Lt. Tung arrested him.

∽

"I want to know why I'm being held against my will!" O'Connor demanded, sitting across the interrogation room table from me and Lt. Tung. "What's the charge? I have the right to know!"

"Use of a Falsified Identity, for starters," Lt. Tung said, shifting her position in the down-push of the overhead force field that simulates earth normal gravity in Mars habitats. "Star travel offworld using false papers is a major offense these days. Might even put you in league with the Terran Separatists. Maybe you're a terrorist. Sounds like it. Want to tell us why you were fleeing Mars under an assumed name?"

"I didn't want to get tossed out an airlock. I was a corporate security chief. I saw what the mobs did to the others."

I stuck my nose in. "Perhaps you should not have armed your security personnel with chainsaws for crowd control. That might be why the people of Mars want your head served up to them on a platter."

Lt. Tung leaned forward. "The Revolution was two years ago. Why wait until now to leave? Why leave today?"

"No reason. I had to save up enough money to bribe my way offworld. That's all."

"Want to tell me about Ms. Lukashenko?"

"Who?"

It was my turn to lean forward. "Nadezhda Sergeyovna Lukashenko," I said, stressing her given, patronymic and family names. Lt. Tung watched me stick my nose in further, but said nothing. "She worked as a secretary in your department." I used my fieldcomp to float a holo of the paperwork up into the air between us. "She disappeared just before the Revolution broke in Draper City."

O'Connor leaned back in his chair, scraping it across the floor. "Yeah, I think I remember her. She was in my department, but I don't remember anything about her. It was years ago. A lot of people worked in my department."

"Really?" I opened the file in my comp and floated up additional holograms. "Let me refresh your memory." I lit up the first one, then changed to light up the next holo after it. "She was the junior secretary in your department for just three weeks before you took an interest in her. Within a month, she jumped four pay grades. Reason why, not listed." [new holo] "You and she became sexually involved. Various people from your department made statements regarding your interoffice liaison." [new holo] "Shortly thereafter, she went missing." [new holo] "How is your memory now? Any clearer?"

"Yeah," O'Connor said, his eyes wary. "I slept with her. So what? She was one of ten, twelve women I slept with while I was security chief. Is it a crime to have sex with someone so boring you don't remember them clearly?"

I continued. "On the day that she was last seen by any of her friends, you went to the Draper City Outport and put in a request for a Butler Trans-Stellar Foods company floater." [new holo] "You purchased eight liters of liquid-H fuel." [new holo] "You signed off on *all* of the corporate responsibility and insurance forms you could get." [new holo] "You filed a flight plan listing your trip as an unannounced inspection of the BTSF facility at

McKinley Station." [new holo] "You departed Draper City Outpost at 1137 hours, outbound across the surface."

"You got a thing for old work files?"

I highlighted the last page in the cluttered wall of holopics hovering between us. "1137 hrs. Is that correct?"

He shrugged again. "How should I know the exact time after two years? Anyway, so what? I was Security Chief. We did unannounced inspections all the time."

"Sure you did," Lt. Tung said. Her Chinese eyes narrowed dangerously. "It's 600 kilometers from Draper City to McKinley Station. A long, boring flight. You didn't take anyone with you?"

"No. I went alone."

"Uh-huh. Sure you did." She lifted up a holopic of her own, one detailing the floater he'd used. "You checked out a KaVo 155. That's a luxury model. Actual leather imported all the way from Earth. A stocked minibar. Fully autonomous computer control. TwinPower engine, can cruise at 200 kph, gets 50 kilometers to the liter, AND IT SEATS FOUR! Why would you take a vehicle that seats *four* if you were going there *alone*?"

"I like to put my feet up."

"Sure you do." She slid the holopic aside with a wave of her hand. "A KaVo 155 is a pretty fancy choice for a mere sec-chief just making a routine inspection. Why didn't you check out a Tatra L200? Or even an Espra one-seater? Was it because they're just commonplace work floaters?"

"I like the feel of leather, okay?"

"I don't think so." Lt. Tung enlarged the holo of the KaVo 155. "You chose a fancy floater because you were going to be taking a woman with you. Someone you wanted to impress. Someone you wanted to lull into a false sense of security. Someone like Nadezhda Lukashenko, for instance."

"I flew alone," O'Connor said through clenched teeth. "I took the KaVo because I had corporate privilege. I wanted to ride in real leather seats and listen to a sound system that cost more money than I made in a year. Is that a crime?"

"It is when dead bodies turn up where you crashed!" Lt. Tung shot back.

I dissolved the floating wall of documents and put up a new set from the data file. "The floater you were in — it 'suffered a breakdown'?" [new holo] "You crash-landed on the surface roughly 375 kilometers from the Draper City Outport, yes?" [new holo] "The global positioning transponder aboard the floater went out at 1349 hrs. That was when you impacted the surface, wasn't it?"

He put his hands on the table, leaning forward. "Gee, I don't know. I was so busy crashing that I guess I forgot to check the time!"

"1349 hrs." [new holo] "Oddly enough, you didn't activate the floater's emergency locator transmitter until 1511 hrs." [new holo] "Why was that?"

He stiffened at the question, leaning back away from me. "I — was knocked unconscious during the crash. When I woke up, I was confused. I had an air leak, I had to get into my suit and then I tried to fix the floater." His voice leveled as he found his excuse. "I didn't want to have to call for help because the company would take the wrecked floater out of my hide, so I tried to fix it. It was only when I knew I couldn't make it fly again that I turned on the beacon."

"That doesn't make any sense," Lt. Tung said. "You took out insurance on the floater. *Full and complete insurance*. So why would you have gotten into trouble?"

Dots of sweat marked O'Connor's forehead. "I was so shook up by the crash that I forgot about the insurance," he said, not meeting Lt. Tung's hard stare. "Once I remembered it, I turned on the beacon."

"Oh, when you 'remembered' it?"

"I had just crashed! I wasn't thinking clearly!"

Lt. Tung's eyes narrowed. "It wasn't because you had to kill Lukashenko, put on a pressure suit, strip her nude so there wouldn't be anything to identify the corpse, then drag her dead body out of the floater, over to the crevice you deliberately crashed alongside, and dump her where she would never be found?"

"No."

"So, you *didn't* kill Lukashenko?"

"No!"

"You didn't lure her aboard the floater, fly her out into the middle of nowhere, crash-land the floater, and then kill her?"

"*No!*"

She came up out of her chair. "*Kill her*, then drag her corpse across the sand and heave it into the crevice?"

"NO!"

"*You killed her!*" Lt. Tung yelled. "She knew about the funds you embezzled and you had to get rid of her!"

"I DIDN'T KILL HER!"

"Oh yes you did. And it was a great plan." Lt. Tung smiled but shook her head. "You chose the perfect spot to dump the body, Dhiren. Would never have been found if that railway tunnel hadn't gone right through the crevice at that spot."

" '*Crevasse*,' not 'crevice' " I said.

Lt. Tung's smile turned devious. "You only messed up by five meters. Just five! If you'd tossed the body in just five meters further north or south, the tunnel dig would have missed her corpse entirely. But you screwed up royally, Dhiren."

"I DIDN'T DO IT!"

"*YES YOU DID!*" she yelled back. "You deliberately crashed that floater because you knew that any unscheduled touchdown on the surface would be logged by the GPS satellites, so you gave yourself a perfect excuse to make a 'crash landing' right there next to a nice, deep hole in the ground. You chose that spot ahead of time because it was the perfect place to hide a body. You killed her, Dhiren. You killed Lukashenko and you hid her body in that crevice, didn't you. *Didn't you!*"

"NO! I DIDN'T KILL ANYBODY!"

I blinked, looked back through the files, and then killed all of the floating holopics, causing the two to stop and stare at me. "This has gone on long enough," I told them both. "You've wasted enough of my — of the ministry's time with all this. Is this conversation being recorded?"

"Of course," Lt. Tung said, confusion in her eyes. "Why?"

"I don't appreciate when an innocent man is harassed by the police. Citizen Dhiren O'Connor, this conversation is being recorded and constitutes a legal declaration on your part, not only to the Martian Police Corps, but also to the Ministry of Police Oversight."

Lt. Tung came up out of her chair. "Agent Granitski —"

"I'm ending this farce!" I declared. "*And*," I snarled over my shoulder, "I don't need your help to know when a man is innocent!" I focused on his face. "Citizen Dhiren O'Connor, you have been questioned by a representative of the Martian Police Corps, and you have been shown evidence of your actions two years ago as documented in corporate files. Do you swear for the legal record that the physical evidence shown to you by the MPC is correct, and also that no act of guilt has been made proven?"

"Yes!" O'Connor declared, grinning hard at Lt. Tung.

I smiled. "There you go."

"What?" both Lt. Tung and O'Connor asked.

I smiled hard at O'Connor. "You just incriminated yourself. You swore that all the corporate records shown in evidence to you are true. That's proof enough for a conviction."

A glint of red flashed into O'Connor's eyes. " '*Proof*'?! What proof? You don't have any evidence! Not one damned thing in those files proves I killed that bitch. Yeah, all right, so maybe I crashed near where you found a dead body. *So what!* Sheer coincidence, that's all!"

"WRONG!" I screamed, leaping to my feet. "The vehicle you checked out was a KaVo 155, which has leather seats, computer control, seats four and can do 200 kilometers an hour. And *it gets 50 kilometers to the liter.*" I flipped up the holopic of the receipt from corporate records and shoved it at his face, pointing at the line. "You purchased eight liters of fuel. Just enough for 400 kilometers of flight, for a surface flight that, *one way*, is 600 kilometers long. That 400 kilometers' worth of fuel wasn't nearly enough to reach McKinley Station, but it was just far enough to reach the crevasse where we found Lukashenko's corpse. It not being an officially sanctioned trip, you had to purchase the fuel with your own money, and you're so damn cheap you only bought enough fuel to fly to the burial site, and no further. That is proof beyond any shadow of a doubt that you deliberately planned both the murder *and* the disposal of Nadezhda Sergeyovna Lukashenko. *And you just swore to that in a recorded legal declaration.*"

O'Connor fainted dead away.

Lt. Tung's mouth hung open, and she looked from me to O'Connor and back to me before she found her voice. "You — " She glared at me. "But why did you say he was innocent? It's on the record! He'll claim entrapment, and the judge — "

I stopped her. "What made you think I was talking about O'Connor when I said those things? I simply chose that moment in the conversation to inform you that I do not appreciate it when an innocent man is harassed by the police, and that I do not need your help to see where a man is innocent. You can check the recording: I never stated that O'Connor was the person I was referring to. It is not my fault at all if he drew a wrong conclusion from my statements."

Lt. Tung grinned and made a remark quite inappropriate from an officer of the law. "Have you always been this big an ass?"

An ass? I stared at O'Connor. I had just brought a murderer to justice and avenged the woman he killed in cold blood. I hadn't stood by watching; I'd gone in after the bastard and taken him down face-to-face. My hatred for the whole world had been sharpened down to a hatred for the monsters hiding among the populace, and catching Lukashenko's killer had made me feel better in a way nothing else had. Maybe that was the answer. Personally defeating that arrogant murderer had put fresh O_2 in my tanks. For the first time in months, I didn't need a drink.

I liked how that felt.

"An ass?" I asked her. "No. But I'm going to be one from now on. You can count on it."

I picked up my fieldcomp and walked out of Interrogation, smiling.

J.F. BENEDETTO

J.F. Benedetto (www.FoulPlayWriter.com) writes short fiction in five different genres (mystery, science fiction, historical, adventure, and ricepunk) and his stories have appeared in print from America to Australia. He worked three years as a writing mentor for the Mystery Writers of America, four years as assistant editor of the Triangulation speculative fiction anthology, and nine years as a contributing editor for American Mensa's Calliope — a career he sums up via Hemingway's Dictum: "We are all apprentices in a craft where no one ever becomes a master."

The Good Thief

Mary Sophie Filicetti

Normally, I would never break into someone's house. I'm overall a pretty law-abiding person, but sometimes curiosity leads you in unexpected directions, and you can't worry about the consequences.

I had driven past 699 30th St. during the first month of my commute without paying particular attention to the property, unremarkable from the front. It wasn't until I started jogging through the neighborhood, when I took in the view from behind, that questions began to eat at me.

The back yard held grass high enough it had turned to hay. Vines of ivy crept up a large, dying oak on the property, which retained a few feeble branches sparsely covered with leaves. The side of the house facing the street was painted in a respectable off-white, its shutters and trim black, while the rear and freestanding garage displayed a completely different effect — painted garish maroon with midnight blue framing on the windowpanes. Viewed from the side, the house looked at war with itself.

The property was surrounded by a chain-link fence with "No Trespassing" and "No Soliciting" signs attached.

The rest might be dismissed as neglect; it was the garage which brought me up short, its front windows painted over with a freehand mural — a mound of dirt representing fresh graves, with three crosses atop the mound. Del Ray took pride in its reputation as an off-beat town, but painted graves went beyond quirky. Could I really be the only neighbor wondering whether someone was buried inside?

Back home my housemate, Tracy, called down to me as I crossed the threshold.

"Jess, we're going out for drinks tonight. Are you in?'

I ran up the steps, and poked my head into her room. "Sure. Hey, what's with the house around the corner with the creepy garage?"

"Which one?"

"The garage with the *graves* painted on it? You must have seen it."

Tracy cocked her head briefly before taking in my sweaty appearance. "Oh, yeah, I know which one you mean. We were thinking of hitting Penn Quarter. How fast can you get ready?" She methodically switched essentials from her work bag to a small clutch: phone, wallet, lipstick, keys.

"Wait — you didn't tell me about the house. What's the deal with the person who lives there?"

"I'm not sure anyone does live there. Why do you care?"

Camila walked in, holding two dresses on hangers, her face a question. "What are you two talking about?"

Tracy pointed to the green minidress. "The one on the left, definitely. That decrepit house in the neighborhood."

"Did the guy die?" Camila asked. "I bet he was a hoarder."

"Do you know him?"

"I've seen him in the neighborhood. He's like an older

version of that guitar player from ZZ Top — tall, long beard, always wearing headphones. Can you imagine being the relative who cleans out that house?"

I couldn't steer them back to the topic of the garage; all conversation was thwarted as they hustled me towards the shower. Wiping the steam from the mirror, I stared at my reflection, unwilling to switch gears. The paint job on the rear of the house wasn't finished yesterday. Other people passed by the garage, yet no one took time to investigate its meaning. Crimes were committed every day while people went about their lives ignoring the signs, until the cops are involved and a neighbor says, ". . .we haven't seen his wife lately, but we never dreamed anything was wrong."

Tracy's offhand "why do you care?" prickled in the same way as my mother's famous. "mind your business, Jessica." As an always distracted child, my teachers declared me to be "attention deficit," while my mother found me merely too curious. I provided my mother multiple opportunities to wield her scolding phrase, whispered harshly in my ear when I stopped to stare at a melee breaking out in a parking lot, or someone spray painting graffiti on the side of a building. What were they writing? What did it mean? "Mind your business, Jessica," was the answer.

I wasn't present at L'Enfant Plaza the time violinist Joshua Bell decided on a lark to busk, incognito, in a metro station at rush hour. About ten at the time, I'd have no doubt joined the small audience of children who slowed to the strains of Bach, only to be hustled past the virtuoso violinist by their too-busy parents without a second glance. One young boy, entranced Pied Piper style, stopped and turned repeatedly until his mother took it one step further and placed her body in between to block Bell from her son's line of sight. You miss things, minding your business, in this case a free performance by a world-class musician.

The house on the corner generated questions that called out to me. I had no intention of minding my business.

~

After an hour spent searching online, I wasn't far along. For a house dating back to 1939, the absence of sales listings struck me as off. I couldn't find a listing for the owner or renter, which annoyed me no end.

The house needed work, but if a developer ripped out the garage, renovated, and expanded, it would be worth a half million dollars or more in this neighborhood. Camila and Tracy methodically shredded realtors' offers that came in the mail, afraid our landlord might get the bright idea to sell the house out from under us. Why would the old guy rattle around in a ramshackle house when he could sell for a fortune, maybe head down to Florida? If it were me, I'd be tucked away in a sunny little condo near the beach.

I ran a favorite scenario by my housemates. "Let's say the family buys the house before World War II, the father returns in 1945, and our neighbor is born the next year. He marries, moves off, and returns with the wife when his parents die. He inherits the house with a sibling, but he's down on his luck. He decides to do away with his brother for the house. The wife is appalled when she uncovers the crime, she can't live with it, and now he has to kill her, too."

"So your saying he's bumped off members of his family, buried them in the garage, and painted the scene to

The Good Thief

highlight the fact?" Tracy's eyebrows arched, her expression incredulous.

"What is she basing these theories on?" Camila asked, turning to Tracy.

"Nothing. This is all coming straight out of her vivid imagination."

My premise might need work, but I couldn't understand their lack of interest in the possibilities.

The frequency of my runs picked up, varying the time of day, always passing that house. I'd approach from one side or the other, then round the corner to survey the front. Each time, I noticed something new. The windows in both the house and garage were blocked from view with blinds or heavy paper. A porch light came on at night, but the interior ones remained off, leaving the rooms in darkness. A humming sound coming from the window air conditioning units meant someone was inside. The surrounding metal fence was rusty but sturdy looking, though its locked gate was hardly a deterrent. At about four feet tall, it would be easy to hop over. Not that I saw any reason to be jumping the fence.

A few weeks later, finishing up a run with an extra loop past the property for my cool down, an idea came to me. I paused inside our door, stretching, sweat running down my body, heat radiating off of my face in waves, and called out to Tracy.

"Hey, Trace, who's the guy that organizes the neighborhood watch?"

"I think his name's Ted. He lives a block over on Custis."

Camila closed her laptop and looked over. "Did something happen in the neighborhood?"

"No, I want to ask him about that house's owner."

"Were you running past again?" Tracy asked. She stepped outside the kitchen to stare at me, spatula in hand. I picked up a scent that might be chocolate chip cookies, if I was lucky.

"What is it with you and that place?" she demanded. "You've become obsessed! He's just some weird old guy, and you've concocted this whole drama in your mind."

"At least she's using the obsession for her own betterment," Camila said. "Look at the muscles on her thighs."

I sighed loudly walking upstairs to my room. 'Attention deficit disorder' my ass. Really, my ability to focus was far superior to most people I met.

The next week, armed with a description of Ted and his house, I created an opportunity to "bump" into him, expanding my running route to include his street. On the third trip, I spotted our neighborhood leader out weeding a large flower bed.

A half-block away, I made a show of finishing my run, checking my watch, shaking out my legs, while inspecting the flowers displayed along his walkway.

"Your yard is amazing. I've never seen tulips this tall."

Ted looked up at me, shading his eyes from the sun.

"Hi, I'm Jessie; I live on the next block." I gestured vaguely across the street. "My housemates said you run the neighborhood watch; is that right?"

Ted stood up and removed his gardening gloves to shake my hand. He looked younger than I expected, his hair more reddish-brown than grey, handshake firm. "Hi, Jessie. Ted. Is there something wrong?"

So much for my attempt at small talk.

"No, not really. Do you know the house on the corner of 30th street? The one with the garage?"

He pulled out a handkerchief from his pocket, and I shifted from foot to foot as he wiped his forehead.

"Oh, yeah, the old Peterson place."

"Mr. Peterson's the owner?"

Ted nodded, his attention diverted by some rogue weeds. "I met him a few years ago at a block party, and see him walking to the Catholic church on Sundays, but that's about it. Why? Has he said anything to you?"

"No. . . it's his garage — I find it a little disturbing."

"You mean the Calvary crosses?"

"Yeah." *Calvary crosses?* I had no idea what that meant.

"Mr. Peterson is a bit strange, sure, but he's always coherent. He's a retired accountant, or auditor, something like that."

"Is he married? Does anyone else live there?"

"No — I assumed he's widowed, but I'm not sure that's particularly based on anything he's said. Oh, there was someone who used to visit him — a nephew on a motorcycle. We'd hear it revving at all hours; eventually someone called the cops about the noise, which seemed to take care of the problem."

We stood for a moment as the conversation stalled.

"Ok, thanks for the info."

"Is there anything I can do for you?"

"No, I was just curious. . .I'll let you get back to your weeding."

The *Calvary Crosses*, Google informed me, represented the three crosses at the crucifixion. I suppose if I'd paid better attention in Sunday school, this might have occurred to me. I switched to Google images to confirm the theory, and found multiple scenes that displayed three tall crosses in a watercolor style, sunset in the background. The resemblance to the garage appeared minor.

I lost a few minutes sidetracked by commercial products sprinkled throughout the images. The Calvary cross nail art required a closer look. I zoomed in on the photo, cropped to show only three fingernails, each painted with a cross, and tried to picture the woman at work writing mundane emails, all the while faced with that gruesome scene from the Bible. This is why I don't talk to people on the Metro. You never knew when you might be pinned in your seat by some zealous stranger preaching reform.

Scrolling further, a more relevant image popped up: three simple crosses on a hill. Still, my neighbor's crosses were shorter, more like tomb markers, missing the sunset. I wasn't convinced Peterson's were meant as Calvary Crosses. A link on the page led me to the website of a Catholic priest who lectured about the two thieves on the cross — the bad thief who blamed others for his bad choices, versus the good thief who accepted his wrongdoings.

"What are you working on?"

Startled, I slapped closed the laptop cover. "Just checking the news."

"Why do I suspect it has something to do with our neighbor down the street?" Tracy asked, setting her lunch on the table.

"Did you know approximately 30% of Americans have

a criminal record?" I asked. "I'm not sure if that's convictions or arrests, but basically the same number of people have records as those with 4-year degrees."

Tracy followed me into the kitchen, undeterred. "Can I ask you something, Jess?"

"Sure." I opened the fridge, scanning the shelves for something edible. I couldn't remember when I'd shopped last.

"What do you hope to get out of all of this? What's your end game?"

I looked up at her. "I don't have an 'end game.' I just want answers to my questions."

Sunday morning I woke early, leaving time to properly dress in a blouse and skirt. I hadn't entered a Catholic Church in a few years, and didn't want to draw attention by my appearance. My housemates were sleeping off a late night out together. Their lack of invitation, a not very subtle message, didn't affect me. I'd survived an entire childhood with teachers desperate to point out the consequences of my actions, a pointless waste of energy. Tracy didn't know what she was up against.

I sat in my car, parked down the block, watching his house. Sure enough, at 7:45, the front door opened, and Mr. Peterson stepped out, leaving on foot. I had pictured a slim, wiry figure, but Peterson in the flesh was broad-chested, solid. I drove the few blocks to the church, then waited until he entered. Congregation members greeted one another and formed small groups at the front entrance; Peterson skipped the introductions and walked straight in.

I was skimming the missal to find my place, when

welcoming remarks were briefly disrupted by someone speaking in the pews. I looked up in time to find Mr. Peterson talking aloud. Everyone ignored the remark. In my experience, commentary from the audience during a Catholic mass is neither expected nor appreciated.

I had ample time during the sermon, or homily, to thumb through the gospels and find the good thief/bad thief passage the online priest had referenced. The only difference I could see between the wrongdoers was in the way the penitent thief, facing his death, had the good sense to apologize for his actions. 'It's better to beg for forgiveness, than ask for permission' was my takeaway. Words to live by.

After the service ended, Peterson turned in the opposite direction of his house. Perfect timing for a little peek into the garage.

One side of the structure was sheltered by bamboo trees, allowing me to slip around without notice. The windows were clouded; a small amount of sunlight filtered into a garage crammed full of junk: furniture, rusty tools, rolled up rugs. It was hard to see, but the floor appeared to be hard-packed dirt. Against the far wall, a motorcycle was propped up, its fenders reflecting the light. Well, well, well. If this was the nephew's motorcycle, where was the nephew? I moved to the front of the garage cautiously, wishing I'd changed into my running clothes, to fake a stretch break if a neighbor walked past. The ancient door looked heavy, but there was a relatively new padlock attached.

I turned towards home, about to cross the street when I saw Mr. Peterson approaching. Crap. My heartbeat sped up — I was not nearly as crafty as I thought. Had he noticed me checking out the lock on the garage door? It was time to ask about the crosses straight-on. I glanced his way with a big smile.

"Hi there! I'm new to the area — "

"I've seen you," he said.

"You've seen me? Do you mean at mass this morning — or in the neighborhood? I live around the corner."

At mass I'd not been close enough to notice, but face to face his appearance was less than tidy. He wore a button-up shirt, but the collar was frayed, and there were stains on the front, the suit pants wrinkled and ill-fitting.

While his expression remained impassive, I felt him mentally shaking a finger at me. "Where did you come from, girl?" he asked, leaning towards me.

I stared at him for a long moment, and then walked away. I wasn't sure when Ted last talked to the man, but I was pretty sure 'strange' had developed into something a little more sinister. Not that it mattered to anyone else.

A plan took form before I'd walked in the door at home. I'd need to find some bolt cutters, and a new identical lock — and I should probably bring a shovel.

There was no way of knowing the best time to break into the garage. I certainly couldn't do it in broad daylight while Peterson was in church. A late night was my best option.

It wasn't like I hadn't considered breaking and entering before. There was that time back in middle school when I came across a neighborhood home covered entirely in industrial-sized black tarp. Wide awake that night, full of questions generated by the 'Keep Out' postings, I snuck out of my house to search for answers. I'd almost reached the heavy tarps when a disembodied voice from the darkness called me off. Like a chastised pup, I turned tail and slipped away. My parents, always on alert to my 'impulsivity issues,' either never knew, or decided to let one small mishap slide. Whatever the outcome, it was worth the risk.

The following Sunday night, prepped and ready, I eased out of the house. The bolt cutters, kindly loaned by a neighbor, made short work of the small padlock. Much more challenging was lifting the warped door, a feat of strength to raise high enough to duck under. Once inside, I turned on my running headlight. I was right about the dirt floor, which was uneven and rutted. Tripping over something on the ground and barely catching myself, I looked down to see a shovel. A lucky break, since I'd failed to score one. I'd focused my light to pick it up when I heard the creak of the door behind me. The noise gave me a few moments to choose: hide or talk my way out. Instead, I froze.

"What are you doing in here?" Face shadowed, Mr. Peterson stood silhouetted by the streetlight behind him. His voice — low-pitched, gruff — punctuated the air in short bursts.

"Oh, hello, remember me from last week? My housemate's cat is lost, and she thought he might have snuck in here." There was no way he would believe me, but I didn't see what else I could do. Stuck at the back end of the garage, I waited for his reaction. His considerable bulk blocked the exit.

"Who sent you here?" He cocked his head to the side. "How did you get in?"

I deflected the questions, plunging ahead with the story. Conjuring an image of a cat, my brain called up the pet from The Brady Bunch, "No one sent me. Tiger — that's Tracy's cat — he's pretty good getting in where he doesn't belong," I said, "I'm sorry, sir, it won't happen again."

"You're right it won't, because I'm putting a stop to it."

I didn't like where this was going. I reached for the phone in my pocket, one eye on the man, the other punching in 9-1-1 and hitting send.

"You've been watching me, watching this house. I've seen you run by."

A shiver ran up my arms. His words last week now made sense. He'd watched me, too.

"I know about you," he said, moving into the garage, scanning the floor. What was he looking for? I followed the direction of his gaze, which landed at my feet. The light from my beam picked up a dark stain in the ground beside the shovel.

"Where is your nephew, Mr. Peterson? Isn't that his motorcycle against the wall?"

Peterson's head jerked up towards me, his brows knit. "Jeremiah should have listened to me. 'Now reform your ways and your actions and obey the LORD your God.'"

"Jeremiah was your nephew? What did he need to repent?"

Peterson shook his head. "He was an impertinent young man. Said I was crazy, that I couldn't take care of myself."

"He asked to move in with you?" I asked, stalling. At least his forward movement had ceased.

Peterson bristled. "No, girl. He wanted to dump me into 'assisted living.' Put any fancy name on it, it's still a nursing home."

Maybe his nephew's idea wasn't so off-base. My phone vibrated in my pocket, but I didn't move.

"I own this property," he said, more forcefully. "I worked thirty years to pay off the damn bank. What right did he have?"

"He was probably concerned about you."

"Or about the money."

A siren sounded in the distance, grew louder. Peterson's words were drowned out, his attention deflected by flashing lights.

I jumped as car doors slammed in succession and two of Alexandria's finest made their way to the garage. One cop flipped the light on by the door as his partner looked around with an expression of distaste.

"What's going on here? Did one of you contact 911?"

I spoke up, retelling my lost cat story, but Peterson interrupted. "This girl broke into my garage. Aren't you going to arrest her?"

The cops focused on me. "Is this true, miss?"

"Well, yes — but I suspected something was wrong with his nephew, and I was right. His nephew, Jeremiah is missing — that's his motorcycle against the wall. And he threatened me, too," I said, stumbling through my words in the face of the cops' unflinching stares.

They asked Peterson for identification. Satisfied he was the legitimate homeowner, the older officer said, "Sir, we'll certainly investigate the break-in, but we need to consider any threats made as well. Maybe you'd like to make a statement?"

"It is not for man to judge one's deeds," Peterson said, and turned away, heading for the door of the garage.

The first officer reached out his hand to stay him. "Sir, if you could just — "

Peterson yanked his arm out of the officer's reach, his face diffused with red, eyes bulging. "Whoever commits sin transgresses the law, for sin is a transgression of the law." His voice rose to a bellow. The cops took a step back. Peterson continued "Rather than making amends for his transgressions, Jeremiah died with his sin." He turned towards me, his glare pinning me in place. "And which sinner are you? Are you penitent?"

I flicked my eyes to the cops, who exchanged a look, silently deciding our fate.

"We're going to need to call this in," the first cop said. They escorted us gingerly out of the garage. Lights flicked on in nearby houses; a few neighbors stepped out to stare. With luck, no one would recognize me.

Peterson seemed to shrink into himself. "Why couldn't you have left me alone?" he asked.

The cops frisked us; the discovery of the lock and bolt cutters in my bag earned me a trip to the police station. I heard one officer calling for a psych evaluation and a second car. Forget the good thief and bad thief, I was more concerned about which one of us required the psych eval.

The police station at the courthouse was less intimidating and better lit than on the crime shows Camila watched. I spilled my guts to the police officers without a lawyer or much in the way of resistance; I was shivering, and suddenly felt exhausted. An officer printed a statement for me to sign, cited me for criminal trespass and remarked I was lucky it wasn't for breaking and entering. I chose not to argue over the redundancy of the two terms.

The call to my mother I later recognized as an error in judgement.

"Do you realize you may end up with a record, Jessica?"

"Everyone has some kind of record nowadays," I replied. "Everything we do lives online, forever."

"We'll talk about this more when you can be serious," she said, and hung up.

My next call was to Uber, an effort to forestall the 'I-told-you-so' from Tracy. There would be plenty of that to come later, but I needed space to mull my recent choices and formulate a back-up option in case I was forced to find new digs.

~

Months later, I turned the corner to 30th Street and found the crime scene tape removed from 699, replaced by a "For Sale" sign on the lawn. I wished the realtor luck. On the surface, the property appeared transformed, with a new paint job and freshly planted grass on the site of the former garage. The ugly history remained. I felt conflicted by the removal of the crosses. Somehow, it felt callous to wipe away that marker of Jeremiah's last moments.

The block was quiet. The county vehicles had moved off to the next crime and the satellite-mounted news vans were stationed at the courthouse to cover the trial. Peterson was declared competent for trial, as reported by Camilla, who devoured every detail on the news and pumped me for information. I made peace with her need to know, since she'd smoothed things out with Tracy at home. Besides which, her fascination with the case outweighed any desire to lecture.

The charges against me were dropped after a long tongue-lashing from a judge, who briefly acknowledged my part in Peterson's arrest before he railed about the 'reckless disregard' for my own safety, for authority, blah, blah, blah. I bowed my head obediently and responded with a "yes, sir" at the right times, but wasn't particularly sorry. If it wasn't for my "wrong-doing," Jeremiah would have remained a missing person, his family uninformed, his case left to gather dust in some file room. Regardless of Jeremiah's motivation or character, he didn't deserve his fate, and I felt a kinship with his lack of penitence. Given the chance, I'd follow the same path over again. Minus any mistakes along the way.

They say the third time's the charm. I'd certainly keep my eyes open for the next opportunity.

Mary Sophie Filicetti's *fiction has appeared in* AEL's Locked Room *mysteries,* Montana Mouthful, Every Day Fiction, 365 Tomorrows, Nightingale and Sparrow, Toasted Cheese, The Phoenix, *and the* MacGuffin. *She is a first reader at* Little Patuxent Review, *and is currently completing her MFA in Fiction at Spalding University.* Tweeting at @marysfilicetti

Tuckerizations

A huge thank you to Kickstarter backer Benson Calure who selected Tuckerization for his reward. Kevin A. Davis made sure that Sheriff Benson Calure helped catch the murderer in "Route 90."

Thank you, Benson Calure!

Acknowledgments

Detectives, Sleuths, & Nosy Neighbors became an idea as we identified our interest in good, short mysteries that our authors offered in anthologies such as *Hidden Villains*. Our *Noncorporeal* editor, A. Balsamo, supported this love and we moved forward to bring new writers and stories to the world.

We must thank Heather Lewis, Tony Cioffi, Kristi Barnes, Heather Norris, April Davis, and Kevin Davis for the hours spent reading through almost one hundred submissions to bring a selection for A. Balsamo to select from.

Inkd Pub could not afford the publication cost alone and we love our Kickstarter backers. Join me in thanking them for making this and future anthologies possible.

Kickstarter Patrons: Robin Collins, Kristi Wallington, Ed King, Matthew, Ron Miller, Kathryn, Amanda Eschmeyer, Mary Jo Rabe, Norbert Grygar, Boris Veytsman, Heidi Cunningham, Michael Barbour, crystalbrier, Kathy Waller, Victoria Tait, Jessica Enfante, Jackie Sharp, Margaret Curelas, Patrick Kelly, Amanda Balter, Alexandra Corrsin, Isaac 'Will It Work' Dansicker, Michelle L, EricV, Benson Calure, Tiffany Smith, Timothy C Hanifen, Jason Martinko, Tiffany Seitz, Christina Fernandez, Michael Axe, Zachary Fissel, Sohrab Rezvan, Heather Lewis, Regina Federico, Sara Jordan-Heintz, chris William mobberley, Heather N Christian, Thomas G. Tellefsen, Lise McClendon, Tikiri Herath

Also by Inkd Publishing

Hidden Villains by Robyn Huss - our original anthology with David Farland as lead author

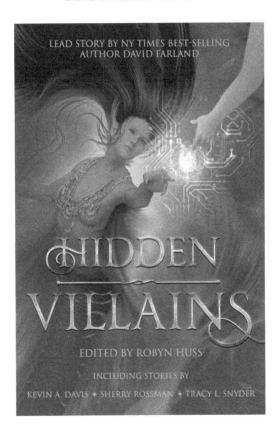

Hidden Villains: Arise by Robyn Huss - with Jody Lynn Nye as lead author

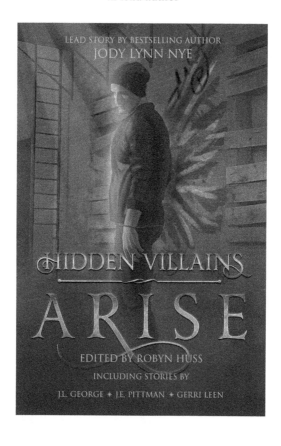

Behind the Shadows by Sara Jordan-Heintz - our horror anthology

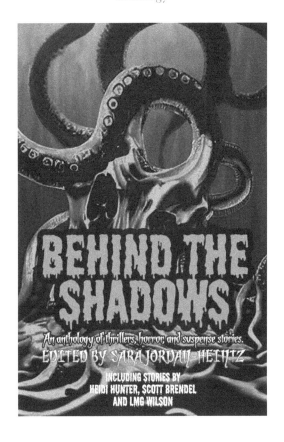

Noncorporeal by A. Balsamo - our spooky anthology

Books are available in paperback and eBook; please visit us at InkdPub.com to find locations. Join us on Facebook to keep up to date.

Sign up for our newsletter at our website for open call announcements, Kickstarters, and launches.

Inkdpub.com

Milton Keynes UK
Ingram Content Group UK Ltd.
UKHW010901080524
442402UK00004B/122